just to watch them die

just to watch them die

CRIME FICTION INSPIRED BY THE SONGS OF

JOHNNY CASH

EDITED BY
JOE CLIFFORD

www.gutterbooks.com

JUST TO WATCH THEM DIE

CONTENTS

Foreword

Micah Schnabel

There's something about a person dressed all in black, barreling through the speakers with the stories of desperate humans doing desperate things in perilous times. And in 1954 Johnny Cash stood in Sun Studio in Memphis, TN, attempting to bring these songs outside his chest and into this world. But aside from the stories there was something else that connected, mainlined to punk-rock hearts everywhere in a time before such a term had been coined. There's an ever-present pulse to those early recordings.

Inside the Sun Studio control room, listening to the playback, everyone is hearing the sound coming out flat and gospel-like. Like they were supposed to in those days. But everyone in the room recognizes the life of the song is somehow being sucked out of the stories. The band is tight, the voice perfect, yet, somehow, something is missing. Hollow reproductions of the real thing.

It's life in a pre-Ramone-d world. Short-wave radios with small, tinny speakers producing smooth angelic gospel songs on the AM dial promising the poor salvation. While back in Sun Studio, Johnny Cash is sliding a dollar bill behind the steel strings of his acoustic back near the bridge, where the strings meet the body of the guitar, hoping to inject some urgency into the lifeless recordings. And just that small action of George Washington scraping against steel and wood of the acoustic guitar while he strummed wrought a whole new sound. The sound of life being breathed into the songs. All of a sudden there was a pulse. The songs felt alive. They were no longer just simply listening to a song; they were *feeling* the sound-waves wash over them. That small bit of friction being produced between the steel and wood had created a sound that would soon rip through those small transistor radios and into the heart of America. The songs were no longer willing to be backseat passengers on a Sunday drive with nothing much to say. They were now demanding to drive up front, with the windows down and the radio turned way past it's usual noon o' clock existence. That small amount of friction had turned those smooth gospel tunes into the very first punk rock anthems. That Drive! We had never heard anything like it and we jumped at the chance to feel like all of a sudden someone was speaking to *us*! And *for* us. Telling our side of the story. No house made of gold, pie in the sky, jingoism here. But truth. Honesty and sincerity. A hot shot of post-modernism into the still unaware modern times. We are out here! I am not alone in the frustration that comes with the American workaday selling me apple pie and road side peaches; telling me I should be happy to spend my days nameless and faceless. These were songs for the rest of us. And you could feel it!

This is the reason you can still to this day find Johnny Cash tee shirts anywhere and everywhere, from the studs and safety-pin leather jackets of Oakland to the Applebee's in Des Moines, Iowa. Those songs brought a voice into the world that proclaimed *I am not one of them.* There is something more inside of me. I have a name and a voice and it is not the same as everyone else. I am aware that I am being duped and even if I can't find the words there is someone out there speaking for me.

There is a reason these songs continue to bring people together. The sound of anger and loneliness. It's all there in that scratchy pulse. Sneaking that percussive beat into those AM radio stations pumping directly into our hearts. There have always been people like us. But this gave us someone to rally behind. Something we could connect to and call our own. To this day there's some kid in a basement somewhere in the Midwest hearing that friction for the first time and the message is just as urgent and important as ever.

Johnny Cash was able to break down all of the false walls we tend to build around ourselves. Gender, race, nationality, all broken down by the drive and crackle of that guitar put up against that voice and the stories of us. The forgotten. And this is why people continue to be drawn into these songs. Because we all have that fire in our hearts.

So do yourself a favor and go and listen to the Sun recording of "I Walk the Line," pay attention to that percussive pulse happening and think of how that subtle slide of that dollar bill into those guitar strings guided so many into the punk rock records and buzzsaw guitars that have grown so near and dear to our hearts.

This is where it all began.

You are not alone.

just to watch them die

Like the 309

Rob Hart

This close to the water, the wind was sharp. Ophelia clutched her jacket tight. Empty roadway and blank industrial buildings receded into darkness in both directions.

She couldn't remember which way would take her toward the heart of Manhattan—to people, cabs, sanctuary—and which direction would take her to the Hudson River. She pulled out her phone and exhaled, her breath blooming in front of her. As Google Maps hunted for her location she turned to look at the steel-and-glass building behind her, nestled in between two warehouses.

The sight of it made her so angry she didn't feel cold anymore.

Preston had seemed nice. Funny and sweet and kind of adorable, with the way his long brown hair fell in front of his eyes and he had to keep brushing it back. When she said her name was Ophelia, he asked if her parents were fans of *MacBeth*. She let the mistake slide because at least he was correct that it was a Shakespeare reference.

After three drinks together he invited her back to his place, and it sounded so innocent. Sure, maybe they'd fuck, or maybe they'd just talk, and Ophelia was curious to find out which.

As soon as they crossed the threshold of his apartment, his attitude shifted like tectonic plates. Gone were the witticism and side-eye glances, replaced by a bold sense of entitlement. He'd succeeded in getting her back home and that meant it was time for her to disrobe and accept him.

Ophelia gave him the benefit of the doubt, that maybe it was the booze getting the better of his mouth. But when his gaze dropped to her chest and he advanced like a hungry animal, she put her fist into the soft part of his throat, then her knee into his balls. Two years of Krav Maga finally paid off. She'd only been doing it for the cardio.

She left him writhing on the floor, calling after her, begging her not to call the cops. She took the stairs instead of the elevator and wondered if she should call them. Technically, Preston didn't do anything illegal. Creepy and threatening, sure. And anyone would see that what she did was self-defense.

But it would be a game of Slut Shame Roulette: Best-case scenario, she'd get a female cop, or a male cop with a daughter. Someone with a sympathetic ear. Worst case was she'd get a troglodyte with a badge who'd wonder if her blouse was too unbuttoned, if maybe she should have thought better than going home with a strange man.

Ophelia prided herself on being the girl who didn't cry. But the pressure and stress of the long week, on top of this, had filled her to a bursting point of emotion. It had to come out somewhere.

Ophelia closed her eyes. Took another cold breath. Looked at her phone. As the blue circle shrank, zeroing in on her location, she saw a flash in the corner of her eye.

A cab cruising down the block, the top of it lit like a beacon.

She stepped to the curb and put her hand up. The blinker came on and it drifted her way. It was an older cab, with the rounded top and checkerboard pattern running down the side. It'd been years since she'd seen one like that on the street.

That made her a little worried. Maybe the years hadn't been kind. Older cabs were sometimes ripped apart inside, reeking of food and body odor and who knew what else. She tried to make out the driver, but with the way the glare from the streetlights reflected on the windows, he was just a dull shape beyond the glass.

She opened the door and was greeted by the thick scent of evergreen. The seats were cloth, not leather, and the interior was immaculate. She climbed in. Up front was an overweight man with dark thinning hair, wearing a light tan jacket. She caught a flash of his eyes in the rearview mirror. Old eyes, tired and brilliantly blue.

"What can I do for you, miss?" he asked. His voice was rough and heavy as a piece of lead, the kind of New York accent you only develop if you were born here, raised here, and never left, even for a long weekend.

"Do you go to Brooklyn?" Ophelia asked.

"My dear, I will go wherever it is you wish of me," he said. "I know some cabbies don't like going to the outer boroughs, what with the difficulty in getting return fares. But that's the nature of the profession. Maybe they shouldn't be cabbies if it's such a bother."

Ophelia smiled. "Driggs. On the corner of North Ninth Street."

"I know that neighborhood well," the man said, as he flipped on the meter and pulled away from the curb. "Do you have a particular route you would like for me to take?"

"I trust your judgment."

"Thank you. Though this late at night, it ought to be smooth sailing."

The cab coasted to the corner, coming to rest at a red light. Ophelia inspected the inside. "I didn't think any cabs this old were still in active service."

"I get special dispensation," the man said, carefully sounding out the syllables of "dispensation." "Been driving this for going on thirty years. They're going to have to drag me out of it. Anyway, I don't like those new ones. I know they're better for the environment, but they look like electric razors, don't they?"

Ophelia laughed. "That they do."

The light turned green and the cab turned down 10th Avenue. The driver cleared his throat and said, "Ma'am, may I ask you a question? And please don't feel compelled to answer."

Strange cab in a remote part of Manhattan, an over-eager cabbie when she was used to drivers who ignored their passengers. It was so far from the norm as to be vaguely unsettling. But there was a kindness to his voice that compelled her to say, "Sure."

"Is everything okay?" he asked. "Because you sound upset."

Ophelia thought for a moment. "I don't think a cab driver has ever asked me that."

The driver was silent for the length of a block. Ophelia wondered if she said something to upset him when he asked, "Do you know why I do this job?"

"Why?"

"The money isn't so bad," the driver said. "The schedule is flexible. I get to literally sit on my ass all day—excuse my language. I wasn't built for manual labor. So that's all good. But above all, I'm a people person. And I don't intend to pry, if you don't want to talk. But we've got another twenty or so minutes together, so I just thought I'd ask."

Ophelia sighed. "Everything's . . . fine. Just . . . it was a rough night."

"Rough nights," the driver said, shaking his head, like he knew exactly what she meant.

Ophelia watched the back of his head, getting only the stray glimpse of his profile as he scanned the street. His hair seemed to be fighting a losing battle against his white scalp. She searched the inside of the cab for his medallion, because she was curious to see his face. She found it in the corner of the glass partition, but it was so yellowed and faded she could only see the outline of him.

"There was a guy, and he got a little handsy," Ophelia said, a little surprised at the words jumping out of her mouth. She looked into the rearview mirror and the driver met her glance, raised his eyebrow.

"Want we should go back, tune him up a little?" he asked, and Ophelia couldn't see his mouth but could tell he was smiling. "That's not the type of behavior I like to abide."

"I left him crying on the floor," Ophelia said.

"Good for you, sweetheart. Good for you."

The way he said it: Sweetheart. That was the kind of thing that usually lit a fire in Ophelia. It was a word men tossed around to infantilize women. Make them feel young and small. But there was something warm about it. She liked the way he said it.

"Do you want we should call the police?" the driver asked.

"No, I don't think so," Ophelia said. "I'd like to think he learned a lesson tonight. As for right now . . . I just want to go home."

"Your wish is my command," he said.

"Actually," Ophelia said. "I don't want to go home. I want to sit somewhere quiet and have a drink. Someplace where assholes won't hit on me. Someplace where the music isn't too loud. It's too bad. Places like that don't exist."

"Ah, but they do," the driver said, taking a hand off the wheel and sticking a thick, stubby finger into the air. "Have you ever heard of Rita's?"

"I haven't."

"It's a few blocks from where you live," he said. "Rita is a ballbuster. If you are not a proper gentleman, you get the boot. I stop in there every now and again. Nice and relaxed. Not too pricey. I would be happy to drop you there."

"Thank you."

"So, miss, might I ask your name?"

"Ophelia."

"Ah, you mean that poor girl in *Hamlet* that got drowned," he said.

She smiled. "That's the one."

"I'm not so much into the tragedies," he said. "I prefer the comedies. *Much Ado About Nothing* is my favorite."

The driver turned the cab onto Delancey, wending its way toward the Williamsburg Bridge, traffic growing heavy and causing them to slow down.

"Why are there so many shitty people in the world?" Ophelia asked. Then she laughed. "I'm sorry. That's such a ridiculous question. It's like a question a child would ask."

"It's not a ridiculous question," the driver said. "I spend a lot of time thinking about that. I can tell within a few blocks whether a person who gets in this cab is nice or not. Do they say hello, do they ask me to take them somewhere or demand it? Nowadays people talk on their phones like I'm not even here. I learn a lot about people. And you know what I've learned?"

"What's that?"

"That I do not understand anything about people."

Ophelia looked back at Manhattan as it disappeared behind her, the shorter, darker buildings of Brooklyn coming up ahead.

She leaned back into the plush seat, thought for a moment she'd like to stay there forever. Someplace warm and safe, which is all anyone could ever ask for.

"There are good people in the world and there are bad people in the world," the driver said. "After thirty years of doing this, that's the best I've got for you."

"Which one are you?" Ophelia asked. "Good or bad?"

"I don't know that it's for me to decide, Miss Ophelia," he said. "But I try my best."

As they exited the bridge, traffic thinned out and they fell into a comfortable silence. The lights were in their favor and it wasn't long before the cab pulled to the curb in front of what Ophelia never really knew was a bar.

She rarely walked in this direction—the subway that took her to work and the main thoroughfares where she spent her weekend were in a different direction. Even still, it wasn't much to look at. A long dark window, a green door, a small bench and bucket for smokes. No real sign to speak of, other than the word "Ritas" in those gold and black peel-and-stick letters sold at the hardware store.

"That'll be eighteen-fifty, Miss Ophelia."

Ophelia reached into her purse and pulled out her wallet, found two crumbled singles. She bit her lip and cursed herself. She thought she had more, but remembered she paid for dinner in cash.

"I'm so sorry," she said. "Do you take credit?"

"Machine is busted," the driver said.

"Do you think they have an ATM? I can go inside . . ."

"Their ATM has been broken for as long as I've been coming here," the driver said. "I'll tell you what, though." He reached into the console for something and, without turning, held a ten-dollar bill through the window.

"The ride is on the house," he said. "Go get yourself that glass of wine."

Ophelia stammered. "No . . . I couldn't possibly . . ."

"Sure you can," the driver said, waving the bill. "Sometimes a good conversation can be payment itself."

Ophelia hesitated, but reached up and took the bill, her breath heavy in her chest. For a second time that night she wanted to cry, but held it back.

Twenty minutes ago the world seemed like a very dark place. Now it took a moment for her to remember why.

"I don't know how to thank you," she said.

"You're going to pay me back," the driver said. "And this is how you're going to do it. The next time you come across someone having a rough night, you give them a hand. Pay it forward, as they say. You got me, Miss Ophelia?"

"I will . . . " She started to thank him again and realized she didn't know how to address him. "I never asked your name. That's so rude of me."

"Think nothing of it. My name is Joseph. Like of Arimathea."

"That's very specific."

"My mother was a devout Catholic and wanted everyone to know I was named after that Joseph in particular. But everyone calls me Big Joey."

"I kind of prefer Joseph, if you don't mind," Ophelia said. "It suits you."

"Well thank you, Miss Ophelia. When you see Rita, tell her Big Joey says hello."

"I will. And . . . thank you."

Ophelia climbed into the cold night air, her skin tightening in protest to the change in temperature. She leaned down to the passenger side window. She wanted to see the man's face. It felt very important to her, in that moment, to see his face. More than those kind eyes flashing in the rear view mirror. But the glare of the streetlight distorted his features.

She put up her hand, and he put up his hand in return as he drove away from the curb. Ophelia caught the numbers 309 on the license plate before the cab disappeared around the corner. She committed them to memory. Tomorrow she would call the Taxi & Limousine Commission, to leave a good word about him. She didn't know if it would mean anything, but she wanted to at least try.

Ophelia turned to the bar and it didn't look open, but she pushed through the door and found a small, cozy space that was quiet and old without being dingy. There were a few people scattered across small tables and booths, and music playing somewhere low. She couldn't make out the song but it sounded pleasant.

To her left was an ATM. It appeared to be in working order. Maybe it was fixed recently.

Ophelia sat at the bar. An older woman with frizzy red hair going white, presumably Rita, asked, "What'll you have, dear?"

"A glass of cabernet," she said.

The woman stepped to the end of the bar, reappeared with a clean glass and a bottle. She placed down the glass and offered a heavy pour. Ophelia slid the ten-dollar bill across the bar.

"You live in the neighborhood, dear?" she asked.

"I do," Ophelia said. "But I've never been inside before. It's nice. Big Joey dropped me off here. He said to say hello."

The woman raised an eyebrow. "That's not funny."

"What's not funny?"

"Don't put me on like that," she said. "It's not nice."

The woman pursed her lips, spun on her heel, and disappeared to the end of the bar. The ten-dollar bill was still sitting on the bar.

Ophelia wasn't sure how to take that. She thought of calling the woman over, asking what she meant. Something uncomfortable was roiling around her stomach. She gazed into the mirror against the far wall, behind the row of liquor bottles. She stared at herself as she sipped the wine.

A newspaper article caught her eye, taped up in the far corner of the mirror. She stared at it until she was able to make out the headline.

CAB DRIVER DIES IN TRAGIC ACCIDENT

Though it was warm in the bar, Ophelia's blood dropped to match the temperature outside.

With shaking hands she took out her phone and searched for the headline, her fingers slipping on the touchscreen. The result came back immediately. It was an article from the *New York Post*. She skimmed it quickly, her heart constricting in her chest. By the time she got to the end she realized she wasn't breathing.

Joseph Marino was known for driving a classic style of cab, and was beloved by the community. One afternoon a little girl ran in front of his cab while chasing a ball and he swerved to miss her, hitting a telephone pole in the process.

He died on impact. The girl was unhurt.

Ophelia looked at the date the article was published.

One year ago today.

She placed her hand over the ten-dollar bill. Picked it up and turned it over, the paper worn and dry under her fingertips. It was real. Real as anything.

Real as the cab that brought her here, and the man who spoke so kindly to her. Real as the warmth and the safety she felt just moments ago.

For the third time that night tears approached her eyes, and for the first time that night she allowed herself the indulgence of crying.

God's Gonna Cut You Down

Jen Conley

I was outside smoking a cigarette when the call came. It was my father.

"Tomorrow night," Pop said. "Six. Matt will get you."

I flicked my smoke ashes on the small wooden deck, a deck I'd recently stained for my landlord.

"Eric? You listening to me?"

"All right," I answered. "I'll be there."

"Park your car in the old A&P lot," my father said.

Inside my garage apartment, I sat in the silence, finishing a soda. I didn't drink anymore and my father never said much about this fact, although Pop never said much about anything, until he did. The man was seventy-three, alert, wiry with long arms, his grip as strong as it'd been thirty years earlier.

My father had two living sons and a deceased daughter.

I grew up down in Ocean County, in a bi-level house Pop still resided in, my mom dead ten years. It was a typical neighborhood, nothing grand, but four blocks away there was a small park along an inlet of the bay. A narrow path opened up from the edge of this park, a trail which had been cut in the 1980s and used by us kids and teens—a way to get out further into the woods along the water, to one of the clearings with a hidden beach. Bring a fishing pole, a blanket, beer, your girl. Last year before I'd quit drinking, I'd brought my young wife—ex-wife now—out to the second clearing where my sister Dawn had lost her life.

"I don't want to be here," she'd suddenly said, hugging herself, her eyes darting between the open water and the dense woods behind us. "Get me out of here, Eric! Fucking get me out of here!" I was annoyed. It had been her idea. *Show me, show me . . .* Over the years, I'd been out to the spot several times myself, looking for something that my sister might have lost—one of those barrettes I'd always found in the bathroom, the tube of mascara she kept in her jacket pocket, even the mix-cassette tape she'd made for her best friend, Renee Delgo, because nobody ever found that.

It was a long time that I sat on my couch, in my crummy apartment above a detached garage, thinking. I thought about a lot of things as one does when they live in a crummy apartment, but mostly I thought about my ex-wife. Pop had helped me move in after Emily gave the break-up speech. *"We had three good years together but I can't be tied to a man who has a drinking problem."* At the present moment, she lived in a townhome in Jersey City with a new man and a cat. I worked in Newark for Horizon Blue Cross, and the apartment I rented was owned by a co-worker's cousin.

"That wife was too young for you," Pop said the day he helped me move in. "I'm sure the pussy was good, but she wasn't doing much of the housework, was she?"

The pussy. My father would've never used that word if my mother was alive.

"She was not into housework," I'd answered. "You got that right."

Emily had been twenty-six when she left me, twenty-three when we met, too young, I know. "I can't do toilets," she'd whispered one night in bed. "I just can't." Once a month, I sent Emily a check, even though by law I didn't have to—we weren't married long enough. But she'd asked.

I got off the couch and went back outside, where I smoked several cigarettes, my throat growing ragged and pained. The autumn sun was deep orange. I wanted to think about Emily but she kept pulling away from my mind, like a boat drifting from the dock. My father's voice, that phone call, and my sister's killer, David Ward, who had been released six months earlier—that shit settled in my head like concrete. David Ward, the goofy older kid who had played army men with me when I was nine, that stupid dumbass had returned to my childhood neighborhood to live with his mother. His mother who lived nine houses away from Pop.

It's been a long, difficult road with the ghost of David Ward hanging over my family. And nobody was angrier than my younger brother, Matt. Back in June, two months after David got out, Matt came up for a visit. "Motherfucker is waving to people!" We spoke inside my apartment, Matt with a beer in his hand—he'd bought a six pack from the local liquor store. "He's got a used car and a fucking job, dude! A fucking job!"

I opened a soda.

"That ain't all," Matt went on. "I've been trailing him, right?"

"Sure."

"So the dickhead hits Wawa every morning. Gets his coffee and a fucking doughnut with sprinkles. Then he talks to the women behind the counter. Just chats, like '*Gonna be a nice day.*'

And the women, they talk back, like '*You stay cool!*' Fucking bullshit."

Matt paced the room, raging a thousand times wilder than the average infuriated person because my brother couldn't sit still. He couldn't stay faithful to one woman, couldn't hold a job long. He was a perpetual teenager, rebellious and hot-blooded—but it was all due to his ADHD. When you're handed that card, there's not much you can do but live it. Matty had the same wiry build as our father, the same long arms, broad shoulders, rectangular built but not tall. The Irish side, my mother used to say. I was the big one—tall, broad shouldered also, but I was thicker, wider, stronger. The Dutch side, Mom would say. My sister, Dawn, she was just small.

In August Matt came back with more news. "He goes over to Spirits at Happy Hour. I went in, sat at the end of the bar. He don't recognize me, the dumb fuck. He's just some mushy fat pathetic loser, man. I don't think anyone knows him. The boys let him play pool. Play pool! And Jessica, that hot bartender I was nailing? She fucking buys him back drinks. Nobody recognizes him anymore."

It'd made the local papers that he was getting out after thirty years, and there'd been some uproar—Facebook postings of his prison picture, letters of outrage. But David Ward had followed the rules: registered as a sex offender, was in the house by ten o'clock, had his job at a fish market. He did good things, too. He volunteered to walk dogs at the local animal shelter and took his mom shopping. Within a few months, the outrage had died down.

"I ain't forgot nothing," Matty said.

Just a week ago, there was one last visit from Matt. "I saw him talking to some females, teenage girls, you know?" Matt lowered his voice but he was still aflame in fury. "The fucker was outside, mowing his mother's lawn, and these two teenage girls come walking up and he says, 'How's it going, ladies?' Like they're gonna respond to the mushy fat killer that he is. Anyhow, those girls, they just looked at each other, 'cause they know. The kids, they know who's no good. 'Cause we always knew old David was no good, remember?"

I'd been eleven, Matt ten, David Ward fifteen, Dawn fourteen. David hung with a guy named Chuck, always a big hulk of a man-boy, and they'd had a thing for Dawn. She had the downstairs room in the bi-level, the entire lower level to herself in fact, and they'd been caught looking in her window, jerking off together. Matt caught them. Because of his ADHD, he was always up, poking around his room, sneaking off to the kitchen for cookies or anything with sugar, and he'd been sitting at the kitchen table in the dark, looking through the window at the backyard, the full moon illuminating our yard with the above ground pool. He'd seen the shadows moving, two figures leaping over the chain-link fence, and he saw them skirt the edges, moving deftly through the night, until they disappeared from Matt's eyesight. In those days, Matty was in Scouts and he always had a flashlight clipped to whatever he was wearing, even his pajama bottoms. He went down the front stairs, slipping into his sneakers, and went out the front door. He moved around the side of the house, opening the back gate quietly, and snuck around, suddenly finding these two with their dicks out, their hands over them, shaking furiously. The light from Dawn's room shined brightly through the window. Dawn was asleep, but she slept in a tank top and underwear, no bra, no sheet or blanket over her, and the police would later find out Chuck and David had been jerking off to her for weeks.

"Disgusting," my mom said to Dawn. "You can't sleep with

pajamas and a blanket over you like the rest of us? Why didn't you just take your clothes off and dance for them?"

Pop took a piece of plywood and covered her window with it.

"I didn't know they were there, honest," Dawn said to me a few days later. "You believe me, right?"

Matt took a beer from his six-pack. "Wish they got both of them." To that, I nodded. Chuck had been beaten to death in prison, murdered by his cell mate. David, he'd survived and now he was driving around, buying coffee at Wawa, playing pool, getting a buy-back beer from hot Jessica. Dawn, she was dead.

The night was just what Pop had predicted—clear, dark, perfect. I got into Matt's white pick-up and we drove over to Spirits. It was dark, and Spirits was a liquor store with a secret bar in the back, where bar customers parked. David Ward was staying on after Happy Hour ended, enchanted by Jessica, Matt explained. "But he leaves before nine. It's like clockwork—8:47. Must be all that living by rules in prison," Matt said. "You get all institution-like, right?"

My brother handed me a small flashlight, told me to hold onto it, and got out of the truck. He disappeared around the corner of the bar, and I took over the wheel.

David Ward came lumbering out the back door at exactly 8:47. Matt trailed behind him, then broke into a whip-like charge, snapping a long arm around David's neck, a knife at his throat. Matt's truck had one of those narrow back jumpseats and he'd shoved David inside, the knife at his neck, telling him he better keep his fucking fat ass still. I drove the white truck out of the back parking lot, onto the highway, turning off into our old neighborhood. The same neighborhood where for a time, David and Dawn and Renee Regalo and Matt and me—we'd all played Manhunt together the summer before Dawn was killed.

We'd ridden bikes together a few years before that. And during all those years, David, always a dull-witted kid, had played army men with me in the backyard near my above ground pool, drawing lines in the dirt, digging trenches for our men, making machine gun noises when we shot each other down.

The park was desolate. I turned the truck off and got out, opening the side door for Matt. David squirmed and whimpered. The inside lamp of the vehicle glowed dimly and I caught a glimpse of the guy's face. I barely recognized the boy I'd played army men with all those years before.

Using Matt's flashlight, I led the way to the trail, then through it, Matt with his arms around David, dragging him along the earth, the fishy stink of the inlet strong and putrid. We hit the first clearing, then arrived at the second, where several cinderblocks were piled off to the side—Matt had stacked them earlier in the day. David whimpered and blubbered, awful desperate noises coming from his mouth, but no real words. We stood by the inlet, listening to the water quietly lap along the shore. David struggled, tried to move, but Matt pushed the knife into his throat harder, puncturing skin, and in the dark night, when I shined the flashlight on them, I saw the glistening liquid drip down David's neck. "You fucking stay still," Matt warned, his face tight and gruesome. "Stop your blubbering." My brother's fierce and brutal focus unnerved me. I lowered the flashlight.

The sound of a small motor echoed quietly in the night. It was Pop, cutting through the water, moving the boat close to shore, stepping out in his high clamming boots. He held a loop of hemp rope that he chucked off into the sand, and stood before us.

"Come here," Matt said to me. He took my flashlight, handed over his knife, told me to hold David. "You're stronger." I did so but was shocked by David's fleshy body, soft and useless. He had no chance. Matt stepped into the chilly water, soaking his white sneakers and the bottom of his jeans. He leaned down and yanked the boat halfway onto the shore. He shined the flashlight on David.

"Hold him up," Pop said now, taking the knife from my hand. "Hold him with both arms."

I had my hands hooked around David's arms, my front against David's back, but keeping him from buckling to the ground was difficult. David kept sinking, his body dropping. He was squirrely with his relentless whining.

"Boy, hold him up!" Pop snarled at me.

I wanted to let David drop. I wanted to let go, but I did as my father ordered. I jerked my old army-playing buddy up to attention. David whimpered and cried but he did not apologize, or beg. He only whined, *"My mom, she's at home, my mom . . ."*

It's human nature to feel sick when someone is about to die—no matter how awful they'd been in life. They've done movies about it, books too, maybe it's even in the Bible. I'm not a religious guy, never paid attention in Catechism classes, so I wouldn't know. Still, there is this part and if you're at a certain age, like I am, you probably can just guess what it is.

Renee Regalo had promised my sister there'd be a party at the second clearing, or "the second spot" as the kids called it. "Bring that mix tape you made me. They got a boom box." She promised Dawn that Anthony Martino and Joel Rutherford would be there, because that's what she'd heard. "They were cool, you know, cute," Renee told the police. "And we just wanted to hang with them." But Renee had overheard the story wrong. The party was planned for Saturday night, not Friday. When she found this information out, she called my sister but my mother answered and Renee couldn't leave a message like that with my mother. So she assumed Dawn would figure it out once she got to the second spot.

Chuck and David happened to be out that night, sitting on the wooden picnic benches. The moon was full, bright, and they were smoking cigarettes, and they noticed Dawn, noticed her go into the brush, and they followed her because Chuck said they should. At the second clearing, they found her sitting on a log, waiting for the phantom party to happen. When the two boys showed up, she said hello, said she thought there was a party, and that she had to get going. The boys took their moment. Chuck grabbed her and knocked her to the sandy ground and both boys did what opportunistic young men and grown men had been doing to women for centuries. They kicked and punched and raped her and did other ungodly things with sticks and an old bottle that had washed up on the sand, Dawn's screams echoing across the inlet, the bay, but it was a windy night, the water choppy, the splashes against the shore loud. Even so, the teenagers who came out to party always screamed and cheered, and the people who lived along the inlet concluded that her cries were just that. My sister was alive when the boys finished and dragged her into the water. But she was unconscious and she quickly drowned.

Pop took the knife and held it up, the metal glimmering in the light Matt shined on us, and as I held David tight, so tight I knew that God was just as conflicted as I was with myself, my father drew the blade across David Ward's throat, deep and gruesome. David jerked, shook, then caved in on himself. I looked into the dark sky as I let the dying man slip from my arms onto the sand.

While Pop held the flashlight, Matt and me tied rope around

David's body, and looped it through the square holes in the cinderblocks. We did this quickly, without speaking, then loaded the body into the boat. It was Pop and Matt who waded out in the chilly water, waded out until they were chest deep, and then yanked David Ward overboard with his cinderblocks, and put him in a dark grave.

At the house, Pop drank whiskey and Matt drank beer. I stuck around until midnight, when I could no longer resist the urge to drink. I drove back up to my apartment, the moonless night alit with bright stars.

The dreams were relentless. Sometimes I found Dawn's barrettes and I gave them back to her and she smiled. *"You believe me, right?"* Sometimes I was a boy, playing army men with David, drawing lines in the dirt. Sometimes it was me who drew the knife across David's throat.

"You got no inner strength," Pop said one night, a few months after the killing. Things had died down by this point. Sure, Mrs. Ward had begged the police to find her son, reaffirming that he was feeble-minded, yet no one seemed to care. Newspaper articles on Facebook were a flutter with righteous comments of Karma's wrath and God's retribution. The cops, many who had either known my father from my sister's murder, or were the sons of cops who had handled the murder, questioned Pop, but they didn't question him hard.

"I'm just concerned," I said. "That they'll come after me and Matt."

"You ain't concerned about shit," Pop said, standing up and taking two glasses from the cabinet. He returned to the kitchen table where the bottle of whiskey sat. "You're just worried 'cause you can't handle it, can you? You felt sorry for the man."

"He was dumb, Pop. Low IQ. Stupid. He always was."

"You're too goddamned soft." Pop poured whiskey into both tumblers and slid one halfway across the table towards me. Saliva watered in my mouth. "Your former wife," Pop said, "she tell you you had a drinking problem? Was that the reason she gave?"

I glared at him.

"And you believed her." I'd never told him that I still sent Emily $300 a month, but I could tell he knew.

Pop reached across the table and pushed the glass closer to me.

"I know you're having inner struggles," Pop concluded, "but what we did was right, justified and moral." He nodded at the glass in front of me.

I wanted to get up and walk out, but I didn't. I picked up the whiskey, smelled the ferocious stink of booze, sipped it, felt the burn in my mouth. Then, with my father watching me, I drank the rest.

One Piece at a Time

David James Keaton

A week before I quit, I was balancing on the corner of a dance floor and getting drunk at another wedding, when the flower girl ran up to me, swinging a glow-in-the-dark sword in my face. She yelled, "I'm a superhero!" and I asked her, "Did you know superhero films are destroying American cinema?" And then she pretended to cut my arms off. That night I learned that the punishment for trying to dash the dreams of children was not knowing how long I was expected to pretend I had no arms. Apparently it was forever, because the flower girl started screaming when I didn't use my elbows on the steering wheel instead of my hands.

I drive a bus, shuttling wedding guests from the hotel to the ceremony, and finally to their endless receptions. But when the last of the wedding's stumbling revelers piled onto the bus after midnight and I pulled away with a hiss and watched the half-lidded eyes in my rearview mirror, I counted up the forgotten cameras and wallets and cell phones I would be plucking from the cracks of their seats, and I understood that stealing stuff from this job was entirely too easy. I was getting soft.

I've had fifteen or so jobs so far, and found a way to steal from every one of them. I'm not particularly evil or broke. Okay, at first I was sorta broke, making gas money by running an "open drawer" on the register of my first job, a rundown Putt-Putt where I handed out clubs and candy-colored golf balls. I considered it a public service to make sure guys who looked the most desperate around their dates knocked blue balls into the holes all night. But by the time I was chewing open corners of peanuts at CVS so I could throw them in the "loss" bin, I realized somewhere along the way this had become a ritual. I think this urge was hereditary, as my dad told me a story about my uncle stealing a car from a factory, actually stealing a *ton* of cars, or parts anyway, then reassembling a hybrid beast in our garage once he retired. Rumor had it he put it together all cockeyed with the ill-fitting, ever-changing styles of so many models, but the truth was he didn't have any idea how many parts a Cadillac needed when he first started this game at seventeen, and knew even less at sixty-five.

They tell me I look like my uncle, which isn't much of a compliment. He was a big guy, sporting one of those flattops that were so popular in the '50s, more due to the shape of our family's heads rather than our hair. My uncle was smarter than he looked though, and he got upset when people called him "Frankenstein," but even more upset when they called him "Frankenstein's Monster."

"I'm Frankenstein's Monster's *car*," he would correct them, which makes me a car's nephew? Something like that.

So I got the job in the fertilizer factory at my dad's behest. He said it was good money but long hours. Now, when I say "fertilizer factory," you might be dreaming of a conveyor belt of asses defecating into boxes nonstop or something. You're not?

My point is, this was chemical fertilizer, not fecal. Just these little toxic yellow pellets. My entry-level job was on "The Box Line," where I operated a hot-glue gun and sealed boxes once they were full, positioned under a monstrous metal chute where the pellets poured out. Every so often, one unlucky soul would climb the stubby ladder on the side of the chute and shake the grate over top the ragged steel maw until the build-up of pellets was broken loose. I say "unlucky" because even though the grate could be unhooked and rattled fairly easily, the heavy frame tipped in an alarming way, and if you were daydreaming, you could get a hand pinched right off. And this musta happened more than once, judging by the two prominent signs, one with the dog that warned, "Watch Your Paws, Assholes!" and the other that simply read, "3 Days Since Our Last Accident."

That last one was not an erasable board.

So it was easy but dangerous work, but because there were only two of us toiling at any given shift, I was hard-pressed to come up with anything worth stealing yet. It didn't have to be a big heist or anything. In fact, the least *tangible* thing I'd ever stolen was "time," but I was already doing this, at the urging of the old hand who trained me. So I just kept on squeezing my glue gun and laying lines of hot glue on the box flaps like heaping stripes of toothpaste, then sliding it to my partner who squeezed the flaps and counted to ten, finally shoving them down the conveyor and through the doggy door out to the trucks. My partner's name was "Joon," like the month but spelled wrong, an odd name, he admitted, and unusual for a boy, but according to him, not nearly as tough to grow up with as you'd think. He said made-up names these days were too goofy to bother deciphering genders for any effective teasing.

So me and Joon built boxes at a pace just barely above "inert," and we had a lotta time to get to know each other. Time I didn't need because I knew Joon's entire life story after day one.

Whenever I dreamed of factory work, I always thought I'd be given a pointless job (check!) that was mind-numbing and tedious (check!) that would position my body in a swirling cartoon of Rube Goldberg machinations, a nightmare for most, which would, ironically, inspire me in its solitude . . . and this is where things were rotten in Denmark. I'd never figure out what to steal from this joint if Joon wouldn't shut the hell up.

Did you know Joon had three cars in his life, but was never in an accident? Me either. Did you know that Joon once saw a man eat an entire wedding cake while hiding in the bushes? Prove it, right? Did you know superhero films were destroying American cinema? Joon was unconvinced. Did you know Joon was the most unessential human being ever to squeeze boxes and count to ten?

We did talk about his collections a little, as I had my own collection in my garage, where nothing matched, no rhyme or reason (which usually disqualifies something from being a collection). Just a little something I'd managed to smuggle out some doors. And with the uptick on loss-prevention these days, it was typically the back door you had to smuggle things out of, after you first threw it in the trash, then later rocked up in the dead of night to do some dumpster diving. This is how I got some good music out of Media Play, before internal theft bankrupted 'em, and how I got fifty boxes of Godiva chocolate out of Barnes & Noble—my most uncharacteristically lucrative operation. All that took was a fine-tipped marker (snatched from CVS), and one teeny number altered on some expiration dates. Then after a routine inventory, the manager became my unknowing accomplice, instructing me to roll the candy to the curb. I kept one box for the garage, now long expired for real, but managed to sell at least twenty boxes on eBay for fifteen bucks a pop. Godiva was popular around the holidays. Or "Go Deeeva" as the dumbasses called it. I tried to eat the rest but it gave me diarrhea.

Though it was worth essentially nothing, just to keep with tradition, I decided to swipe a box of fertilizer. But a box of fertilizer was too big to squirrel out with the trash, even if I managed to walk it past the security guards (security was surprisingly tight due to pharmaceuticals stored in the other end of the building). And filling my pockets with pellets wasn't just unambitious, it was unremarkable. Most men there shook fertilizer out of the collars and pants cuffs every night, judging by the dusting of yellow marking their paths like sad treasure maps through the parking lot.

So I'd have to think bigger. But on the box line Joon never stopped talking, not even to breathe. Joon probably developed this skill to acclimate to a lifetime of dull-ass work, but it was no less excruciating. I understood this was also a side-effect of two men doing a job meant for one, but this told me that my uncle had been wrong. Robots would be replacing us soon. And Joon would no doubt talk them into a rusty grave.

A week later, I figured out how to clog the grate. All I had to do was come in early and splash some of my coffee up there to make the mesh a little tacky. Then I convinced Joon that I couldn't shake it loose anymore, even when it was my turn in the rotation. You know how in movies when someone has to tell an elaborate story to convince someone to do something, and their acting is too good? I didn't have that problem. In this instance, my untrustworthiness worked in my favor. Because just how the audience wants a character to be convincing, it was easier for

Joon to go up and shake the grate rather than listen to me string together a bunch of half-ass excuses.

So I was well into a mental diagram of how to fold one of our long boxes into a complex, body-hugging origami and sneak it down the legs and arms of my overalls and home to my garage when Joon finally pinched his hand.

He squawked, and as I scrambled up the ladder to pull him loose, I would love to tell you that I didn't know what was going to happen up there, and that it was all in slow-motion and an out-of-body experience or whatever. But there was a good thirty seconds of me just watching as I saw the chute pitch to the right, then roll to the left, and head straight for his skinny neck. Maybe I could have stopped it, but I was too busy studying Joon's severed hand, which was holding my hand tight but free from his body. I could feel the pulse of its last muscle memory trying to squeeze an invisible box, and I couldn't help but wonder how it might look in my garage.

Then the squawking stopped, and when the grate slammed down again, Joon's head came off so clean, at first I thought there would be no blood at all. Then the blood came like a fire hose, and when I kicked a box into position under the chute with my foot, those yellow pellets soaked up the blood so fast and clean, it was as if there was never any accident at all.

When the dripping stopped, still in shock, I came down off the ladder, took my glue gun in my hand, and laid a big stripe of glue on the flaps of the box. Then I took five steps to the left where Joon used to stand, and I sealed it up. I counted to ten like he always did. Then I counted to twenty. Then I counted to a hundred as I finally had some quiet to figure out what I was going to steal.

Thinking back, I probably turned on Joon on Wednesday.

Wednesdays are bad enough, but that day I'd pumped some hot glue on my glove and it started to burn through to the skin. Joon reached over and yanked off the glove, smiling like he was the superhero I needed but didn't deserve. That might have been when I was officially sick of him, but I swear I never wished him dead.

But I had to act fast, and this meant some brutal decisions. I knew that simply by spinning his body around at the top of the chute, that careful tips of the grate would clip him into bite-sized pieces as easy as you'd nip the cheese corners to round off your burger. So I did this, and the blood poured down into the boxes pretty fast, but not too fast that I couldn't keep up with it. I sent parts of him out the cat door, sealed and soaked up and on his way to help some poor farmer's corn grow nice and tall. I daydreamed of Joon's ghost rambling in Kevin Costner's ear until he was finally convinced to build a hockey rink in a cornfield during an Iowa heat wave and ruin his life forever.

Some of Joon would go out the door in boxes, but the rest of him was a real problem. You couldn't leave with more than a reasonable bulge in your pockets, but I knew I could leave the factory three times that day without arousing suspicion. We were allotted two breaks and one lunch, and it was early. I didn't smoke, but I would today.

I hit the big red "Stop Line" button and started with the head. Go big *and* go home, I told myself. I put it under my shirt, giving myself a beer belly, and the guard didn't bat an eye. Then I found a soggy cigarette on the ground and fired it up in case I had to breathe on anybody. In my car, I worked Joon out from under my shirt and threw him in the trunk without even getting back out. That was the beauty of '80's Mercurys and their drop-down back seats. Easy access.

On my lunch, I took out his hands and his arms next. I was surprised to find those were the easiest. Hands in your pockets make shapes in your pants that are so recognizable that they're completely ignored. The brain can't see anything wrong, even if your actual hands are still visible and the math doesn't quite add up outside of a Hindu painting.

After that, I took my last smoke break and brought out his legs, stuck down my pants, then I ran past the guard like I was having some intestinal distress, which was true. But if he didn't wonder why my shirt was bloody, he sure wasn't gonna care that I might be dropping deuces in my car.

Last up was the torso, the hardest and the easiest. I didn't need it for my collection. Only a crazy person would keep a torso around. So for this I just propped it up on the toilet in the bathroom stall, locked the door, then crawled back out. No one used that bathroom but us two, so I figured I'd bought myself a week before the smell hit the rest of the warehouse. And the torso balanced on that seat perfect, too. Turned out our heavy butts were the most important part of our gyroscope, legs and tails be damned.

When I hit the button for the last time and the box line resumed, I got back on double duty and finished out the day. It was easy.

Like I said, this was never a job that needed two people.

I took all his spare parts to my garage, which had been my uncle's old garage, and where he still stored his car. By "car," I mean his rolling junkyard masquerading as a car. And it didn't look like anything of this world, of course, but that shouldn't mean you couldn't start the engine on any cursed thing with four wheels. Or at least that's what I hoped. It just needed to eat something first, a little fuel in the tank. Or the trunk. Either way.

Counting up all the pieces, my heart skipped when I realized I was somehow missing a foot.

I was a little nervous about going back to work the next day, but I knew that any foot would do. So I slunk back to the warehouse at 7 a.m., and when Joon didn't clock in, they sent me a twitchy WWII vet to stand in for him, some psycho named "Billy," and it only took half the day before I could sucker him up there to shake out the grate. I warned him to watch his hands, that kicking it loose was the only safe way, really, and when his foot was almost pinched off at the ankle an hour later, only to be removed at the hospital that night, I made sure to put in a job application at the Emergency Room. Orderly, parking attendant, whatever. The job is never important, just the collection. And if that World War II flipper was gone by the time I infiltrated my new job, I'd swipe someone else's foot. One thing I learned from my uncle was that once you realized you weren't bound by the rules of building the right thing with the right parts, you could dream of building any damn thing you want.

Despite all that hustle, our family legacy of completing the job finally got the best of me, and I was pulled over in my uncle's Cadillac on my way home from my first day in the E.R., busted for stealing medical supplies. The joke is, they didn't even notice the foot at first. The cop knew something was up right away though, even without the stethoscope around my neck. It's true that people will overlook an extra hand, maybe even an extra foot, but cops will sure notice an extra taillight.

A Boy Named Zoë

Lynne Barrett

Well, no wonder I grew up sneaky, with so much of me a lie.

I was Billy Carlow, a freckled Carolina boy, but there was a dreaming self inside me who shouldn't, couldn't, exist, yet somehow slipped out. I'd be on the playground in dungarees and a Tar Heels T-shirt when I was eight, and something about me said to other boys, you can kick that kid and call him girly when he cries. That'll be hilarious.

Ma got the idea I might be smart because I'd rather stay inside and study. I was good at memorizing Scripture, and for a while when I was ten I thought I'd be a preacher, because they weren't expected to be tough. My daddy, Bill Senior, wasn't much for religion, but Ma took me to the hard-shell Baptist church way out in the country where she'd grown up, and she was excited that the preacher thought I had potential. Daddy worked making cigarettes at Lorillard, and Ma answered the telephones at an office downtown, which didn't pay much but was "nicer." So when she said that if I wound up a minister I'd be a man to be proud of, Daddy just grumbled and had another beer.

That July our preacher took me on a trip to a revival up in the mountains in Virginia to show off my memorizing. I stood up and recited a bunch of Isaiah, and people made a fuss. But then that night, where we were staying, in a motor court cabin with twin beds, he started talking about temptation and showed me some naked lady pictures, and when my boy parts responded, he petted me some and then he hurt me, and everything was confusing and frightening. Everything was wrong.

And no way could I tell my folks. I was sure they wouldn't believe me. Or if they even believed me, they'd blame me, because I was weird and must have brought it on myself. So, after the trip, I said I'd found I was off religion and didn't want to memorize Scripture anymore, and Ma was upset, but Daddy slapped my back and said that was okay with him. He told me I could help him do carpentry in the garage on Sundays, where he liked to build shelves and benches, with the radio playing country music. I didn't like carpentry, but I did it and learned to use my hands and could recognize which song was whose. Daddy's favorites were Merle Haggard, George Jones, and especially Johnny Cash.

Ma switched that fall to the big brick Baptist church on Friendly Avenue, where her friends from work went, which, only much later, made me wonder if she'd suspected, but she never said a word to me. I endured carpentry and school sports and kept on memorizing schoolwork and tried to stay away from other kids. There was no one I trusted.

Then in middle school, I had Miss Freemantle for English. She wore her dark red hair pulled back into a braid she twisted up, and had thin, round metallic eyeglasses, which if you looked close had a lilac tint. She wore skirt suits with padded shoulders (this was the late '80s), and her well-polished high heels emphasized her ankles. I loved to look at her. We had a unit on myths.

I liked ones where characters got turned into something else. Like Ariadne, who bragged she was a better weaver than Athena which angered Athena, but then Athena acknowledged that her weaving was pretty good and instead of killing her turned her into a spider, so she could still make webs. Which I liked—it was a dark justice. I wanted to do real well on my myth report, so I read our whole book looking for a topic and saw it mentioned, just casually, that Tiresias, a prophet but not a Bible prophet, a Greek one, had turned into a woman for a while and then went back to being a man, a blind man who could tell the future.

When I asked where I could find out more on Tiresias for my project, Miss Freemantle loaned me a big hardcover myth book of her own. (It had her name written inside, Anna L. Freemantle, in beautiful purple script.) Tiresias was scattered across other stories, so I followed him through the index. I learned that he angered Hera because she caught him striking a pair of mating snakes with his stick, and she turned him into a woman as punishment. I didn't learn why it was bad to hit mating snakes. I was sure a lot of boys in my class would have done the same. Hera's husband Zeus was very unfaithful, which made her bitchy, so I guess she thought being a woman would bother Tiresias, but he seemed to have a good time and was a famous courtesan, it said. I looked up "courtesan" in the middle school library's big dictionary on a stand. It said a prostitute with high-class clients. I guessed a woman who'd been a man would really know what men liked. In another story, Zeus and Hera were arguing about who gets more pleasure from sex. She said a man, and he said a woman, and Tiresias, who'd been both by then, said, oh, a woman, far more, which for some reason pissed Hera off and she blinded him. But then Zeus, to make up for it, gave him the ability to understand the birds' songs and see the future. Or another version of the story was that Tiresias saw Athena naked, which nobody was supposed to do because she was a warrior girl goddess, so she blinded him, but then she gave him the foresight and the bird interpretation and also the ability to read visions in smoke. In the only illustration of him, he just looked like an old blind man talking to Oedipus, so you'd never know he'd had such an interesting life.

Anyway, just reading about Tiresias made me feel sneaky, so I could tell I shouldn't write my report on his stories, even though Miss Freemantle already knew it all. In school where we were, it seemed like it was risky that she was even teaching non-Christian myth.

So I did my report on Hercules. He was like a superhero, but there was one episode where he was forced to be a slave to a princess, Omphale, and she made him dress like a woman and do a woman's chores, so I got that in, but tried not to let on that even that excited me. Which it did.

When she gave my paper back, Miss Freemantle had written "Excellent" on it beside the A, and she looked at me with her big eyes watery behind her cool glasses. Kind of like Tiresias, she could see things, I thought. I wondered what she saw in me.

By then I was a thief. It started with smoking. I took singles from Daddy's packs and sometimes a whole pack from a carton. He got them at discount at work, and he drank too much to keep good track. I also would steal newspapers people left lying around, or sometimes a magazine from a doctor's office, and take them into the woods to read—not really wild woods, but out at the edge of things where we lived we still had wooded areas that hadn't been cut down for developments. So I smoked and read about far-off places and tried to imagine myself there, impossible as it seemed. And I'd look at pictures of female models and movie stars, studying their clothes and bodies and how they tilted their heads and used their eyes.

Of course I couldn't just go buy girl clothes. And a boy couldn't shoplift on the female side of a store. So on a Saturday I took a bus to the university part of town and found a laundromat that college kids used. I'd brought some clothes of my own in my knapsack, and quarters for a washer. The college kids sat outside, talking, not keeping watch on the dryers. So I nabbed a bra. Not a pretty one, just a white one that seemed like it wouldn't be missed. When I got it home, I knew it was too dangerous to put in with my school stuff where I kept my magazines, so I poked it up through the hatch in my closet that led up to the attic crawlspace where we stored things like winter coats and Christmas lights.

The next day, when Ma was at church and Daddy was doing carpentry, I arranged an old stool and my suitcase in my closet so I could boost myself up there. Late at night I'd go up and put the bra on (I stuffed socks into it), and sit by the old painted shut window at my end, and imagine I was Andie McDowell. I thought she was the prettiest, Andie McDowell, who was, like me, Southern. I wanted to be her, and I wanted to be with her. Or Isabella Rossellini. Or, sometimes, Miss Freemantle, now that she wasn't my teacher anymore and I'd moved up to the high school. I didn't imagine girls my own age, because a girl my own age would expect me to be a regular guy.

I'd started to smell bad and gotten hair on my body. And grew taller, though I was never really tall. The fuzz on my face changed, and I looked more masculine, but I also felt more sure I wasn't masculine, really, because I didn't like it. Still, I tried to be stronger in case I needed to fight to defend myself. I pretended to be a regular guy. I imitated them. They imitated each other, anyway, trying to be like whoever was the manliest. Guys are always fighting off their softness—though I didn't realize that then. I was sure I was the only messed-up person in the world. I grew my hair as long as I could get away with, which wasn't too hard. Grunge had reached us, and we all looked kind of ratty. Sometimes late at night I'd go up through my closet and get changed in the crawlspace. I'd stolen other clothes—blouses—no skirts. And then I'd slip out the window at my end that I'd worked on with Daddy's tools to open wide and not squeak, and sitting outside it on the little roof over our side porch I would be a girl, a girl with a dick, yes, but I'd brush my hair and put on some lipstick that my mother thought she'd lost and look up at the moon through pine branches, and sometimes, if the wind was strong enough that I could get away with it, I'd howl.

Of course, before long, I roamed. I got afterschool work bagging at Winn-Dixie, so I had spending money. I found a vintage shop on Spring Garden where two older girls worked who were into Goth stuff. They introduced me to Siouxie Sioux. And David Bowie. And many things. My new friends put powder over my freckles to make me pale and advised me on clothes and introduced me to other people, so I learned my way into a world I hadn't known existed all around me, though it wasn't what it would be in places we talked about, like New York and California and London. Let's not take too long on this part. The point was that my parents hated just the day-life parts they saw, that I had long hair and was wearing all black to school, which my mother said was Satanic. I told them this was because I was deeply into Johnny Cash, the Man in Black (who was kind of Goth, really), and that I wanted to sing, and could I take a girl I liked to a concert? And what could they say? I was turning sixteen. That was one advantage of being a boy. Boys were expected to get a little wild.

Until one suppertime about six months later, I came home

from work at the Winn-Dixie, and my parents were waiting for me at the dinner table, with no food out, and told me to sit down. Some friend of my mother's said her son (I immediately knew who) had gone to a party in Raleigh and had seen me dressed as a girl, prancing around. I had learned how to tuck my dick up, not with a gaff, just something friends showed me how to improvise, and wore fishnets. I was calling myself Ariadne right then, but of course I wasn't fooling anyone. And I sang, which was stupid since it made me more noticeable because I had a very deep voice by then. I was scared, but I couldn't find the words to deny it. My father, drunk and wild, raged at me, then pounded me, then threw me onto the floor of my room and told me to stay there and slammed the door so hard everything rattled.

I was glad to be in there. I put my desk chair against the door to block it. I could hear them: Ma said it was the Devil's doing, and my daddy said I was just a faggot and there was no changing that, but Ma said I needed prayer and guidance and she'd heard they had church-run places they sent you to fix you up so you suppressed the bad thoughts and felt the right things and were normal again and Godly. I could tell she'd win, because these days she always won the arguments because he drank himself into giving up. While they argued I quietly gathered up everything I could think of taking. Kids I'd met who'd run away had told me not to go off without thinking. You needed money and your driver's license, social security card, comfortable shoes, and things you wouldn't think of like extra underwear and socks. So I changed and filled my knapsack and gym bag. I waited till things quieted down to just my mother sobbing. Then I went up the hatch into the attic and out the window and onto the roof. I tossed my stuff down and jumped and took off running. I knew a girl who'd take me in for a night, and after that, I could only think about getting far away, before the church cure got me.

Well, the years after that I won't go into. A lot of adventures sound like fun, but generally it's one damn mess after another. The one thing I would never do, I vowed, was go back home. I learned to survive and figure out who I could trust. I was not the craziest person out there—in fact, in my world I was on the conservative (ha ha) side. By twenty I was living in New Jersey, working at a grocery store and getting my GED. Then—because I'd learned, helping friends, that I really liked to work with hair—I went to beauty school and got a job in a salon. I saved up to begin having electrolysis, which costs a lot and takes a long time to get through, and was worried that just that first step towards transition was going to be beyond my means. But then I thought, that means there's money to be made doing it. So I saved up to become a licensed electrologist in New Jersey, hundreds of hours of training in practice and theory, which included psychology, which I took to. I saw that electrology was a front line of transition because you can do it as a first step and see how changing your outside feels. So it's not just the technique. You have to understand people, as I try to do. My job is about being thoughtful and open to other people's confusions and gentle about different sorts of pain.

Today I call myself Queer and Trans. I had work done on my jawline, but when I tried hormones they changed my body in ways I found, after all, didn't feel right. I can speak only for myself here—you have to know yourself, as I tell clients. I backed off on laryngoplasty and kept my voice. As a kid I thought of myself as essentially a she, because the she in me was so forbidden, but I've found that the she where I am, she's in between. I'd like another pronoun. Of course, I've met people who disagree with my choices and how I view them, in all sorts of ways and from every direction, but growing up as I did, I distrust all orthodoxies. Legally, still, I am a male, but in my work and private life, I'm Zoë Carlow. (After Ariadne I tried other names that started with A, like Andie and Anna, then switched to the other end of the alphabet and found what feels right to me.) I'm striking—pretty would be the wrong word. Sometimes beautiful. But my voice is deep, and I'm not really passing. I'm simply Zoë: just turned forty, fit, and healthy. I gave up smoking when I took up electrology. I'm married to a woman—she's bisexual—who is cool with who I am, and we've discussed having a child, and it's nobody's business how we manage.

Once I left home, I never told my family where I was. If they wanted to, they could have found me once I was working under my social security number, my last name unchanged. But not long ago, when things got nasty in North Carolina and they put in the crazy bathroom law, I found Anna Freemantle was a librarian at the university in my hometown, with a listed email. So I wrote to thank her for introducing me to myth and told her about my life. She responded, saying she'd started getting her master's in library science soon after she taught me. She had married but kept her name, and now had three kids, one in college. I had to adjust my thinking. When she taught me, she must have been in her mid-twenties, because somehow she's only fifty-three. She told me that she sometimes saw my mother in the supermarket, and a while after that, she wrote again saying she'd heard my father was at home with advanced COPD, and wouldn't I want to see him before he died?

It seemed a terrible idea, at first, but then I thought, well, if Anna Freemantle is down there, maybe. And heard myself praising my clients' bravery all day. So I went. My wife stayed home. She told me she'd heard enough about them and wasn't willing to spend a penny in the state till it undid the law. In fact, she thought I was crazy to go, but I drove down, eight hours. I got gas just before I left Virginia, as I'd promised my wife, and touched up my lipstick and hair. And drove on. I was to spend the night at Anna Freemantle's house, but first I had to go home.

There'd been development all around, but I found my way to the house, still white but looking battered. I got out of the car and walked around to look up at the window I went out of. Then I knocked on the front door, and an old lady with silver hair opened it. I said, "Ma?" I was dressed in a black suit and pumps. (I've always liked that look.) She recognized me. She said that Anna Freemantle had called and paved the way. And that she'd had a lot of years to pray and think, and she couldn't approve of my lifestyle, but she'd let me in.

And there was my daddy. No longer big Bill Senior. He was thin and droopy and wheezing. Sitting in an old lounger, with oxygen nearby. I perched on the sofa and looked him in the eyes and said, "Daddy, my name is Zoë, who used to be Billy your son."

And he laughed with a wheeze and said, "I knew you were queer, didn't I?" And laughed again and blotted his mouth with a tissue he threw on the floor. "No praying that away, is there?"

And I said, "No." Thinking, you're going to die. Nothing funny about it. And I said, "I just came here to thank you, Daddy. I work with precision hand tools every day in my job, that's one thing. And you gave me your love of music that tells rough truths, that's another. And you and Ma made me sneaky and tough enough to get away from you."

And my mother stood up and told me to leave, but my daddy laughed and looked me up and down and said, "My boy."

Rusty Cage

David Corbett

One thing you learn quick in prison: Do your time, or it'll do you.

Some guys team up to pump iron. Others put the "con" back in economy, trading soups for smokes, coffee for sweets, maybe even dealing smack or hash. Others hook up with the appropriate tribe—Aryans, Spanics, Blacks—and eye-fuck each other.

Me, I ain't much of a joiner, least not since my village idiot of an accomplice decided killing a cashier might just motivate her to open the register. Earned me a Class A felony, minimum fifteen years. All of which seemed reason enough to keep to myself.

One day, about two months into my stint, I wander myself over to the library, pick the fattest goddamn book I can find, and decide to school myself in whatever the hell it says.

Book was titled *The Modern Mind: Philosophy from Descartes to Derrida*. Written by some professor at UT in Knoxville.

Yeah, yeah, I know. But like I said, inside prison, time messes with your mind. Keep it occupied or watch it come unhinged. I sat down at the table and applied myself to the pages.

Took me two months to read the thing cover to cover, and

that was just to plow through the words. Couldn't say I understood a tenth of what I read. So I went back and went through it again, and then again, then again and again. Two years on, something just kinda clicked.

First thing that truly, deeply registered was a phrase damn near everybody's heard: Descartes' _cogito ergo sum._ I think therefore I am.

Wasn't till I read that book for the zillionth time I realized what that actually meant.

Turns out it was a response to something Augustine said: _Fallor ergo sum._ I am deceived, therefore I am. Assume, Descartes says, that all our sensations and all our ideas are just a vast and intricate illusion created by some Evil Genius.

Now, you can imagine, for a guy in prison, that's a pretty goddamn apt analogy. Everything I think and feel and taste and smell is wrong, and there's a conniving mastermind behind it all.

Oh yeah. I'll see your Evil Genius and raise you a life of crime.

But that's not the kicker. Descartes points out that even if all that's true, the mere fact that you're thinking—_regardless of what actual thoughts run through your head_—proves you're really alive. You exist. That pinpoint of consciousness is your salvation. Your freedom.

Imagine the power of that idea to a man behind bars. It's more than just the usual rigmarole that the real prison is inside your head. Your whole mind is a prison, a cage, there ain't no escape, except for that miniscule, all but invisible flicker of light way back there. That's you. That's me.

The next big insight came from William James: What's true is what works. To me, that meant: Don't over-think it. Whatever you do to get out of Riverbend and stay out, fine.

That and everything else I read began to calm me down. Like

a weight got lifted—not quite like I was flying, but not like I was just clawing at air, trying to stop my fall, neither.

Come year fifteen and my first parole hearing, I aced it. They released me back into the world, by which I mean Tennessee.

Luckily I got a sister with a churchy streak who considered it her duty to take me in. Lives in this nice, forested neighborhood along the ridge overlooking Shoal Creek Valley just outside Loretto, about three hours east of Memphis.

Name's Joanne, big-boned girl with a heart to match, reliable, careful, kind. How she and I came to be kin, go figure.

I'd studied up on car repairs inside—man does not live by philosophy alone. Joanne's Silverado screeched like a gutted owl every morning when she cranked it up. I told her the serpentine belt had loosened up on her, and I'd fix it.

Took me less than an hour, guided by a video on her cell phone as I worked.

That pleased her no end. She had her little brother back, and he was different. He was quiet, calm, helpful.

Which meant I got to work on her points and plugs next.

I was out there in the driveway, fussing around under the hood, when a neighborhood girl drifted on up. Maybe eight or so, shy child, tomboy type, no bigger than a minute. Wore her short black hair in a Prince Valiant cut. Add to that picture a plaid shirt, overalls, hightops.

Didn't even bother to say hello, just hunkered down behind me, silent as a stone, watching as I went about my business.

From time to time, I'd turn around, gesture for a tool I'd laid out on the blacktop—torque wrench, boot puller, spark plug socket—and she'd pick it up, wait for my nod, then hand it to me, like a nurse to a surgeon.

Glancing up and around at the nearby houses from time to time, I could tell we were being watched. Ex-con in the neighborhood, folks spend a lotta time at their windows. 'Specially when I'm standing right there in the open, a child within reach.

This may sound strange, but I sensed in that little girl's silence an echo of my own. Sensed as well—can't say how I knew it—that she had a cage all her own, and was hoping I'd show her how to break out and run.

Come noon I was getting hungry, but with Joanne at work and no one else at home, I knew better than to let the girl follow me inside. I'm rehabilitated. That don't make me stupid.

Thinking I'd prime the pump, I wiped some of the grease off my hands and said, "Name's J.R. What's yours?"

I might as well have posed a riddle. She cocked her head, brow furrowed, eyes narrowing into mine.

"You don't need to tell me, you don't want."

That earned me a nod. "Rella." Her voice a musical little whisper. "Rella Finley."

I did this kinda shrug-and-nod toward the neighborhood. "Which one of these houses along here belongs to you, Rella?"

She pointed—three mailboxes down, across the street.

"How about I walk you on home so you can have yourself some lunch."

She shook her head like there was a bug in her hair. "Momma's not home."

"What about your daddy?"

"He don't make lunch."

That right there, ya know? Shoulda framed the whole damn picture right then. Instead: "Fair enough. Tell you what. I was gonna make me a sandwich, PB&J with some hackberry jam my sister put up. I can make two, you're interested."

Her nose wrinkled up like a curled finger. "Don't know what that is."

"Hackberry jam?"

She nodded.

"Kinda tastes like sweet tea. I probably got grape jelly or strawberry preserves you want that instead."

The nod acquired a bit more vigor.

"Which one?"

"Grape."

"Grape what?"

"Grape, please."

"You got it," I said. "Wait here." I turned toward the house with one last over-the-shoulder peek at all the busybodies keeping score, and went on in to fix lunch.

I dug four slices of wheat bread outta their packet and slathered on the peanut butter, slopped on the jelly and jam. What's the point of being free if you can't get messy? Grabbed two sodas and a fistful of napkins and headed on back outside.

Girl was sitting right where I'd left her. Don't get me wrong, I knew all this was risky, but think about the spot I was in. I just shoo her off, she might get resentful, and the resentful tell tales. Or say she digs in her heels, stays put, then what? I told myself: Don't fight it, go with it.

Sure enough, things turned sloppy. Wasn't thirty seconds before that girl had jelly glopping down her chin onto her overalls. I pointed to the spot, nudged a few more napkins her direction. No way I was touching that girl. No way I was letting her come in to clean up, neither. We both washed up with the garden hose, splashing our faces, scrubbing our hands.

After that, took me maybe two hours to wrap up, checking

the gap on each plug, connecting the vacuum lines, straightening the wires so none of them crossed.

Engine turned over fine, no backfire, no warning lights on the dash. Felt kinda proud, to be honest. Couldn't help myself—I lifted my palm, Rella did likewise, we high-fived.

So natural, so innocent a thing. And yet: palm-to-palm. Skin-to-skin.

I could feel it instantly, that lightning bolt of terror flashing through me. Who was watching? What would they think?

"Tell you what, Rella." I started gathering up my tools. "There's stuff I gotta do inside, make some calls, that kinda thing. But thank you for the help, keeping me company. It was fun."

Damn that little girl. Looking straight at me. Smile like a sparkler.

Wasn't till that moment I saw the bruises on her neck, like purple fingerprints where someone had gripped her by the throat.

I felt like reaching out, taking her hand, asking: What happened? But that, I knew, could not happen. Just thinking such a thing—given who I was, given the circumstances—was madness.

"Why don't you go on home now. I'll see you around. Okay?"

Imagine what it felt like, watching all that joy drain away, first the eyes, then the rest of her face. Like I'd just picked her dog up by the scruff, pitched it against a wall.

She spun herself around, darted off, running toward home.

You can imagine how that looked. To somebody outside the immediate situation.

"Rella! Walk, okay? Don't run. Can't have you tripping over whatnot, hurting yourself, hear?"

She didn't, or if she did it didn't make no difference. She tore down that street like I'd said something awful. Asked her to do something for me. Just this once. Our little secret.

Took a couple hours, but sure enough, just before supper, doorbell rang.

Her father was one of those soft, hefty men who think their anger makes them tough. Minute I crack the door he's got a finger in my face. "I know about you." Heat coming off him like a grease fire.

"Don't see as you could know much about me at all," I said, "since we never met."

"What did you do to my daughter?"

I remembered the marks on her neck. "Do? Not a damn thing. I made her lunch, since she said you couldn't be bothered. I let her help me fix my sister's truck. Then I sent her on home."

"That ain't what she says."

You learn to read a man's energy in prison. His was all over the place, like an overhead wire swinging free of its pole. Which meant he was hoping for something to latch onto, wanted me to give him good reason to take the next step. And normally, no way I'd've given him the pleasure. I woulda let him flail and fume until all that energy burnt off. But given what he'd said, the vagueness of the accusation, I couldn't just stand there, say nothing, do nothing.

All I could think of, though, was: "What exactly does your daughter say I did?"

"You know what you did."

That settled it. He was bluffing. Didn't even mention the bruises, which meant . . .

"You think I did something bad to your child you call the law, you have them come on out here. I got nothing to hide. Otherwise, we're done."

I stepped back to close the door. The finger flew up again. "I'm watching you. Hear me? This thing ain't over."

Yeah, I thought. I know. Nothing's ever over with your kind.

When my sister came home I laid it all out, told her what had happened and, even more important, what hadn't. By the end she had her fingers to her lips. They were trembling.

"You don't know that man," she whispered. "Ain't no end to his spite."

As though on cue, we heard a pickup rumble to a stop outside, engine idling. My sister went out to the living room, edged back the curtain alongside the picture window.

"It's him," she said. Her voice, like despair was too gentle a place. "Passenger-side window's down, and there's something pointing out. A rifle barrel. Oh, J.R.—"

"Call the police." Lofty word. Loretto's got like fifteen-hundred souls, served by four cops. Come nightfall, only one's on duty. "What he's doing out there? That's harassment."

My sister let the curtain drop. She wouldn't turn and face me.

"Maybe it'd be wise for you to go away for a while. Till this blows over."

So much for the thickness of blood. "This kinda thing don't blow over, Joanne. You gotta stand up, or it just becomes the way things are."

Finally, she turned my direction—wide soft face, framed by her straw-colored hair, pale as the moon.

"Joanne, I leave now, I might as well tattoo *Pervert* across my forehead."

"Please, J.R. Try to understand. Send me a number where I can reach you. Once you settle. I'll let you know when it's safe. To come on back, I mean."

Comes a point, further talk just postpones the inevitable. "All right," I said. "I'll pack up. When I'm ready to head out, I'll need you to go out and keep him occupied."

Like I asked her to set him on fire. "I'll try," she said.

Wasn't much to pack, I had maybe two pairs of jeans, three

shirts, a parka. Whole time, I'm thinking: He's the one marked up that girl. God knows what else. Small matter. What's true is what works. And sometimes a lie works just fine.

Once I had my duffle squared away I gave Joanne the nod, and she opened the front door, headed out to his truck like she was heading off to die.

I slipped out the back door and got my bearings, figuring if I headed through the trees, sooner or later I'd hit Route 64, where I could thumb a ride to Memphis.

Never made it that far. Turns out Ol' Fat Finley had friends.

I'll make this short, because it ain't pretty. They knocked me to the ground with their rifle butts, bound my hands, and put a noose around my neck, which they used like a lead to drag me through the pines to the next road over, where another truck sat waiting.

They threw me in the back onto a rough wood palette, slung a tarp over me and kept on hammering me with their gun butts, kicking me for good measure as we drove off, southeast by my reckoning, probably out Rascal Town Road past where Gable Branch joins Bluewater Creek.

Been raining pretty hard for several weeks that spring, and the creeks were running high. I heard the rapids once the truck stopped and they drew away the tarp, dragged me and the palette out through the pines and hickories and cottonwoods to the creek bed.

They beat me to my knees, blood running down onto the smooth wet stones, then beat me unconscious. I came to when the first spike drove through my palm. They were nailing me face-down to the palette, like a cut-rate Jesus. Each hammer blow, my mind went white. When I screamed they stuffed a rag in my mouth. Smelled like turpentine.

Once both hands were nailed fast, Rella's old man came

forward. Over the roar of the creek he shouted, "You think you can make a mockery of folks around here? Diddle our kids, laugh in our faces? Guess again, jailbird. Enjoy the ride."

Took four of them to pitch me into the water. How and why I didn't drown right there I don't know. But I bobbed up long enough to snag one breath before the current caught me and sent me spinning like a whirligig, slamming into rocks, desperate for breath, electric with pain.

I can't tell you how long it took because time became an abstraction, a thought in somebody else's mind. But I realized if I didn't tear free I was a dead man. I ripped first one hand then the other free from the rough wood, tearing holes in each palm big as nickels. Somehow got my legs beneath me and stumble-dragged myself to the creek bed, soaked to the bone. Collapsed face down onto the rocks while my lungs heaved.

Took a moment before I heard the snarls.

Took all my strength just to lift my head. A pack of wild dogs stared down at me from a low wooded bluff overlooking the creek, eyes yellow from hunger, teeth bared.

I felt around for a rock, one big enough to do damage, dragged myself to my knees, because I knew any sign of weakness would only invite them to attack. Then I reared back my head and howled, dragging the sound out of my gut like I wanted them to hear me in hell, feeling the raw sound tear up through my lungs and into my throat, daring the alpha and the rest of them: Come on. I got absolutely nothing to lose.

Or maybe it didn't happen that way.

Maybe nobody grabbed me outside the house. Maybe I got away clean.

And maybe I'm the one put those bruises on Rella's neck. Maybe that's not all I did. Maybe every word I've said here's just part of an elaborate illusion, a con, a scam, I'm messing with your head. I'm your Evil Genius. And the only thing that proves you exist is the fact that you're deceived.

Pick the version you think is real. Either way, whatever you're thinking, whatever you're feeling, let it settle in, let it lock in place. Because those thoughts, those feelings, they're the bars of your cell. That's your rusty cage.

What do you intend to do—break free and run? Or just do your time.

The Ballad of Forty Dollars

Tom Hazuka

Mickey Dykstra is an addict, not a murderer. The plan was never for old lady Duerson to die, or even to get hurt. She was supposed to be at the Senior Center food pantry collecting the weekly free groceries she could easily afford to buy herself. The last thing Mickey expected was for her to come home so early. No, not true—the last thing he expected was for a sweet, stupid grandma to not only have a .38, or whatever the hell it was, but to pull it from a kitchen drawer like it was a cheese grater and try to go Dirty Harry on his ass. If her reflexes weren't ossified by fifty years of Pall Malls and Southern Comfort the slug might have torn through his throat instead of hers. But a pop of adrenaline at the sight of that gat flashed out his fist like some badass ninja's. She shot herself and crumpled to the scabby linoleum, blood spurting from her carotid artery like some snuff money shot.

She lies in a heap beneath a grinning Garfield clock that's four minutes fast.

Mickey was an undersized linebacker in college, and the hit he put on Julius Robertson (who played a season for the Colts till a crackback block turned his knee into linguine) was the highlight of his career. Stopped him at the goal line on fourth down to preserve a win. Mickey jogged off the field with an ice pick of pain in his spine, made more vicious when his teammates mobbed him. Vicodin helped a little, Percocet maybe a touch more, but Mickey never played another down, lost his scholarship and didn't graduate. Two years ground past and the pain remained, like a houseguest from hell who moves from the ratty couch to your bed, drooling on your pillow.

So a simple robbery has bled into a simple murder, and so far Mickey isn't a nickel richer. He's not even sure where to look for money. Where do old bats stash the shekels when they cash their Social Security checks? They don't trust banks, right? It would be just his luck that this one did. He sees a ceramic cookie jar with a handle that can't be true, but somehow is: a grinning man in blackface with huge lips wearing a tight, too-short tuxedo, cradling a huge watermelon in his arms. What's in her back yard, a noose? Mickey checks in the jar for loot but finds only stale Fig Newtons. He eats two, and feels like a competent criminal as he wipes his prints off the handle with the Iron Maiden T-shirt he got at Goodwill for a buck.

Mickey congratulates himself for being smart and doing this job a few hours before the sickness will start. But suddenly he's shaking and sweating, heart burping against his breastbone as if he needs the stuff now. He stares at the crumpled crone on the floor. What he has done is beginning to register; this isn't some surreal video game he can reset.

He pukes the Fig Newtons on his Chuck Taylors.

Rinsing his mouth at the old-fashioned white sink with rust stains around the drain, he wonders if anyone heard the shot. How did he not think of that till now? His blood freezes as a siren blares up the street—oh Jesus, no Jesus—then Dopplers into the distance. Just an ambulance, fuckface, get it together. What's done is done so just get on with it.

He's almost out of the kitchen before he backtracks and wipes his prints off the tap. He rips four paper towels from the old lady's roll to sop up the puddle of vomit and clean his sneakers, then stuffs the wadded towels in his pocket so not to leave any DNA in the trash. He's seen the TV shows.

The wood paneled hall smells like an attic. Crooked, framed photographs line the walls. Creeping by, Mickey stifles an urge to straighten them. A few are in color, but most are from ancient times when the world was black and white. In the last photo before the bedroom, Mrs. Duerson looks about Mickey's age. She's sitting on a blanket at the beach, wearing a one-piece swimsuit and cat's eye glasses, sticking out her surprisingly stacked chest and trying to smile like a movie star.

Mickey tries to swallow but can't.

He wonders what his life would be like if he hadn't made that great play on Robertson, if he'd tripped or gotten blocked to the turf instead of being a hero for one afternoon. Instead of a monkey on his back, would he have a college degree? A good job instead of working nights behind the counter at Gas 'N' Go, alert to every sketchy character who bumbles in at four a.m., wondering if this will be the one who pulls a gun and robs him, or worse?

Somewhere he has a newspaper clipping celebrating his game-saving tackle, with a few humble quotes from him.

Why oh fucking why did that old bitch have a fucking pistol?

Searching through drawers he remembers the joke Kathy told him a few months ago, shortly before she dumped him.

"Why don't Mexicans like blowjobs?" she'd asked out of nowhere in the McDonald's drive-thru line.

"I couldn't tell you." This was surely going to be a dig at his friend Marisol, who Kathy accused Mickey of fucking every time her back was turned. Unfortunately, her jealousy was unfounded.

"Because they don't like any kind of job."

Mickey laughed, sort of. With a thought like a paper cut he realized he didn't like Kathy much.

"For sure *you're* not Mexican," he said. "You love blowjobs." She punched him in the arm way harder than she had to.

There's not one penny in the dresser, just scrapbooks and yellowed old lady clothes.

Mickey has to piss like Secretariat. The bathroom has a powder blue toilet with three cigarette butts floating in dark yellow urine. He lifts the seat, and with a grateful sigh adds his long, hefty stream to the vile mixture. He thinks about leaving it that way, but decides to wrap toilet paper around his fingers and flush.

Mickey would never carry a gun. He *hates* guns. Why oh fucking why did goddamn Mrs. Duerson have a fucking pistol? It's her goddamn fault. Nothing would have happened—

If you hadn't broken into her house.

Nothing would have—

If you hadn't been a hero.

Nothing—

Mickey notices a wooden headboard behind her bed. He slides the door and finds a Bible with a worn leather cover, a box of CVS facial tissues and half a dozen prescription bottles. Hope rises at the sight of the meds, but a quick check shows no drug he's interested in. He picks up the Bible, which might be an antique and worth something. A green piece of paper pokes out like a bookmark, zero clearly visible. Heart hopping, he flips to the page.

It's a twenty-dollar bill. Actually it's a pair of twenties atop each other, one as crisp and clean as a new beginning, the other wrinkled and stained like it spent a month in a carnie's underwear. He stuffs them in his pocket. Before closing the book he scans the page where the bills were. If this was a movie he knows he'd read some line that would change his life.

His eyes fall on Ecclesiastes, chapter 11: *Do good and give to them that need—God will bring all men to judgment.*

Are you shitting me? Really? Okay, so what. Probably every page in that damn book has some ironic line in it. Anyway, who's the one in need? That would be me.

He drops the Bible on her pillow. He figured on scoring a couple hundred bucks or more, but forty dollars isn't the worst thing that could have happened. Forty dollars will make life bearable for a day, maybe two.

The lady was old. Time wasn't on her side. Her fault for having that gun. Stupid, stupid, fucking stupid.

Mickey recalls meeting Kathy for lunch at Denny's, when she slid into the booth wearing a tight I'M WITH STUPID T-shirt.

"Trying to tell me something?" he asked.

"What? Oh, this. I'm only wearing it because it's pink and matches my nails. Don't you know anything about women?"

"I guess not."

"Stick with mama Kathy and she'll teach you everything."

"I just might," he said. Then the day after Easter she told him they should take a break to see other people, which of course she was already doing—in particular, doing his best friend, Joey Porter.

It was Joey who inadvertently put Mrs. Duerson in Mickey's mind as a source of income. Last summer they were smoking weed in Joey's Mustang and talking about high school. Mrs. Duerson's son was an assistant principal, a fat, balding prick named Richard who the kids of course all called Dick. Joey coughed out the dregs of a monster hit and smacked the steering wheel.

"Dick Duerson's the perfect name for that cocksucker. I bet his mama likes to do her son. No way he gets laid otherwise."

"Incest is best," Mickey said.

Watching a Cheech and Chong movie in his parents' basement last Sunday, Mickey thought of that night in Joey's car: that stupid pun, that son who's a sonofabitch and his mother who must keep cash in her house, and goes to the Senior Center every Tuesday to scam her free food handouts like some welfare queen she'd scorn.

Which is why he's here now.

Goddamn, his back hurts. So, he realizes, does his heart. The idea of passing poor dead stupid Mrs. Duerson on the floor is too much to take, so he decides to go out a back window. Before he does, though, he pulls the wad of paper towels from his pocket and covers his fingers to straighten that photo of her at the beach. She was young once, she really was, with a pretty smile and even prettier tits. Maybe she was even a cheerleader.

Crawling out the window Mickey knows he might get caught, might go to jail for a crazy long time. And he knows that the rest of his life will be a fight to remember a laughing girl in black and white, instead of a ragdoll corpse in living color.

Sunday Morning, Coming Down

Mike Creeden

The sun warm on his face, white light prying open his eyes, for a second, Tower thought it was finally over, that he'd died and gone to the other side. Focusing, he stared out the windshield at the ocean. The docks. The New Bedford waterfront—one of the few places he could safely park when he was loaded.

He stumbled out of the car and into the biting cold wind and walked toward the water. Late October, a few days before Halloween. His clothes reminded him of the date: old black jeans cut six inches too short and frayed at the bottom, construction boots blackened with shoe polish, a spot of blood on the toe, suit jacket inches short at the sleeves—Doctor Frankenstein could animate a dead body, but he couldn't find it clothes that fit. The stiffness in his walk didn't mean he was still in Halloween character; it was more the twenty beers and half as many shots he'd downed to scare away the ghouls. And the blood on his hands, which he saw as he bent to pick up the flyer.

He smiled, already preparing a story to share in testimony service. Of all the trash riding on that cold wind—the dead leaves and crunched-up cigarette packs and smashed Dunkin' Donuts cups—the one item to wedge into the fringe cut of his undersized jeans, a postcard flyer from the Bible church where he almost married the preacher's daughter and got out of this life.

Five minutes before ten, Tower was in his old seat: third row from the back on the aisle. Attendance was light that morning, which made it all the sadder. Back in the spring and summer when he'd been coming on the regular, you could count on no less than six doable and easily seduced ladies. Still, he got a handful of backslaps and greetings when he stepped into the foyer:

"Nice to see you, Brother Russ."

"Great to have you with us this morning."

"Well, praise the Lord, the prodigal Number Fifty-Five has come home."

Ten minutes into service, the church band did what two large coffees and a shot of whiskey couldn't: it woke him up. They kicked in hard to the last chorus, the snare drum popping like a .25, guitars chugging through a boogie rhythm, piano tinkling out the melody, bass throbbing, hitting you *right down there*, and the ladies—those tasty church ladies all bound up and sheathed in silk and smooth cotton—they showed Tower what they needed. Saint and sinners both, Russ Tower loved them all. The church girls, bubbling over with a lifetime of suppressed urges, they could just wear a guy out with sweaty nights full of screaming and clawing. You had to promise them a lot: go steady, get engaged, do a dozen street meetings before they'd consent. But the new converts—the deliver-us-from-evil-but-not-just-yet crowd—they reformed their ways more gradually. He picked some crusty blood from his knuckles as he watched one move.

Her name was Kristine Fernandez. She'd been coming around when Tower was with Mira Moody. Kristine was friends with

Leanne, the middle Moody, so Tower thought it best to stay away from her, but she'd brushed up against him on her way in, looked back and said "excuse me" with spark in her eyes and some tease in her voice.

It couldn't be that easy, could it?

The pastor strode to the pulpit. He pounded it with his fist and the vibrating wood thrummed until the mic squealed with feedback.

"Well, glory!" he said in that whiskey baritone. "Today is the day that the Lord hath made. Let. Us. Rejoice. And be *glad* in it."

Tower liked Jack Moody, and when he allowed himself to dream a better life, it resembled Jack Moody's. Jack was forty-five to Tower's thirty-six, but they had some things in common. Both big, handsome lugs who effortlessly charmed the ladies. Both had played football. Both had done things they needed Jesus to provide cover for: drugs, battery, armed robbery on both their sheets, a few sexual assaults that no one knew about on Tower's. It was in the later chapters that the stories diverged: Jack Moody married a prime Texas filly, fathered three gorgeous young church ladies, and pastored a working-class congregation big enough to tithe him a living. Russ Tower continued robbing and beating people and occasionally woke up in his car by the docks. But that flyer: maybe it had been a sign from the Lord. Maybe he could change. Starting today.

During testimony service, Tower shared last. He didn't go into a lot of detail because he didn't have it. He just told them he drank too much and maybe got into a fight and woke up on the docks.

"And I got out of my car and I walked toward the sea and I tell you, brothers and sisters, I thought about throwing myself into that ocean." Tower paused, milking the moment the way he'd learned to do. "And then I felt something blow up against me," he said softly, looking down the leg of his dress pants. "I bent over and I picked it up and—*Praise God!*—it was this flyer."

Tower reached into his suit jacket pocket, and pulled out the folded-up postcard. The crowd hooted in ecstasy.

It was only then that Tower allowed himself to look toward the front. Kristine was turned toward him, offering the sexiest, most promising smile he had seen in some time.

Pastor Moody waited for the shouting to die down. Then leaned into the mic and said, "My daughters are going to do a special. Mira, Leanne, come on up."

Tower felt the need to adjust himself as the Moody girls walked up to the stage. His year-long fling had led to his baptism, his tongue-talkin' and to a not-quite-public promise to marry Mira. It was there he formed the idea of becoming a minister. He felt some guilt for the way Mira had to lie to her father—to the whole congregation really—but she'd have been in a ton of shit if she admitted to screwing out of wedlock. It took considerable talk and bit of physical persuasion to keep her quiet. The abortion had been a tragic coda to the whole sad song.

"What's up, y'all?"

Leanne was at the mic, flashing her sexy smirk at the congregation. *Someday*, Tower mused, *you will lay with me.* Leanne was the one Tower really wanted. But she was with Kenny, the Keith Richards wannabe who directed the church band. She beckoned him over with a jerk of her head, leaned into him—an unnecessarily sexy gesture here in church, but the kind of shit Leanne could get away with. Kenny's eyes widened, then he nodded and walked back to his spot and cued the band. The song started with single notes on the guitar, the drums tapping lightly behind him, bass stepping slowly into the line, creating a dark soundtrack, a *Gimme Shelter* short of vibe that sounded nothing like the bouncy church tunes the band usually played.

The melody was still poking around inside his brain when Jack Moody walked up to the mic.

"Turn in your Bibles to the book of Judges. Chapter four, verses nineteen to twenty-one."

The crowd murmured. Jack Moody gave his *I hear ya* nod. "Leanne told me I needed to preach on this. Said folks here need this message. I don't usually do requests, not even from my daughter, but maybe the Lord's fixing to do something this morning."

Tower spent most of the sermon thinking about what he was going to do to Kristine Fernandez after he plied her with a chain pub hamburger and five or six beers. He ignored the altar call, watched a few regulars walk up and kneel and beg forgiveness, probably for jacking off to images of sinner girls while their fat wives lay a humpable distance away in bed.

Kristine approached him at the coffee fellowship after church, grabbing and no doubt enjoying his rock-hard triceps. "Kenny and Leanne are going for a picnic this afternoon. Lloyd State Park. Wanna come?"

He smiled and nodded. *Today is the day the Lord hath made.* Indeed motherfucker.

After church Tower went to the gym, then to the supermarket to get supplies for the picnic. In the parking lot, he noticed another church flyer on his car under the passenger side wiper. Another on the rear passenger door. Weird.

Driving down winding and rustic Old Dartmouth Road, he kept the driver's side window open despite the chill, blasting *Back in Black* to warm the air. Mira used to feel guilty listening to the devil's music, but she loved her some AC/DC, especially "Hell's Bells."

The park was quiet as Tower took the dirt path toward the picnic area. Dead leaves crunched underfoot, the air getting colder and colder. He'd weakened regarding the booze, bought a pint that he intended to mix with the cokes if they wanted any but, out of respect for the pastor's daughter and his dream of building his own church, drank the pint on the road. He sniffed, caught a faint burning smell in the distance as he stepped off the path onto the soft, silky grass of an open field.

Finally, he saw them. Two hundred yards across the field and to the left, a volleyball net, ropes loosening with disuse, the net sagging. Next to it, a fire on the ground, around which stood three people, dressed all in black with hoods. Tower's body gave an involuntary shiver.

What the hell is wrong with you? Tower thought. *Why are you acting like a little kid lost in the woods?*

One of the figures stood and turned toward him. The hood came down, dark hair tumbled out.

Kristine waved. "Come on," she yelled. "It's about time."

After they ate, Kristine wedged herself between his arm and chest, coaxing him into putting an arm around her. The whole thing seemed pat, put on, no hunt in at all, no fun.

Leanne's eyes moved from Kenny, to the fire, to Tower and back. She started kissing Kenny's throat. Tower got hard. Was he about to have a Christian orgy? He watched them kiss through the flames.

"Behold the flames of hell," Kristine said.

He turned toward her. She wore dark brown lipstick and lots of black eye liner, not exactly a holy look but a familiar one all the same. Light brown eyes with a promising spark of crazy. She was exactly the kind of woman he went for but he wasn't thinking about screwing her. In fact, somewhere on the drive over his purpose had evolved into something strangely wholesome.

He wanted to be like them, if only for an afternoon.

"Is it time to get drunk yet?" Kenny produced a fifth of whisky, three quarters full. He took a small tug and passed it to Leanne, who took a healthy drink. Kristine sipped and passed it to Tower.

"Just be yourself, man," Kristine said.

Tower drank as Kristine slid her hand down his pants. He turned and ran a hand up into her hair and pulled her head back and kissed her. She resisted briefly and then they went at it for a good thirty seconds.

When they took a breath, Kenny flashed Tower a sarcastic wink.

Leanne said, "Bra-vo" and produced another bottle. She and Kenny stood on the other side of the fire. She took a tiny pull and offered it to Kenny, who shook his head, as did Kristine. Leanne looked at Tower through the flames, her eyes drawing him toward her.

"Looks like it's just you and me."

She reached across the fire with the bottle. The flames singed the hair on his wrist as he took it. He drained half of it in one drink.

He woke up shivering. Above him, Kenny held the empty cooler, water dripping out, soaking Tower's face and hair and shoulders. Leanne stood behind Kenny, watching silently.

Tower grunted apologetically. He went to stand, but something pulled in his shoulders. His right arm was pulled diagonally away from his body, along with his left. His feet were spread and tied in similar fashion. What the fuck?

"About time." Kristine stepped into view. He looked over to where the net had been. Only the poles remained. They tied him up with a volleyball net?

"You can't hold your liquor either, can you?" Kenny said. He'd grown some balls now that Tower was tied to the ground.

"Gracious, I thought he would hold it all night." Leanne looked at Kristine. "How many did you put in there?"

Kristine shrugged. "I don't know, two?"

Leanne stepped toward him.

"How many did you give my sister?"

"I don't know what you're talking about," Tower said weakly.

"Yes, you do. How many roofies did you give Mira before you fucked her?"

He'd only given her one, the first time. The other times she'd done it willingly. But there was no way Mira had figured it out. Tower didn't want it to, but his old cockiness flowed. "I didn't have to drug your sister to fuck her. She wanted it. It was easy." He stared at Kenny. "She wants it too. Don't let her tell you otherwise."

"Shut up," Leanne kicked him in the ribs. Tower winced. Of course she'd hit one recently broken. He pulled but the ropes held fast. His shoulder sockets crunched. Be calm, he told himself. He'd been beaten up by thugs, cops, and once by the Providence mafia. No way three Christian kids could best him.

"What do you want?" Tower said.

"Justice," Kristine said.

"Judgment," Leanne corrected.

Kristine dropped to a crouch beside him. As she leaned over her breasts spilled into the 'v' cut into her sweatshirt. Her breath was hot with whiskey and anger. "We want judgment, Mister Frankenstein."

She reached into her sweatshirt pocket and pulled out a phone. She swiped and held it in front of his face. The photo showed them standing at the bar, him in the stupid Frankenstein outfit, her in some goth/bondage getup.

"Do you remember what happened next?"

He shook his head as if to swipe the memory away.

She pulled her sweatshirt down. "You put your face there. You licked my breasts and then . . ."

"A man tried to help her," Leanne said.

Tower twisted his arm, felt the scabs tear off his knuckles. "We had a fight."

"Some fight," Kristine said. "You punched him in the stomach and pounded his head on the bar. You led him outside, arm over your shoulder like he was drunk friend. In the alley, you threw him into the wall and he hit his head and fell forward and you hit him in the face four or five times as he fell."

"There was blood on my shoe." Tears welled in Tower's eyes. If this was what repentance felt like, he welcomed it. "Is he—still alive?"

Kristine looked over the trees. "I don't even know who he was. Some guy I'd been flirting with. I called the ambulance. I waited with him."

"Then she called me," Leanne cut in. "She'd been coming to church, starting to get right with God. The men out there aren't like the men in church. Although some of them pretend to be."

Suddenly Kristine stood up. She wore the same shiny Doc Martens she'd worn the night before. He begged for one of them to stomp his face. She got him square in the mouth, busting his lip and loosening a tooth.

The fire crackled. The blood flowed fast and he nearly choked on it. He turned his head to let the blood pour into the grass. Blood could purify; that's what they said. He pulled at the ropes.

"They're tight, Sisera," Leanne said. "The stakes are buried deep."

Sisera. What the pastor preached on that morning.

"We brought extra," Kristine said. "In case we needed them for . . . anything else."

As she reached behind her he couldn't help but think about the curve of her ass. He could never stop. She held a yellow stake sharpened to point, shaved off edges like hair along the blade.

"Call the police," Tower said through puffy lips. "I'll confess."

"And you'll get off," Kenny said. "Guys like you always get off. I got a buddy who's been in jail three years for hitting a guy with a baseball bat. You probably beat guys up every weekend."

"And assault women," Kristine said.

"And rape them," Leanne said. "Sisera."

Tower opened his mouth but Leanne held up her hand. "Mira called it a rape. I begged Mira to report it but she wouldn't. I told my father, said it was a friend of mine. You know what he told me?"

Tower shook his head.

"Vengeance belongs to the Lord." Leanne said. "You've done that shit with other women in the church." He shook his head, but she smiled. "They all talk to me."

"We didn't set you up," Kristine said. "God wanted this to happen."

Leanne continued. "When she showed me the picture and I saw that it was you, I thought about calling the police. You'd maybe do a little time, but that wouldn't make a difference."

"Because you've been in jail," Kenny said. "You were in Dartmouth with my buddy."

The baseball bat guy. This was more awful than he'd imagined. He knew it would end randomly, the wrong person crossed, revenge coming as a quick flick of the knife or a gunshot.

"Pat Harrington. He was doing OK. In for a simple assault. You got him into other stuff. Added three years to his sentence."

"Cute story you told this morning, Sisera," Kristine said. "The postcard blowing up against your leg. You didn't notice the one on your windshield?"

"What's Sisera?" Tower's voice came out in a whine.

"You never did pay attention in church," Leanne said. "Kenny, what did we read this morning?"

"Judges four. Nineteen to twenty-one."

Tower shivered. "Stop. It's enough. I'll go away. I'll turn myself in. Whatever you want."

"You will." Kristine bent down to him, kissed his bloody lips.

"You wanted to be like my father," Leanne said. "But couldn't pay attention to what mattered."

Kristine picked the whiskey bottle off the ground and uncapped it.

"*Please give me a little water to drink, for I am thirsty,*" Kristine recited. She squeezed his cheeks until his mouth opened. Beyond her, the sky was clear and dark blue and dotted with stars, vivid as a painting. She poured in the booze and he opened his throat and let it roar in. She tossed the empty bottle into the grass at his feet.

"And then," Leanne said, "the Lord tells Jael to stand by the tent where Sisera is."

"Sisera being the asshole who does what he wants and always gets away with it," Kristine said. She reached for something over his head. A hammer.

Tower moaned. "You're not going to do this."

She turned him toward her and placed her knee on the corner of his head, pinning it to the ground. The weight of her along with the booze and the terror created a rush as he imagined as a black, smoky cloud.

She placed the sharpened stake on his temple. "*And she took a tent peg and seized a hammer in her hand—*"

"Or volleyball peg." Kristine smiled.

Tower's eyes darted toward his feet. Leanne had a phone in her hand.

"Just call," Kenny said. "It's enough. He got the message."

"OK, fine," Leanne said. She looked at Tower as if he were a small boy who'd just shit himself. "I'm calling the police and we're getting out of here. The Lord can take his vengeance in his time."

But who can know the Lord's time?

Engrossed in the dramatic role she'd been playing, Leanne lifted her finger to tap the first digit of the number, and as she tapped, the phone flew out of her hand. Reaching to grab it, she stepped on the empty whiskey bottle and fell toward Kristine, still holding the spike at Russ Tower's temple.

The Lord's vengeance unfolded, swift and precise.

Rose of My Heart

Nik Korpon

His name was Ross but I called him Rose. I never thought to ask if he minded.

There were a lot of things I never thought to ask, things I should've before letting him hitch a ride on my train:

Will a bad person go to Hell?

Can you load a revolver with one hand?

Do you know how to drive a stick?

Do you plan to abscond with my money and leave me shit out of luck?

But now, with the barrel of a Remington .29 nestled between my lips, I really wish I'd asked.

"You got any idea who you fucked with, *puta*?" the man says.

I'd shake my head but it might chip my teeth.

"No, you don't. You don't even know that you don't know. What we do to people like you, *gringa*, we chop them in five pieces and leave them in the *zócalo*. Then hide the head to make people wonder." He's missing a finger. The remaining knuckles read LA REGLA—"the rule"—the ink more green than black.

"You got till sun up to bring me my shit. It's not in my hands by then, I kill you and your *güero* both."

Guess I'll get the chance to ask Rose in person.

Assuming I can find him.

I met Rose two weeks ago, at a roadhouse called The Painted Horse outside Amarillo. I was day-drinking mescal, the hang-dog Indian bartender keeping my glass full as long as I kept the bills coming. I asked him how he braided his hair so nice but he ignored me. At that point I was still pretty flush after hitting a check-cashing stand in Lawton, Oklahoma, four days earlier.

Rose sat two stools over, shuffling a deck of cards, ropes of muscle turning on his forearms, his thick blond hair curling out from beneath a Stetson. I was drunk enough to wonder what else he could do with those hands.

"You going to deal me in?" I said.

"I would, but it'd be impolite to take money from a lady." He pushed the brim of his hat up with his index finger.

"You think I can't play cards?"

"On the contrary. You could probably take a man's wallet, watch, clothes, and car, then have him borrow money to buy you dinner afterward." He gave me a big smile and I ground against the stool a little when I got a look at that jaw. "But I never lose."

"How about you drink with me instead?"

"I'm Ross," he said, holding out a hand. His forearms were covered in rose tattoos, all of them different styles—from traditional to jailhouse—and all of them terrible.

"Valerie," I told him. That wasn't my name.

"Pleasure's all mine."

"I like the way you talk."

Forty minutes later, I fell back against the vinyl backseat of my Cutlass, wrapping up my hair in a bun on top of my head to cool my neck.

"You learn that on shore leave?" I said between gasps.

"Nah." He lit a smoke, handed it to me then lit another for himself. "Catholic school."

I made the sign of the cross. "I might fall in love with you, you make a habit of that."

He held his cigarette between his teeth while he buckled his belt. "Was that a nun joke?"

After our cigarettes were finished, he held the back door open so I could climb out. I stretched my arms above my head, bent backwards and felt the Texas sun bake my skin.

"I'm going to wager you don't have a job," I said.

"Should I take offense to that?"

I shrugged. "The men I like generally don't."

I kicked the front door so hard the top hinge buckled. Scared the shit out of the poor girl sitting at the counter. Rose came in beside me, blond hairs still curling out behind the gorilla mask he wore.

"This is going to be real easy, girlie," I said. "You open the safe, put the money in my bag, then go back to reading sex tips in *Cosmo*. Got me?"

Her lips trembled like she was trying to think of a reason to protest. I cocked the hammer on my revolver. That made the decision for her.

Most times, that's really all you need. People dream about being a hero, jumping over the counter and beating the hell out of the mean ol' robbers. But when the moment comes, they realize it's bad enough they're a pretty girl working in a fertilizer supply store and getting shot in the face over that just ain't worth it.

She grabbed handfuls of banded bills from the safe and

dropped them on the counter. Rose swiped them into a gym bag, never dropping one, while watching for any farm trucks pulling in. Every motion was fluid, like he'd done this a hundred times already, and that thought made me pause as much as it made my blood thrum.

"That's it," the girl said. "That's all we have."

Her tone said that was the truth.

"I told you this could be easy." I stepped backward, heading toward the door without taking my eyes off her, expecting Rose to fall in line. But he rushed toward her and, for a second, a horror struck inside me, thinking he was going to kill the poor girl. Then he yanked the phone from the wall.

"Don't want any calls," he said to me as we cleared the front door.

He tossed the phone in the trunk next to the bag of money and we pulled out of the parking lot like the hounds of Hell were gaining on us.

That night, sitting on a lumpy mattress at the Thunderbird motel in Lubbock, legs crisscrossed and my skin flushed and tacky with sweat, I asked Rose how many places he'd robbed.

"None, why?"

"'Cause you took to that one like a fish to water." I exhaled smoke, pressed my fingertips against my neck.

"Was I too hard?"

"No," I lied. "Long as they don't bruise, it's fine."

"I'm sorry."

"Why? I asked you to." I dropped the butt in a can of Lone Star. "You telling me the truth?"

"About being sorry or robbing stores?"

We toured west and central Texas, hitting another farm

chemical supplier in Odessa, then places in Barstow, Fort Stockton, and Dryden—none of which proved to be worth the effort, as the drought had brought most farming to a halt—before hopping on Route 90 and tracing the Mexican border. In Comstock, I ate some bad carne asada and spent most of my time hugging the toilet. Rose would fill up a washcloth with ice from the machine and hold it against my neck, slicking my hair back off my face. It was about the sweetest damn thing anyone had ever done for me.

It took two days for me to find my feet again. By that time, the cash that had been flowing at the Painted Horse was down to a pathetic dribble. I reckoned we had three days before we were broke again.

I sipped at a warm Lone Star, hunched over a map splayed out on the chipped laminate table.

"I say we head north toward Fort Worth, then pick up 35 toward Oklahoma. Might be a little slower, but it's better than doubling back and risk hitting an APB."

Rose pulled a cheese-and-peanut-butter cracker from the plastic sleeve.

"Let's go south."

I considered it a minute, before shaking my head. "I've always had good luck in Oklahoma. We need something to go our way."

"I used to have friends down this way." His finger circled Laredo and Corpus Christi. "Lots of money to be made."

"We talking about the same kind of money?"

"The green kind?" He turned on that smile that made my knees go to water.

Something in my head said Oklahoma was the way, but then he hooked his finger inside the waist of my jeans and started tracing my hipbone. "You ever swam in the Gulf of Mexico?

Prettiest place you ever seen. Don't even have to wear anything, the water's so warm."

His finger went farther down and slipped inside.

South it was.

We stopped for gas outside of Del Rio, not far from the Mexican border. He went to grab something from the market across the street while I filled up.

The hose clicked off, but Rose still wasn't back. I parked on the side of the squat cinderblock building, scanning the sidewalks for Rose. A twist of black smoke threaded through the cloudless sky, coming from somewhere in Ciudad Acuña. All the problems they'd been having over there, I was surprised the whole damn city wasn't on fire. It was the same in most of the border towns. Laredo. Tijuana. El Paso. Anywhere there was space to fight for, cartels were fighting for it. That had pushed a lot of the crews into Texas, sparking off a whole new round of fighting with the local operations. That was part of the reason I stayed away from drugs—too much violence. The other part was seeing what heroin did to my mother growing up. I stuck to good ol' armed robbery.

"*Elote?*" someone said.

I jumped back and cocked my fist, ready to spread a nose across a face, when I saw Rose standing next to me holding two ears of grilled corn.

"I thought you might want to eat."

I hadn't realized how hungry I was until I smelled the food. "Scared the shit out of me."

"Got something for us." He grabbed my arm and walked half a block away. Still chomping on the corn, he nodded across the street. "Let's get the masks and get paid."

A short man with a thick mustache stood behind a small grill, turning food with a pair of metal tongs. The sign had prices in dollars and pesos.

"We're going to hold up a street vendor?" I shook my head. "I think you misunderstood something."

He set his hand on my chin and pointed my head to the left.

"A bar?" I felt my body sink. "Hell no. There's a reason I stick to small, inconspicuous places. No one I come across in a farm supply store has a shotgun under the counter." I pointed at the bar—which was sketchy anyway. "Those guys definitely do."

"I checked it out, darlin'. Nothing but a couple drunks sleeping and some field hands that aren't going to risk getting shot over a few thousand pesos. That's like, less than a dollar."

"That fast?"

"It's in my blood. My grandfather is Comanche."

I hated the idea of hitting a place like that, but we weren't far from sleeping in the car.

"In and out in less than a minute," he said. "Don't even bother with the people. Grab what's in the register and beat feet. It'll get us two days south and we can find some better places there."

I finished off the *elote*, and like it was a sign from God, my stomach unleashed a primal growl. The corn had only made me realize how long it'd been since I'd had a full meal.

"Fuck it," I said, tossing the gnarled cob into a trashcan.

We parked on the side on the road, then grabbed the masks and guns. Outside the door, Rose kissed me, bit my bottom lip so hard I tasted blood.

"Ladies first," he said.

I kicked the door in and started doing my thing, yelling and flipping over tables. I figured, bigger job, bigger front. The drunks never woke and the field hands just cowered.

But that bartender—six-foot-eleven, skin so dark his teeth looked like stars, thick Pancho Villa mustache drooping over his mouth—he looked insulted. And angry. I forgot what I was doing. Rose kept up his end, slamming stuff and making a lot of noise to show we weren't fucking around. He tossed the bag onto the bar.

The bartender looked at him for what seemed like ages, then said something in Spanish. Rose flinched slightly, then trained his revolver on the bartender. After a minute, the bartender unlocked the safe. "Your funeral, *pinche guero*."

Something passed across Rose's face. On the surface, it looked like a smile, but not happy. Not like it should've been when the job was within reach. This was deeper, darker, covered in blood and filled with screams.

Rose said, "The spirit of Buffalo Hump says burn in Hell."

Then he shot the bartender in the face.

Everything moved incredibly slow but hyperfast at the same time. Rose vaulting the bar. Us busting out of the door. We were on the highway, then a motel room in some town in southwest Texas. It could've been anywhere and it could've been nowhere.

I couldn't feel my body. Everything inside me was vibrating with the sound of that gunshot.

Then Rose dumped the bag on the bed.

There were so many bills they tumbled off the side of the bedspread. And not the stacks I was used to seeing—dirty ones and crumpled fives. These were twenties. Fifties. Some hundreds. More money than I'd ever seen in my life.

"Where did this come from?"

"The bar, darlin'." He said it with something like a laugh.

I pushed the money around, like I was making sure it was real, when my hands hit something buried underneath. I swatted stacks aside, and sitting on the floral bedspread were two thick rectangles wrapped in black plastic, grey duct tape holding them closed.

"Rose, what is—" The room tilted and at the same time contracted, like the walls were breathing. "I need air."

I slapped open the door and started walking. No destination, I just needed the sun to scorch my skin, something to ground me.

So I walked. I remember looking down at the sidewalk when I left the motel—to avoid eye contact with anyone. I had no shadow and thought that was some kind of sign.

I knew what those packages were. I had no contact with anyone in that world but still: *I knew what those were.* But knowing and possessing were massively different.

What the hell was I going to do? Leave without Rose? My money, car keys, and few possessions were in the room. Join him? No way was I was getting into the drug game. Existing on small stick-up gigs wasn't the most consistent way to live but it had worked for the last ten years. And besides: I didn't want to leave Rose. It was lonely out on the road, every motel the same, each room empty when I walked in. I liked watching Rose sleep. I liked smelling coffee when I walked out of the shower. That he fucked like a choirboy twice a day didn't hurt either.

So where did that leave me?

"To do what I do." I startled as I realized I said it out loud. A woman walking her dog stopped to look at me. I had to do the same thing I did during every job. Make them obey.

By the time I got to the motel, I was drenched with sweat and starving. I was going to go inside, lay down the law, then make Rose take me out for tacos.

And as my knuckles rapped against the door, my eyes looking out at the parking lot, I remembered thinking, *Where the hell is my Cutlass?*

Then the door flew open. It was not Rose.

*

The big brown man motions for his men to leave. He stops when he gets to the door.

"You're lucky Osiel called me. I don't kill women. My *abuela* raised me different. But all these *pinches malditos*, they're savages. They fuck you then kill you then maybe fuck you again. ¿*Entiendes?*"

"I understand." My voice quivers. I tell myself to buck the fuck up. "If it means anything, I left as soon as I saw the drugs. I don't cotton to that."

He stares at me for a long minute and his eyes are absolutely terrifying.

"It don't." He points the gun at me. "You find your *güero*. Find my shit. Find your way north. You're banned from Texas."

I stand in the middle of the room after they leave, my legs trembling, willing myself not to puke on the carpet. Then the trembling from fear becomes trembling from rage. That motherfucker ripped me off. Stole from me. I told him I didn't want to go south and he talked me into it. I told him I didn't want to hit the bar and he talked me into it.

But why? I start pacing the room, blood pounding in my fists. Before I realize what I'm doing, I feel a crunch against my knuckles. My arm is sticking through the cheap bathroom door, halfway to my elbow. I definitely need to leave here, like ten minutes ago.

I reach down to grab my purse from the carpet when a glimmer catches my eye. I snatch it up, cup it in my palm. A matchbook with *The Painted Horse* in gold lettering.

And it all hits me. Rose being sure the bar was fine, *his grandfather was Comanche*, the way he handled himself.

Goddamn, you are stupid, woman. Mescal and a good dick'll do that to you, I suppose.

At least I know where I'm headed now.

*

I step inside the Painted Horse. Light streams through the windows, catching the motes of dust. There's a man behind the bartender, a gringo younger than me.

Like last time, the place is mostly empty. One man sitting in the corner, eating a plate of rice and beans with a beer to the side.

And sitting at the bar, shuffling those same cards, is my Rose.

I straddle the stool next to him and order a mescal. "Most expensive you got, and make it a double." I hook my thumb at Rose. "He's paying."

Rose won't look at me but he nods okay to the bartender.

"Didn't think I'd see you again," Rose finally says, hands still moving, arranging cards, setting them wherever he needs to pull off his trick.

"I've survived a lot worse things than a two-day bus ride from Del Rio. Though I think someone killed a chupacabra around San Angelo and left it in the toilet."

The bartender sets my drink down. "Best we got. Made by a woman in town." He goes into the back.

Rose clears his throat. "You told me the day we met that you liked the way I talked."

"I did." I sip at my mescal and it's like *cielo* in my *boca*. "But I should've listened to my grandmother."

Rose finally looks at me, cocks his eyebrow.

"'Silver tongue,' she'd say, 'means coal heart.'"

Rose resumes shuffling. "Sounds like a Catholic thing."

I swallow the rest of my drink. I won't miss Texas, but I will miss this mescal. "I could've loved you, you know."

Rose doesn't have any kind of response. I didn't think he would, but some kind of platitude would be nice. Guess that's his way.

"I just wanted you to know that." I pull the Ruger from my purse and set it against his head. "It's important to know."

I pull the trigger and the bar is splattered with red, shards of white skull, gelatinous bits of grey matter.

The man in the corner falls off his chair, ducks under the table. The bartender comes racing out from the back, an axe handle in hand. I point the Ruger at him. He drops the wood, holds his hands up.

"This is not meant for you," I tell him.

He falters a moment, glancing down beneath the bar.

"Don't be stupid, kid. Go into the back a spell."

Hands still up, he retraces his step.

When he's gone, I vault over the bar and snatch the sawed-off sitting on the cooler, pop out the shells and drop them in my purse, then smash the barrel against the bar until it's too bent to use. I grab the duffel bag beneath the bar, take out the drugs and drop them in the cooler, then sling the bag over my shoulder. I start to leave but pause a second. I nestle the bottle of mescal into the money, then climb over the bar and give my Rose one last look before I head out into the desert.

Missouri Waltz

Sarah M. Chen

Lorraine closed her eyes, the last stanza of "Killing Me Softly" always getting to her. Making her want to laugh and cry at the same time. The whooping of the crowd told her she'd done good.

Baby, I wouldn't do it any other way. That's what she'd always tell Darius. Back in Chicago. Before she caught him with that woman. The last time, not the first.

He was just like her daddy. A sucker for the songbirds. Some would say she had daddy issues, worming their way inside her head.

Turned out they were right.

"Sing 'Lean on Me'!" someone from the far end of the covered patio yelled, jolting her from her thoughts.

"What's that now?" She shielded her eyes with her hand, peering into the crowd. Barely visible with the string lights hanging from the rafters like fireflies. "You know the rules, baby. Ain't no yelling up in here. Use your spelling skills." She nudged the Mason jar with a sandaled foot. It overflowed with folded napkins and torn paper.

Ernie, her keyboardist, reached into the song jar and handed

Lorraine a scrap of paper. She was about to read it when she saw him. Seated way in the back. Her daddy had come to see her. As she'd been prayin' he would.

Lorraine saw her daddy exactly three times in her life. Those moments ingrained in her mind forever, like a nasty scar.

The first time he'd rolled down the street around midnight in a beat-up car that whined and spat. Made her get out of bed and come running outside in her pajamas to see what in the world was hollerin' so loud. When the yellow Chevy turned into their driveway and a tall lanky man with coal-black skin and shiny white teeth emerged from the car, Lorraine thought he was beautiful. He winked and asked her how old she was. He cradled a shoebox in one arm. She held up five fingers.

The man said that was a fine age, and, boy, she was all grown up. When her mama shouted at him from the front door to get lost, hands on narrow hips, the man laughed and said she don't mean that. He handed Lorraine the shoebox, but before she could looked inside, her mama charged down the cracked driveway and snatched it away.

"Don't give her nothin' I don't know about," she fumed.

"She'll dig it," the man said. "I know my baby girl." He winked at Lorraine again and she giggled. He smelled like cigarettes and spices.

Her mama shooed Lorraine inside the house. She peered at them through her bedroom window. They shouted and circled one another like buzzing wasps. Then they got all quiet and her mama started crying. The man wrapped his long arms around her and pulled her close, bringing her inside.

Lorraine didn't sleep a wink that night. She heard grunting and laughing through the thin walls. Then thumping, slapping, and muffled crying. Eventually silence.

The next morning, her daddy was gone. A hint of cigarette smoke still floating in the air. Lorraine's mama refused to get out of bed for two days. Eventually, she got up and shuffled around the musty house, her shabby robe hanging open, exposing a bruised body underneath.

When Lorraine complained they had no food and no milk, her mama told her to go to the store. She reached for the Folgers coffee can on top of the fridge. It toppled to the kitchen tile, landing with a hollow, tinny sound. Her mama tore off the plastic lid and crumpled to the floor with an agonizing shriek. She beat the sticky linoleum with her fists.

"Fucking bastard! I'll kill him!" She threw the empty can across the kitchen. Sobs racked her body.

Her mama pulled that coffee can down every night after dragging herself home from a twelve-hour day cleaning houses. She'd carefully fold up the money, rubber banding it, sealing the can shut. Now they had to start all over.

"Is he my daddy?" Lorraine had to know.

It was the wrong time to ask. Her mama leaped up and smacked Lorraine so hard across the face, she stumbled backwards, crashing into the stove. Her mama's tired face twisted with rage.

"Don't ever call him that. You have no daddy."

But Lorraine didn't believe her.

The second time, Lorraine was fourteen. Again he showed up at the house at midnight, this time in a fancy red convertible. He yelled, "Violet, baby!" Her mama stood in the doorway with a shotgun and screamed if he didn't get off her goddamn property, she'd blow his fucking head off. Lorraine peeked out her window just in time to see him, in an ill-fitting suit, swagger up the driveway with a grin. Violet pointed the gun at his feet and got a shot off. He yelped, grabbing his foot, and staggered back to the car, leaving a trail of blood.

"You fucking shot my foot!" he shouted.

"Next time, I'll aim for your balls, you cocksucker," Violet screeched. "Stay the fuck away from this house and Lorraine or I'll kill you."

Violet died three months later from a brain aneurysm. When Lorraine cleaned out her mother's things, she found the shoebox he'd brought her. She'd forgotten about it. Inside was a mixed tape labeled "For My Sweet Lorraine." She brought it to her grandma's house, her new guardian.

Lorraine played that tape with songs like "At Last" and "Backlash Blues" over and over. They reminded her of her daddy, but when she sang along shame washed over her. What would her mama think? Pining for a man her mama swore was a wife-beatin,' whorin,' thievin,' sonofabitch.

But Lorraine couldn't stop. She sang in her grandma's kitchen. The church choir and school talent shows. St. Louis nightclubs and, eventually, a recording studio in Chicago. That's where she met Darius. A man who turned out to be like her daddy. Only worse.

Ernie nudged her. She turned to him. He raised his eyebrows. "You gonna tell us the song?"

Lorraine realized she had the paper in her hand, holding it in front of her like names for a "thank you" speech. She searched the back of the club where she spotted her daddy. He was shrouded in shadow and cigarette smoke. Then he shifted on the bar stool and Lorraine could make out plump cheeks and a mustache. About ten years too young and fifty pounds too heavy to be her daddy.

Disappointment flooded through her but she shook it off. Reminded herself she was on stage.

"Superstition," she announced. "Last song of the night."

The crowd clapped and hollered in anticipation. The bartender yelled for last call. The drummer started up the beat and Lorraine nodded her head to the rhythm. Same song the last time she saw her daddy. Six years ago. Right here at Bessie's.

Lorraine had been twenty-six then. The prime of her career. She'd noticed right away the man groovin' to the beat, singing along with her. His suit hung loosely on his thin frame like sheets on a clothesline.

It was as if he sang directly to her, like his voice reached out and squeezed her chest. When she finished, he clapped louder than anyone else. He strutted to a bar stool with a slight limp and sat down. He lit a cigarette and gazed directly at Lorraine. Then he winked.

She yelled for a break and threaded through the tables until she towered over him. He leaned back, his bony elbows on the bar propping him up. She wanted to slam his head down on the beer-stained oak.

"My sweet Lorraine," he said. His voice was raspy and when he grinned, she saw his once-beautiful white teeth were mottled brown and yellow. His skin looked dull and ashen.

"What are you doing here?" She didn't want to reveal how much his presence rattled her but her shaking voice hid nothing. She clenched her fists, nails digging into palms.

"You know who I am?" her daddy asked, sucking on a cigarette.

"I know who you are." She wanted to squeeze his scrawny neck until his tongue lolled out and his eyes rolled back. Thrash him around and toss him behind the bar like a dirty rag. Tell him he was a fucking cocksucker for driving her mama to an early grave.

But she also wanted to cry. And hug him and tell him she thought of him every time she sang. How the tape he made her got so worn out that it stretched thin and broke.

He gestured to the stage. "I knew you'd be the best. St. Louis' songbird. Got them pipes from your daddy." He thumped his chest, releasing a strangled cough.

Lorraine stiffened. "You've got fuckall to do with this. This is *my* hard work."

His smile fell and he shook his head. "But that manager of yours. Darius." He continued as if she hadn't said anything. "He ain't good. You gotta get rid of that one."

She leaned over him, the stench of cigarettes and whiskey assaulting her. "You have no right to come up in here and talk to me like that. Tellin' me what to do."

Her daddy didn't seem to be listening. He stared at her left hand and pointed. "What you got there? You marryin' that thug?"

She looked down at her ring finger. The big rock glittering despite the club's dim lights. Darius had given it to her last week. Went down on one knee and everything. "None of your goddamn business," she said. The fact he knew so much about her, about Darius, pissed her off. "Get out. I don't want you in here."

He chuckled. "I ain't goin' nowhere. It's a free country. I came to hear my baby girl sing."

"Then my set's over." She spun around but he grabbed her arm and winched her back. He was strong for such a frail-looking man.

"Hold on there now, girl." His face shone with desperation. "I want to ask you something."

"I don't want to hear nothin' you have to say. All you want is money, am I right?"

Her daddy shook his head. "Nah, it's not like that."

Lorraine pulled her arm but he latched on tight. "The hell it's not. Let go of me."

"Miss Lorraine, there a problem?"

They both looked up to see Freddy, the bouncer, looming over them. His biceps, glistening in the Missouri humidity, bulged out of his tight T-shirt.

Her daddy released her arm, seeming to shrink inside his suit. "Okay, okay. Can we start over?"

Lorraine hesitated. She could say all right. Sit down and join him for a drink. Hear what he had to say. She'd ask him things like, did he love her mama? Did he know she died? They could start fresh. He was here, wasn't he? Maybe he didn't want money.

"He's just leaving," she said, coldness in her voice. Her daddy looked at her with broken eyes. Lorraine pursed her lips. "Right now."

"Gotta finish my drink first." He lifted a tumbler to his mouth and sucked down the rest of the whiskey, ice cubes rattling, making a big show of it. He stood up. "Lorraine, baby. You makin' a big mistake." He leaned toward her.

"Just go!" She spun around and headed back to the stage, the commotion of Freddy throwing her daddy out of the club behind her. She didn't want to look back. She couldn't.

The applause brought her back. Ernie held up the bucket as people crowded to the stage, money stretched out. He murmured thanks to every dollar. People milled around, settling their tab as they made their way to the exit in the back.

Lorraine was exhausted. It was time to head out. Call it a night and chalk it up as a failure.

"Don't look so down, Miss Lorraine. We made a killing tonight," Ernie said. He handed her a wad of cash.

"Keep it," she said. "Buy something nice for your girl."

"What you talking about?"

But she ignored Ernie and the rest of the band as she walked to the side exit. Two men wearing cheap suits and gun belts framed the doorway, faces grim as they watched her approach. She stopped in front of them. One she recognized as the man she mistook for her daddy earlier.

The other one with sandy-brown hair and pock-marked skin flashed her a badge. "Lorraine Knox?"

"Yes?"

"I'm Detective Miscavage. Chicago P.D." He pointed to the other officer. "This here's Officer Brixton. St. Louis." The cop nodded at her.

"About time y'all showed up. I killed the son of a bitch two days ago."

The cops looked at each other. Detective Miscavage cleared his throat. "You're under arrest for the murder of Darius Knox." A pair of handcuffs came out. Officer Brixton gently turned Lorraine around, moved her hands behind her back, and the Chicago detective snapped the cuffs on her wrists.

She caught Ernie and the other band members staring at her, uncertainty and shock on their faces. She shook her head and smiled. *Don't you worry, I'm all right.*

"You sure made this easy for us, Mrs. Knox," Detective Miscavage said. They escorted her through the alley, down to the street. Flyers announcing "St. Louis' one and only, Miss Lorraine, is back!" littered the sidewalk. A St. Louis Police Department vehicle parked at the curb.

"Ain't no point in hiding," she said. "I'm glad he's dead."

The fists had come flying when Darius arrived home early. She'd just walked out the front door, purse in hand, luggage by her car. Fed up with his whores and his terrifying rage.

"Where you think you're goin,' bitch?" With lightning speed, he punched her in the gut until she collapsed, heaving to catch a breath, purse clutched to her chest. He dragged her back inside the house by her ankle as she thrashed and screamed.

All it took was one shot to the back of the head. With his gun she'd stolen, tucked inside her bag. Blood, brain, and bits of bone splattered all over her and the entryway tile.

She'd driven through the night, down to St. Louis. To her home. To Bessie's.

Detective Miscavage guided her into the backseat of the police car. Slammed the door shut. She gazed out at the club. It looked dejected and lonely without the crowds, the applause, the drinks slamming on the tables. She wanted to remember Bessie's but not like this.

Same with her daddy. She'd been hoping he'd come see her tonight. All she could remember over the years was the desperation and hurt on his face. She wanted to change that. If he'd been here tonight, she would have said, "Daddy, what'd you want to ask me?"

Then she would have told him he was right. Right about Darius and a lot of things.

The two cops climbed into the front seat. Officer Brixton sat behind the wheel, turned around.

"You did a good set, Miss Lorraine," he said.

She nodded. "I appreciate it."

They pulled away from the curb and Lorraine leaned back in the seat. Thinking of her daddy and how there'd be another time. There had to be.

Hurt

Terrence McCauley

The tracking device had led James Hicks here.

He killed the headlights half a block before turning into the dark alley between the warehouses.

He took his foot off the gas and let the Buick roll through the darkness. The security lights from the warehouse complex next door offered just enough light to steer by.

He checked his dashboard screen. A live shot from the University satellite miles above the earth confirmed that no one was guarding the alley or on the rooftop. The loading bay gates were chained and had rusted shut decades ago. He toggled the screen back to the city's records for the warehouse. They confirmed the only way into the abandoned building was a service entrance door in the alley. The electricity to the building had been cut years ago. The building was completely dark, yet the beacon on Harriman's handheld had led him here.

Hicks threw the Buick into park next to the service entrance, but kept the motor running. He'd need to get out of there fast in the likelihood that things went to shit.

The Vanguard had taken Steve Harriman for a reason. Hicks knew they wouldn't let him go without a fight.

In fact, he was counting on it.

Hicks slipped his night-vision goggle harness onto his head, but left the goggles pointing up. He wouldn't flick them down until he was in the darkness of the warehouse. He got out of the car as he pulled the Ruger .454 from his shoulder holster, then gently pushed the car door shut with a quiet click. Just because no one was standing guard outside didn't mean someone wasn't on the other side of the service door keeping watch. No need to tip his hand any more than he already had. Steve Harriman deserved every break he could give him. He'd already gotten the poor kid into enough trouble already.

Young Harriman had proven to be a good operative in his short time with the University. He'd been eager to prove himself in the field several times, which was why Hicks agreed to let him attempt an infiltration of the Vanguard two months before. Things had gone well and the kid was a natural undercover man. It was an opinion Hicks had held right up until Harriman missed his first check-in that day. Then his second. And his third.

Hicks knew from experience that field agents often missed a check-in or two for a variety of reasons. They couldn't get away or things unfolded too fast to keep track of time. It was the nature of undercover work. But missing three in a row without any communication at all made Hicks worry. Especially where the Vanguard was concerned.

The signal from Harriman's handheld hadn't moved from the abandoned warehouse in over two hours. The Vanguard weren't fools. They knew Hicks would be tracking him and should've gotten rid of the phone.

Hicks knew something must have gone wrong. The fact that

they hadn't gotten rid of Harriman's phone meant they had wanted someone to come for him.

And that was exactly what Hicks intended to do.

He only hoped it wasn't too late for Harriman.

Hicks moved around the Buick and took up a position against the warehouse wall next to the service entrance doorway. He stopped to listen for sounds from inside like a scuffing of boots on concrete, the click of a round being chambered or a safety being thumbed off. A muffled curse or the squawk of a radio. That nearly imperceptible silence that happens right before the shooting starts.

But all Hicks heard was the chilled night wind in his ears.

He reached out and slowly wrapped his fingers around the doorknob, fully expecting the door to burst open at any second, followed by Vanguard security forces spilling into the alley. He held the Ruger ready for that eventuality. Most people wouldn't have chosen a .454 as a tactical weapon, but most people didn't have James Hicks' training. The Ruger didn't have the power of an automatic weapon, but it was powerful enough to put a hole in anything in front of it. Even with Kevlar, the impact of the bullet would be enough to knock a shooter on their ass and break a few bones for good measure.

But nothing happened when he gripped the knob. And nothing happened when he slowly twisted it and found it unlocked.

Sweat beaded along his upper lip and back. The door should have been locked.

He gripped the Ruger tighter. Either they knew he was coming and this was a trap or they were already gone and left Steve Harriman's phone behind. He wasn't prepared to give Harriman up for dead just yet.

He turned the knob all the way and let the door swing inside.

He pressed himself flat against the building once more, presenting as small a target as possible.

Once more, he waited. Listening for anything that would tell him what might be inside.

And once more, silence.

The security lights from the neighboring warehouse cast an uneasy glow into the building. He stole a quick glance inside. Then another. All he saw was a hallway and a receiving office on the right side. Otherwise, it was empty.

In one fluid, practiced motion, Hicks moved inside, shut the alley door behind him and flicked down his night vision goggles. The goggles came to life, casting everything he saw in an electric green glow.

The building's plans showed the warehouse had a wide-open floor plan except for a small receiving office to his right. But now he saw a narrow cinder block hallway that ran about twenty-five feet ahead of him, where a metal door stood.

Someone had made some changes. *Why?*

He followed his training and broke his search into sections. He checked the receiving office first. Its plastic glass window bore the ancient tags of vandals who had ravaged the place over the years. Filing cabinets had been overturned, papers of a long-forgotten business strewn across the floor. A filthy mattress in the corner proved the space had served as someone's bedroom at one time or another.

The warehouse didn't fit the Vanguard's style. The group—like the University—usually avoided fixed positions, preferring to stay on the move. Facilities left a footprint. They had to be secured, defended and maintained. Facilities ran the risk of drawing curiosity and attention, something both organizations had worked to avoid at all costs over the years.

Nothing felt right about the entire set up, but Hicks didn't have the luxury of choosing his battles. This was where Harriman's device had led him. This was where Hicks would look for him.

He crept down the hallway, Ruger ready, mindful of any traps that may have been left in his path. He picked up his feet, careful not to scrape his boots through the thin layer of dust on the floor.

The Vanguard prided itself on employing security techniques that were as effective as they were expensive. Biometric locks and infrared trip wires, often rigged to either explode or alert a platoon of armed guards if the invisible beam was broken.

But Hicks didn't see anything in the cinderblock hallway to indicate it had been rigged. Not even a security camera. Only smooth lines of thick concrete all around him. Even the ceiling was made of concrete slabs. *Why?*

He couldn't turn back now.

He reached the door at the end of the hallway without incident. It was a thick metal hatch with rivets binding the plates together and a sturdy lock instead of a knob. There was also a sharp smell in this part of the hall he couldn't place.

Hicks took a step back, his mind working. *This door should be on the alley, not all the way in here. What good would it do once someone was already inside?*

The answer came to him quicker than the question.

He recognized the smell. Fresh caulking and paint.

He recognized the set-up, too. A long, narrow hallway. Only one way out. A reinforced door on one end.

He'd been led into a goddamned turkey shoot.

The Vanguard had expected him to send in a Varsity group to raid the building, people who would kick in doors and ask questions later.

The hall had been constructed to lead them right to where the Vanguard wanted them to go. The door.

Why?

Hicks kept the Ruger aimed at the center of the door as he quickly backtracked up the hallway, eyeing the concrete ceiling for air vents as he went, looking for narrow slits that shouldn't be there. With the alley door closed, the hallway would make an excellent gas chamber. Even if the alley door was open, a concentrated blast from the metal door would incinerate anyone in the hallway.

Hicks didn't stop moving until his back foot hit the alley door. He flipped up his goggles and pulled out his handheld. He checked the live satellite feed showing the alley. Still empty.

He opened the door, pivoted out into alley and took up a position behind the Buick.

The door at the end of the hall was new. The hallway itself was new. The whole thing had been installed for a reason.

And Hicks was going to find out why the best way he knew how.

He cast his goggles aside and crouched behind the hood of his car, taking careful aim at the door. He couldn't see the lock well enough to aim at it, but had a general idea of where it was.

He controlled his breathing. He breathed in, took the wind into account and how it would affect the trajectory of his bullet. He saw the door with his eyes and in his mind. He exhaled.

Don't miss.

He fired. A split second later, an orange ball of flame and debris billowed up the hall and out into the alleyway. Hicks ducked behind the Buick as the metal door had turned to shrapnel, buffering the car with thousands of shards of metal.

Hicks' instincts had been right. The Vanguard had expected him to send a team to raid the place. As soon as they hit the door with a battering ram or shot out the lock with a shotgun, the entire team would have been wiped out.

That was the Vanguard way.

The cloud from the explosion vanished as quickly as it appeared. He looked over the hood of the Buick and saw a gaping hole where the service entrance had once been. Burning remnants of the receiving office and doorway were smoldering all around him. No fire alarms had sounded within the warehouse. No sprinklers had been activated to dampen the flames inside.

The Vanguard had set the trap well. Hicks had done a better job of springing it. He was still alive.

He hoped he could say the same for young Harriman.

He moved out from behind the Buick, ignoring the countless dents and scorch marks that had scored the car's paint. The entire car had been armor plated and all the windows bullet resistant. The engine was still running. The damage was superficial.

Any damage to Harriman would most likely be far more severe.

He waited for the night wind to blow much of the smoke away from the warehouse before he went inside, mindful of secondary devices rigged to explode as he moved. He held his breath, but the smoke still stung his eyes.

The cinderblock hallway was cracked, but still intact, but the receiving office had been destroyed by the blast. It looked better aflame than it had when he'd first seen it only minutes before.

The metal door at the end of the hallway was gone. No trace of it except for the scorch marks on the cinderblock walls as it blew down the hallway. Hicks was no demolition expert but imagined the door had been rigged to blow on the slightest impact, the hallway designed to absorb the blast. Hitting the door with a thirty-eight-caliber slug or even a nine-millimeter slug probably wouldn't have been enough to detonate it. But a battering ram or a shotgun blast—or the impact of a bullet from a .454 Ruger—was enough to set it off.

That had been the point. Harriman had been nothing more than bait, a goat staked to a peg in a clearing hoping to draw out a predator they could hang on their trophy wall. And the Vanguard had collected quite a few trophies over the years. So had the University.

Hicks knew they'd most likely be back to collect their prize soon, so he stepped through the smoldering doorway and into the main part of the cavernous warehouse.

He gagged as he let out the breath he'd been holding and tried to breathe. Filthy skylights three stories above cast an uneasy light onto the floor below. He looked for signs of anyone who might be hiding in the shadows, but he couldn't see much.

Instinct told him the Vanguard wouldn't be here, and from what little he could see, he was right. They wouldn't have wanted to risk something going wrong with the explosion and being caught in the fire. They wouldn't have wanted to be on site if the explosion failed and the University's Varsity squad captured or killed them.

As the smoke thinned further, Hicks saw the entire warehouse was empty except for one figure in the middle of the great empty space.

Hicks blinked his eyes clear of smoke as he approached it. He stopped when he realized what he was seeing.

Young Steve Harriman had been tied to a thick wooden chair in the middle of the vacant warehouse floor, his head sagging so that his chin was against his chest. He'd been placed far enough from the blast to be standing upright, but the explosion was the least of his problems.

The amount of blood pooled on the ground around his chair told Hicks the kid was already dead, bled out slowly as they questioned him. Another Vanguard custom.

Hicks drew closer and saw a hint of movement from

Harriman. At first, he thought it was an errant breeze blowing his hair. Then he realized Steve was trying to lift his head.

He was still alive.

Hicks ignored the blood on the floor and slid to his agent's side. Harriman had been tied to a thick wooden chair and cut in strategic places in his arms and legs, places that would bleed steadily, but not kill him quickly.

Whoever had done this to him had wanted him to live to see the explosion. To see his own people destroyed as they tried to rescue him. They'd wanted him to know he'd been responsible for their deaths. To know his own death was imminent and pointless.

It was another tactic of the Vanguard. Breaking the body wasn't enough. Neither was breaking the mind. They wanted to break your soul in the hopes you could carry it into the afterlife. They didn't believe in such things, but their prey often did and that was the point.

Harriman's skin was almost white from the loss of so much blood, but he was still alive. Hicks intended to keep him that way. He reached into his pocket for his handheld to call the Varsity squad to mobilize with a medical truck. They could be on site in ten minutes and maybe give Harriman enough blood to keep him alive until . . .

"No," Harriman rasped. "Can't . . . save me. Gave me something to make me talk. It burns . . . Make it stop . . . Please . . . make . . . it stop."

Hicks leaned in close to his young operative. "Who did it, Steve? Was it Li? Tell me and I swear to Christ they'll pay."

Steve's eyes flickered as he struggled to look at Hicks. "I'm . . . paying. It burns . . . inside. Please . . . end it."

Hicks slowly stood and took a step back from him. He saw the amount of blood on the warehouse floor, the pain in

Harriman's eyes. Whatever the sonsofbitches had given him to make him talk was killing him from the inside out.

The Life was like that. The goddamned Game, killing Hicks as much as it was killing Harriman from the inside out. This job sometimes meant ordering the deaths of the people he loved most. The only people he ever truly understood and understood him. The Vanguard could never be defeated from behind a computer console or by drone strikes. It had to be infiltrated and destroyed from within. That meant people like Harriman had to risk their lives on orders given by men like James Hicks.

Harriman's groans turned Hicks' stomach. How many of the enemy had he ordered killed? How many of his own men had he sent to their own deaths? How many friends had he lost? How many friends had he ever really had? How many friends had he ever really wanted? He knew the answer and damned himself for it. Everyone he knew went away in the end.

The Life, the University, hadn't cost him anything because he'd never wanted anything more than what he was. The Life hadn't made him into anything. It had filled a void that had been there his entire life. Each death on either side had merely been the price of being what he was, the way oxygen became carbon in a single breath.

People like Steve Harriman had chosen to follow him and often paid the price. People in the Vanguard had fought him and paid the price, too. He remembered every person he'd ever killed and every person who'd died under his command. He would remember Steve Harriman.

He would avenge him. A vengeance that would, in turn, be avenged by the Vanguard, thus continuing the cycle.

The Life meant death. And Hicks would survive because that's all he knew how to do.

Hicks raised the Ruger and created a new memory. A new rage.

25 Minutes to Go

S.W. Lauden

"Real country music is like comfort food."

The young reporter didn't give a shit about country music. They'd only given her twenty-five minutes with him before the big event, and the clock was ticking.

Her eyes wandered to the intricate patchwork of tattoos that covered his arms, each one a different name. She had to find a way to get the answers her readers wanted.

"It's the same every damned time and you always leave satisfied."

It was still hard to believe that she was interviewing Twang, the notorious country guitarist who hadn't spoken to the press since 2004. Even now the news vans were parked outside waiting to catch a glimpse, and here she was face to face with the man himself. *I guess it really is who you know*, she thought.

His eyes were as dark and piercing as her mother's old album covers had promised, but his mane of curly hair was cut short. It was disappointing to discover that his famous sneer was really nothing more than a nervous tic.

I wish he'd shut up about those damned guitars.

"If you want that classic sound, you need the right instrument.

Nothing fancy, just a couple of single coil pick-ups and wound nickel strings. The thicker the better."

She finally had the opening she'd been waiting for.

"I wanted to ask you about the strings . . ."

"I figured you might. You hungry? There's no way I'm finishing all this food."

He pushed one of the to-go containers across the table. She knew he wasn't going to make this easy for her.

"What did you order?"

"Barbecue, what else? The full spread. There's corn bread, collard greens, slaw and biscuits. The meat's pretty good, but not near as tender as mine."

The reporter shot him a skeptical look.

"Don't worry. It ain't homemade."

His laughter echoed off the concrete walls while her stomach rumbled. She hadn't eaten anything since they called last night to say her Hail Mary interview request was approved.

If Twang sensed her discomfort, he didn't let it show.

"Your loss. Anyway, it used to be that the rockabilly guys played hollow body guitars. They got that from the blues guys. There was a sense of tradition. These days, who knows? Everybody's got the same spiky hair, or beards, or both. Even the so-called country artists."

She tried to turn the conversation back to him by pointing at a battered acoustic guitar leaning against the far wall.

"That yours?"

"Hell no. It's just a loaner, something I can pick around on while I'm waiting. Give me a Fender Tele any day. You see me in a cowboy hat with one of those babies strapped on and you know what you're gonna get. It's the real deal."

"How big is your guitar collection at this point?"

"I have a couple stashed here and there, but I hocked most of them to pay my legal bills. Easy come, easy go. You sure you ain't hungry? I'm pretty full myself."

Twang popped a cigarette into his mouth and asked for a light. She took a Zippo from her bag and brought it up in front of his face. Her hand was sweaty and starting to shake. The sparks jumped and danced, but it took several tries to produce a flame.

Twang flashed his yellow teeth.

"Nervous?"

A prison guard stepped into the cell. He nodded at Twang who turned back to the reporter.

"Looks like it's almost show time. But you didn't come here to talk about country music, now did you? Tell me what you really want to know."

She flipped her notebook to the page full of questions she'd labored over until dawn. Her eyes went right to the bottom of the list.

"Let's start with the tattoos. Who are all those people?"

He rested his hands on the table palms up. The name "Christina" took up most of his left forearm, but other names spiraled outward from it in every direction. The tattoos started at the wrist on each arm and snaked all the way up until they disappeared into the sleeves of his jumpsuit.

"People have been asking me that question for years. You'll probably be real disappointed when I tell you."

"I'm listening."

"The names on my left arm are like my family. 'Christina' was my first girlfriend, back in high school. I always did have great taste in women. But you already knew that, didn't you?"

She winced. He winked before going on.

"'Mickey' is a roadie that I worked with for years. 'Bobby Ray' is my bus driver. 'Tom' is my drummer. They've all been with me through thick and thin. We're like blood brothers."

"Sounds wholesome the way you put it."

"It's a pretty simple system. You know, 'keep your loved ones close . . .'"

"What about your enemies?"

"That would be my right arm. They say to keep them even closer. I guess I really took that to heart."

He paused to let her laugh. She didn't oblige.

"That's a lot of enemies."

"There's always room for more. I got a new one just a couple of days ago."

She noticed a patch of irritated, red skin poking out from under his sleeve.

"How do people make the enemy list? I hope turning down food doesn't qualify."

He chuckled, relaxing his shoulders. She went in for the kill.

"Who's 'Alan'?"

The question rolled off her tongue and hit him right between the eyes. He balled his hands into tight fists, letting his chin drop to his chest. The chains on the shackles rattled. She already knew the answer from the trial records, but needed to get him off balance.

"Alan was the first one, wasn't he? Tell me. You're almost out of time."

He brought his eyes up to meet hers. A young monster stared back at her through the rubbery mask of an old man's face.

"That's my piece-of-shit brother. I hope he's waiting for me in hell, so I can kill him all over again."

"Are the tattoos on your right arm the names of all your victims?"

"Only the ones I got around to before time ran out."

"Did you eat all of them?"

He took a drag from his cigarette, exhaling a thin white ring.

"You know, there's nothing like a smoke after a good meal. Hard to believe this'll be the last one I ever taste."

She wasn't going to let him distract her that easily.

"The families deserve the truth. Let them bury their loved ones."

"I don't feel bad for the families. They know in their hearts what happened, even if they never do find the bones."

"You're an animal."

He leaned back in response, studying her eyes.

"We all are, darlin'. Only difference is that some of us, like you, roam free. Others, like me, are caged up."

She leaned in to ask her next question.

"And your victims?"

"Destined for the slaughterhouse. Although, I guess that's me now too."

"Must be hard to run a 'slaughterhouse' all by yourself. Who helped you?"

His tic was more pronounced now. *Am I getting through, or is he getting off on all this talk of murder?*

He forced an answer through gritted teeth.

"I'm afraid there are some secrets I'll take to my grave."

"Who are you protecting? Which one of your so called 'blood brothers' helped you kill all those people?"

Tiny beads of sweat formed under her shirt. She had him right where she wanted him. Time was the only thing standing in her way. There were still so many questions to ask with only a minute to go.

"Why did you strangle them with a guitar string?"

"Hmm. I guess it was the one thing I always had with me. Besides, I didn't want to damage any of the tasty cuts. Guns are messy and I like to save my knife skills for the butcher block, if you know what I mean."

The prison warden stepped into the room, a guard on his right and a chaplain on his left. Twang pushed his chair back to stand. He was towering over her and flashing a confident, toothy grin.

"I wish I could read that story you're gonna write, but there ain't much chance of that happening. Right, boys?"

He nodded toward the three men standing in the doorway. She flipped her notebook shut in frustration, sure that she'd failed. There was nothing left to say.

"Don't get down on yourself, darlin'. You damn near got me to spill the beans."

The reporter nodded in response. *How do you say goodbye to somebody who's about to die?*

Twang stopped in the doorway.

"You look like her, you know? Back when we were still kids. You've got the same dark hair and pretty blue eyes. Seems like yesterday we were running around together and raising hell."

A tear sparkled at the corner of his eye. It was a tiny reminder that the monster might be human after all. She was finding it more difficult to deny him her sympathy. Her only defense was to lie.

"I wouldn't know. She never talks about you."

"Can't say that I blame her, but she's the one I'll be thinking about when they put the lights out. Make sure and give her that message."

The guard and the chaplain each took one of Twang's elbows and started the long walk to the execution chamber.

"And eat something before you go. You need to put some meat on those bones. Consider it my last request."

His throaty laugh echoed down the cellblock as he disappeared out of view for the last time.

The warden waited until they were gone before he addressed the reporter.

"I hope you got what you needed. I'm sorry we weren't able to get you in to be a witness. This whole interview was just so last minute."

"Thanks. Not sure I could have stomached it anyway."

"Do you have any idea why he requested you?"

"I guess he knew my mother back in high school."

"Good lord. She wasn't one of his victims was she?"

"No, thank God, or I probably wouldn't be sitting here right now. They haven't seen each other in years, but I guess she still writes him letters."

The warden shook his head. She had a question for him now.

"Hey. How did my request get approved, anyway?"

"Hard to say. Best I can figure, there must be some real country music fans up in the state capitol. I hope it was worth it."

He gave her a knowing look before he left. She sat staring at Twang's empty chair for several minutes, reliving the interview in her mind. She was about to collect her things and go, but popped the lid on the box he'd offered her instead. *It's the least I can do,* she thought.

A folded piece of paper was placed on top of the discarded rib bones and other bits of comfort food. The name "Christina" was written on the front in tiny print. The sight of it almost knocked the wind right out of her.

She turned the paper over in her fingers. The letter was addressed to her mother, but he'd given it to her. And now he was gone.

She opened it a fold at a time, until the creased sheet was spread out in her lap like a menu. There was a single sentence written across the middle of it.

I never told them it was you.

The reporter collected the notebook and recorder, shoving them into her bag with shaky hands. Her heart and mind were racing. It was an hour drive back to the family restaurant. She was craving her mother's famous meatloaf, but knew she would never be able to eat it again.

I Want to Go Home

Gabino Iglesias

Ann Marie coughs twice and turns over yet again. The sound and her shift wake up Garrett. She coughs once more, wheezes, moves again. The old springs underneath her creak loudly as she adjusts her legs under the covers. Garrett groans. The coughing, like a tide, came and went all night long. It wasn't as bad as that night a few months ago when she cracked a rib, but it was bad enough to keep both of them up, tired and angry. Garrett hates himself for being so pissed at her. Poor thing would love nothing more than to stop hacking up a lung, but that seems to be out of the realm of possibility. The cough is always there, and there's apparently nothing the damn doctors can do about it.

Garrett tilts his head to the right and stretches his neck. Thirty years of working his ass off on the deck of commercial boats has taken a toll on his body. Everything hurts. Everything's wrinkled. Everything aches. His joints and lower back push him to stay put as much as possible, but his bills push him out the door and onto more boats. The skin on his arms, face, and neck is leathery enough to make wallets with it. He feels old. Then he remembers half a joke, something about sleeping in the fridge and putting a bit of WD-40 in his morning coffee to stay young. Maybe the funny part is the half he can't recall.

Getting out of bed quietly is easier said than done. Garrett lets his legs slip off the edge of the old mattress, finding a pool of cooler sheet along the way, and then uses his arms to push himself into a sitting position. He stays like that for a few seconds, breathing hard and feeling already tired before his ass is out of bed. He stands up and walks over to the chair whose sole purpose is holding his clothes. He steps into a pair of dirty jeans and fishes out a bent cigarette from a pack that will be empty before noon. He refuses to get on a boat without enough smokes, so buying a few packs goes on his mental to-do list, half of which he knows he'll forget until the boat is far from shore.

The bent cigarette looks like a yellowish worm in the dimness of the room. Garrett wants to light it and suck some warm smoke into his body. That might scare away some of the aches, maybe smooth his anger a bit. But he can't light up. Ann Marie's newest doctor says the chronic cough can be triggered by smoke, so he steps out, crosses the hallway and living room in the dark, and opens the door to the front porch.

There's an old wooden chair that was white a few decades ago and a table with a yellow ashtray sporting the name of a beer he doesn't recall ever drinking. A small radio sits next to the ashtray, looking like a black smudge in the pre-dawn darkness. Garrett walks to the apparatus and feels around for the iPod he knows is stuck in the slot at the top of the machine. His son, Robert, gave it to him a few birthdays ago. The small rectangle weighs next to nothing and contains more music than Garrett ever owned. He scrolls using the wheel and finds some Johnny Cash. Garrett replaces the iPod on the machine and clicks play. Cash's incomparable voice comes cracking through the tiny speakers and Garrett quickly lowers the volume. No need to wake up Ann now that she has finally fallen asleep.

A sound in the street makes Garrett look up from the iPod. A fat Mexican on a bicycle is slowly pedaling along the dawn-soaked street, riding the middle of it as if he were driving a large car. Motherfucker is probably up to no good. Only hardworking men and criminals are up at this hour, and the Mexican doesn't look like he's on his way to a business meeting. Garrett remembers a time when living in Galveston meant you could leave your door open. Now it only means you're closer to the polluted, brown water and have to put up with drunk, annoying rich kids a few times a year.

While Cash croons about shooting a man just to watch him bleed, Garrett thinks about his upcoming gig. In a day he'll be jumping aboard the Carol Sue, a fifty-one-foot white boat, to trudge through the dark waters of the Gulf of Mexico trying to catch as much red snapper as possible. It'll be his seventh trip with captain Joseph "Big Joe" Weiss. They'll be hitting some fishing spots seventy miles off the Galveston shore. It'll take them a day to get there. Then they'll spend two days fishing and one more day coming back. All his life, leaving for four days was no big deal. Now that Ann Marie is sick, every trip is a pain. Garrett wants to be as far from home as possible and wants to spend every minute trying to make his wife feel better. He suffocates in her presence and can't breathe when he's away because worry crushes his chest. He gets the urge to call Big Joe and tell him he's no longer available. Then he remembers the medical bills and any thoughts of politely bowing out evaporate with the last of the morning fog. Inside the house, Ann starts coughing again. Garrett winces, takes another drag, and starts thinking about the beers he'll be having tonight with Big Joe and whoever else will be joining them in the water.

The bar is packed. Big Joe's meaty, calloused paw is wrapped around a large glass full of dark, heavy beer. He's addressing Garrett and three other deckhands. There's Tim, a quiet, short man who's somewhere in his fifties; Rob, a thirty-something man with a dark goatee who's always talking about golf and cars; and a pudgy young man named Joshua who Garrett hasn't seen before. They'll leave from Katie's Seafood Market on Pier 19 at noon the next day.

"Get ready to do battle," says Joe. "I wanna come back with those coolers full of fish. Ice, bait, gut. You know the drill. Everything else can wait. We'll work long hours. Two-hour shifts, teams of two. Stay fresh and we can work around the clock. Y'all know the fish ain't biting like they used to, but we need pounds to bring in the dough. As always, no booze on board. Save that shit for when we come back. I don't want one of you going overboard on my watch. Take care of yourselves and each other. Watch the hooks. Work clean and fast and we'll be okay. Any questions?"

Big Joe stops talking and looks at them. Garrett sees the worry in the captain's eyes. Fishing in the Gulf of Mexico is a billion-dollar industry, but not much of that lands in their pockets. Folks like them catch shrimp, oysters, blue crab, and a number of species of finfish, but the big money happens elsewhere and ends up in hands that have never seen a net or a fishing hook. Big Joe has three kids, two of them in college; he needs money as bad as Garrett does. That's why he now focuses on the American red snapper, the iconic Gulf fish. Its market price goes up every season, and that's a good thing. Too bad the number of fish they catch goes down. If all goes according to plan, they'll catch ten to twelve thousand pounds of red snapper on this trip. That's about $50,000 for Big Joe. Each crewmember will be paid a couple thousand dollars, depending on how much they individually catch. Garrett plans on working overtime and packing his coolers to the gills. He knows it won't be enough.

The man next to him interrupts Garrett's thoughts.

"What do you guys do when you get bored out there?"

At the beginning of the meeting, Big Joe said something about having a greenhorn on the boat and smirked. Everyone knew he was talking about Joshua. Garrett looks at the man's hands. They look like he's never seen a gaff hook. The young man has the loose mouth and shiny eyes of a drunk.

"You won't have time to get bored," Garrett says.

Big Joe finishes his beer and taps the table. That signals the end of the usual speech. Everyone mumbles a goodnight and suddenly Garrett finds himself sitting with Joshua and a lukewarm beer. Joshua gets up and comes back with a glass full of whiskey. He starts telling Garrett a story about his father, a man who owns a used car lot in El Paso. Garrett tries to tune out. Cash is on the jukebox.

Go tell that long tongue liar . . . and tell that midnight rider
Tell the rambler, the gambler, the back biter
Tell 'em that God's gonna cut 'em down
Tell 'em that God's gonna cut 'em down

Twenty minutes later, Joshua's recounted his last six years working for his father and the fact that he swindled $42,000 dollars cash and ran away because his dad is an asshole. The man refuses to sell used cars for the rest of his life. That, he says, is the life of a fucking loser. He's been living in his car and cheap motels since he ran away. He smiles as he says this, apparently proud of having stolen from his father. Garrett knows revenge is a powerful thing, but says nothing. Joshua keeps talking.

"I don't like having the money in the car, but I can't take it to the bank or carry it with me, you know? I need to keep it close until the old man gives up looking for me. I'm gonna jump on some boats and make a few thousand bucks while the whole thing blows over and then use the money to open up my own business in Portland. That's fucking far from El Paso, ha! I'm gonna open up a coffee joint specializing in exotic blends. Portland is full of hipsters, man. They're gonna flock to this place. Portlanders love coffee. I'm gonna be swimming in money."

Garrett looks at Joshua's eyes and sees the pudgy man is sauced, his words pouring from his mouth fast and slurry. He hears Ann cough inside his skull.

"Listen, Katie's garage is a small place, just an old corrugated aluminum-covered shack right on the pier. You don't want to leave your car there with the money inside. Take my garage. I'll drive you down to the pier. You can find some place else to stash it when we get back, but it'll be safe while you're gone."

Joshua pats Garrett on the shoulder and thanks him before asking him for his address. Garrett realizes for the hundredth time in his life that youth and stupidity are synonymous.

When Garrett's cooler has enough ice for the morning's first haul of snapper, he moves to a wooden workstation attached to the edge of the boat. His spot is beside one of the ship's six hydraulic bandits, mechanical reels that allow them to catch thousands of pounds of fish in a matter of days.

It's six in the morning—only orange glowing lights from neighboring oilrigs shine in the darkness. Garrett's head is buzzing. They've been in the water on and off all night. They're starting the trip back home in a few hours. It's now or never. Knowing they're about to start reeling in the hooked line, Big

Joe switches on the boat's floodlights, and after an audible thunk, the bow of the boat is illuminated in a bright white glow. Garrett and Joshua are working together. Big Joe said that was the only way they'd keep the greenhorn from fucking up the equipment, the boat, or himself.

Garrett feels something tightening in his chest. The feeling makes him think about Ann. Before leaving, he sat out on the porch, smoking a cigarette and listening to Cash's *I Want to Go Home*, the song he's been listening to for years before heading out to the water. Inside, Ann, who had managed to stop coughing long enough to give him the kind of kiss that still made him feel things after a life spent together, was coughing again. The memory helps the tightening in his chest to subside.

"You ever eat a snapper tongue?" Joshua asks Garrett, his hands struggling to unhook a fish from his line.

"They don't have tongues," Garrett says dismissively. Then he remembers Ann again and changes his tune. "That thing coming out of their mouths when we pull them up? It's not a tongue; it's their stomach. They get the bends, just like divers. The decompression blows their stomachs out through their mouths."

Joshua looks at the fish in his hand, turns toward the ocean, and vomits. Garrett sees the man's silhouette against the orange-tinged sky and drops his line. In a second, he thinks about getting the car keys from Joshua's rucksack half an hour earlier as the man slept through their two-hour break. That was the first move. He also took his floatation vest and placed it behind a cooler. Joshua woke up and got to work without asking for it. All greenhorns do it. Now Garrett only needs to do the damn thing. He takes two steps and grabs the buoy hook from the wall next to the cabin's entrance while looking at the door to the cabin. Tom and Ron are probably sleeping. Big Joe is in the wheelhouse. The coast is clear. Garrett turns to Joshua. The man is spitting into the ocean. Garrett knows he has to put everything he has into the swing. Joshua has to hit the cold water completely out or he'll scream. Garrett pulls the buoy hook back and swings with all his strength. The thick metal pole hits Joshua's head with a loud thunk that shoots pain down to Garrett's elbows. The pudgy man's head snaps to the side and his left arm flies up as he exhales a strange moan before going overboard.

Garrett leans over starboard and peers into the water. Joshua is face down, bobbing in the dark water and already drifting away from the boat. His clothes will soon pull him under. Garrett will head inside and use the bathroom. Then he'll come back out and scream for Big Joe. Joshua is just another idiot who made a mistake. He wasn't wearing his life vest. Happens all the time. That's why there are ads for commercial fishing accident attorneys all over Galveston. This is a dangerous job and many fishermen lose their life every year. The floor is slippery with water and blood. Lack of sleep wrecks havoc on the body. A tired greenhorn drowning is no biggie. Joshua slipped and cracked his head before going overboard. Garrett was inside taking a dump. Things like this happen all the time.

Garrett replaces the buoy hook on the wall and looks toward starboard again. He keeps expecting to hear a scream or to see Joshua's hand grabbing the boat. Neither happens. He walks into the cabin and heads to the small bathroom. He remembers the fat Mexican on the bicycle. Maybe he was just going somewhere early. Maybe he was going back home after having sex with some *chola* a few blocks down. Everyone has a fucking story. Garrett just wants this one to be over. He wants to hold Ann and tell her they're going to be okay.

Don't Take Your Guns to Town

Danny Gardner

Jenny's body twitched. The large fissures in her chest gurgled. Her bare heels pattered against the hard floor of her bedroom like a child with a toy drum but no talent. Todd held the Tec-9 in both his shaking hands. Rel and Ant held still hoping the white boy wouldn't shoot them next.

"I-I didn't—I didn't mean to . . ."

"Todd," Rel said. "Mah dood, you need to cool out."

"Yeah. Cool the fuck out, Todd," Ant said. He gave Rel a knowing glance. Ant had his piece on him. He meant to use it.

"This is your fault." Todd pointed the gun at them. "Coming here from Chicago. Acting tough to impress my girl so you could tag team her in front of me."

"Nobody knew she your girl, dood."

"She didn't act like his girl," Ant said.

"Well, we talked about it," Todd said, to no one at all. He looked over at Jenny. "Aw, man, my life is over."

Todd lowered the Tec. He paced the floor mumbling to himself as he made footprints in Jenny's blood.

"He tweakin'," Ant said, in a whisper. He backed toward the bathroom door.

"Todd—homie," Rel said, in an appeasing tone. Having grown up in his mother's house, where he encountered more uncles than a family reunion, he knew how to talk down a man on the edge of violence. "Nothing happened between us. We was just cool on Instagram is all."

"Instagram. Where she put those pictures she took of herself in the bathroom. So fucking thugs like you could disrespect her."

"No disrespect, dood." Ant watched Todd's inexperienced trigger finger.

"You guys think you're so cool. Your kind of cool kills people."

The patter stopped. All three looked over to Jenny's lifeless body. Ant dived backward into the bathroom—the same bathroom Jenny had taken photos of herself—and slammed the door. Rel raised both hands. He backed up quickly until he hit Jenny's cheap corner desk hard. He almost cried out, startled by the clatter of her intramural trophies.

He couldn't help but eye her blood-speckled University of Indiana banner tacked to the wall. Ribbons and medals for sporting achievements. Framed photos of her and her white friends looking positively Young Republican. Rel wondered if any of them knew of her fetish for black men from Chicago. Those *'bout that life*. Their Drill music. Their tribal beefs dramatized across YouTube videos. Cheef Keef. Young Pappy. The culture that produced a new kind of rap sound. Lyrics unabashedly drenched in blood and tears, equally as much as the bullets from the clips that inspired the verses. Verses pumped through white earbuds during marathon study sessions a world—universe—away from its source. Rel thought of the black-on-black mayhem that gave such things credibility amongst young whites. Black suffering that flavored the fad of the moment since 12-bar Blues left the Delta.

It dawned upon Todd that he accidentally shot his way out of the friend zone. He began to sob.

"Damn, dawg," Rel said. "I'm sorry."

Todd raised the gun. Of all the thoughts Rel could have in that moment, he suddenly remembered it was his birthday.

Rel heard that muthafuckas in Cali still do that *jumpin' in* shit and just couldn't imagine a circle of dudes, swingin' all wild, hittin' you until you're half-dead, like they do in those corny-ass movies from the '90s. Waking you from unconsciousness. Huggin' you. Callin' you crew after whippin' your ass. All that shit sounded gay as fuck, but Cali had always been real country with theirs. Rel and Ant were from Chicago, the true big city, where organized gang bangin' was invented back when Al Capone needed a place to crash after he got that nasty scar on his face. Where indiscriminate acts of violence, or commerce, were replaced with order, structure, roles, and responsibility. Chicago is where, if you want to be crew, nobody beat your ass. Nobody in a Jheri curl gave you a gun and told you to "put in work." Being 'bout that life wasn't about code, or honor, but business. In the hood, bodies were in abundance. Allegiance is no commodity. To get in, you have to buy in. Dope. Cash. Or guns.

Lucky for Rel and Ant, guns lay in abundance across the Indiana state line.

The third of Dashawn's calls came as Rel swiped his ATM card for the toll onto the Chicago Skyway.

"Nigga blowin' you up," Ant said.

"He wanted us to leave before daylight." Rel hit ignore.

"Dashawn could have done this bullshit himself."

"Cool out."

Dashawn was an elite soldier in the squad since his pops landed in Menard Federal doin' time. Chicago 5-O and the DEA cracked down on old established leadership, which destabilized the gangs on the south and west sides. Man-boys in their twenties became the brand new heavies. Vast territories were reduced to the narrowest span of adjacent blocks. That's how the gun runs that armed twelve-year old soldiers became the charge of two eighteen-year-old veterans.

When they passed through the tollgate, Dashawn called again. Ant answered on speaker.

"Happy birthday, li'l nigga."

"Yep, yep,'" Rel said.

"Y'all there yet?"

"It's a three-hour drive, dood."

"That's why I told you niggas to leave early in the mornin'."

"Durin' rush hour?" Ant said. "Stop tweakin'."

"Stop tweakin'? Tha fuck you talkin' to? Fuck 'round 'n' get violated."

"Cool out, Dashawn," Rel said. "This way, we can get in and get out. That's all he meant."

"Take me off speaker, Rel," Dawshawn said. Rel complied. Ant rolled some weed in cigar wrapper to make the trip a little easier.

"Ay," Dashawn said. "I know he your boy, but I ain't the only one tired of that nigga. Aight?"

"I got you."

"Ninas," Dashawn said. "Wit' 30s for each. Just see my dood Gary. Don't come back without them."

Dashawn hung up.

"Fuck that nigga," Ant said. He blazed up the loud, taking a deep drag into his lungs.

"Ant, you need to relax."

"You need to relax." Weed smoke escaped Ant's lips. He leaned over and put the J into Rel's mouth with the intimacy of a brother, or lover. Rel inhaled deep before Ant reclaimed it and took another drag.

"All I'm sayin' is muhfukas are startin' to talk."

"Muhfukas like who?" Ant exhaled. "E'errbody that matters is locked up. Nobody loves anybody else in this shit. It's just us, dood."

Rel thought he had a reply, but then Ant's weed man always got him fire. He put the sounds of Lil Durk through the Bluetooth speaker in the dash. Corn stalks began waving in the breeze.

They walked into the Evansville National Guard Armory not knowing what to expect, but didn't expect it to look and feel so weird. As they wandered around the gun show looking for booth C19 they were struck by the implied violence. So many angry banners. So many murdered paper targets. Pieces of black thugs here. Tattered Osama Bin Ladens there. Open carry advocates comparing their assault weapons next to the booth that offered cotton candy for the kiddies. So many flags.

So few black folks.

Ant wandered off to enjoy the spectacle. Rel found the booth indicated in Dashawn's instructions. Bankroll in his pocket, he stepped up.

"Yo' name Gary?" Rel kept his voice down.

"What's that?" the middle-aged man said. He wore a bright yellow Indiana Pacers jacket. He had an earring in his right ear, which was the wrong ear, but sometimes white folks just don't know.

"I asked if your name Gary."

"Yes, Gary. You must be Rel."

"Yeah." Rel looked over both shoulders. Gary snickered.

"Relax, son," Gary said, his use of son not because of some New York shit, but some *make sure you water the horses before supper* shit. "You're within your rights here."

"We good?"

"You want *ninas*, yeah?" Gary raised his eyebrows as if he knew what's up.

"Yeah. And *30s*," Rel said, suppressing the urge to laugh at the white man speaking his language.

"Thirty shot clips so you won't be outgunned," Gary said, nodding. He grabbed a black duffel bag. "Just like Ruby Ridge."

Gary put the duffel full of guns on the table. Rel pulled out the bankroll. Ant walked up, giddy.

"Ay, dood, I just shot an AR-15. My dick is hard as fuck!"

Gary smiled at Ant's exuberance. He gave Rel's bankroll a cursory inspection before placing it into a steel cashbox.

"You not gonna count it?" Rel said.

"We're cool." Gary handed Rel the duffle. "You guys are young. Times are changing. Take one of those pamphlets over there. Read it. You're American citizens, like anyone else. Don't tread on me, right?"

"Right," Ant said. He took the bag with a grin.

"I threw in an extra for you," Gary said. "A chopper. Old school."

"Thanks," Rel said.

"Tell Dashawn I say whaddup," Gary said.

Rel and Ant walked away without responding.

They were back on I-65 when Rel's phone blew up again. It was Jenny, a li'l freak down at college he knew from Instagram. Ant posted a few too many weird pics of himself at the gun show and, unlike Rel, who loathed location services, Ant was date/time stamped and GPS-marked and there was no way Jenny could ignore them being so close.

"Y'all should come thru," she DM'd.

Ant searched his phone's GPS app for an alternate route.

"We gotta get back," Rel said.

"We'll just fall through real quick. Get on I-69."

A lifetime of friendship with Ant conditioned Rel to shrug off the drawbacks. As they entered Jenny's idyllic off-campus neighborhood, they passed fraternity and sorority houses. Rel thought of the prospect of college. Ant thought of prospective customers. Jenny was already outside her apartment building when they pulled up. She looked cuter than her Instagram posts, in her low-hung university athletics sweat pants and red crop-top Indiana hoodie. She was so excited she hadn't bothered to put on shoes. As the car rolled up to her door, she ran out to meet them and leapt onto Rel.

"Damn," Ant said. He noticed a guy in the doorway.

"That's my roommate, Todd," Jenny said. "He's cool. Y'all come on."

"Y'all," Ant said.

"Cool out," Rel said.

The three walked to the door. Jenny never let go of Rel. As they walked in, Todd didn't say a word. They made it up the stairs to Jenny's room. As Todd entered behind them, Rel felt his protective intent.

"Benchwarmer," Ant said. Rel nodded in agreement. He saw the duffle.

"Dood."

"I'm supposed to leave it in the car?"

Rel sighed.

"Got that loud," Jenny said, as she pulled a fully loaded weed vaporizer from a desk drawer. She closed her door, pressed the spacebar on her iMac and a Drill mixtape from SoundCloud played over Bluetooth speakers. Jenny sat on Rel's lap as they passed the weed around. Todd took the deepest hit. It was so conspicuous, everyone else stared. Once he started to relax, he tried making conversation.

"Which neighborhood are you guys from?"

"Englewood," Rel said. Ant threw his hands up in a prideful salute.

"Damn. I'm sorry," Todd said. "That's been the worst per capita since the '80s."

"Todd majors in Sociology, if you couldn't tell," Jenny said.

"They probably couldn't."

"I know that shit," Rel said. "You study society and culture."

Jenny laughed in Todd's direction. She then started dancing. Rel joined her. Ant took another hit off the vaporizer before he passed it to Todd.

"Loosen up, nigga," Ant said.

As Todd breathed deep of medicinals, Ant pulled the duffle toward himself.

"We came down here to get them thangs."

Ant unzipped the bag. He showed Todd the haul. Jenny's eyes opened wide. How many times had she heard about _that nina wit' tha 30_ listening to music as she studied?

"Ant!" Although high as a kite, Rel was pissed.

"Stop tweakin'," Ant said. "He talkin' 'bout Englewood 'n' shit. Let him see."

Ant slid the duffle over to where Todd sat. The white boy looked inside at death, sold at wholesale prices. He shook his head. Perhaps it was the weed, or his jealously of the two representations of America's hypocrisy, but he made bold words.

"These guns are for you, you know?"

"Yeah, they are," Ant said. He joined Jenny and Rel. Their dance was seductive.

"No," Todd said. "These are semi-automatic weapons. No

one hunts with these. Weapons dealers sell them to people who want to be prepared in case black people from Chicago infiltrate their lives."

Todd looked deeper in the duffel. He pulled out a Tec-9.

"New Jack City 'n shit," Ant said. He and Jenny laughed. Rel didn't. He watched Todd like a hawk.

"See, this gun ruled the street all through the '90s. Especially on the West Coast. Easy to modify. Essentially an automatic weapon kit. The federal government couldn't care less."

Rel didn't say a word. Ant and Jenny were focused only on each other. Todd wouldn't be ignored. He raised the Tec-9 in Jenny's direction, partly to prove a point, partly because his subconscious had beef. His hands were on the trigger as he turned his wrist.

"To make it a real killing machine, all you had to do—"

The Tec erupted in Todd's hands. Jenny caught at least seven from stem to stern. She clutched her throat as she fell backward. When she hit the floor, she coughed blood in a spray that almost reached the ceiling. Turns out good guy Gary, so down for the struggle in the hood, had made a gift of a loaded gun with a hair trigger.

Rel's morbid fantasy was to ponder whether getting shot was truly painful. He imagined himself taking a bullet and it not feeling like anything. Every man in his family died from gunshot wounds, as did countless friends, but it wasn't until slugs violated his abdomen that he knew goin' out hard was all bullshit. The impacts threw him backward. His arms flailed. On the way down to the floor, he knocked over all of Jenny's belongings. Ant, if he hadn't escaped out the window, remained in the bathroom. Rel grabbed his perforated guts. The squishing sounds his fingers made in his own blood scared him so much, he began to cry. It made eerie sense. Todd shot Jenny with a gun meant only to kill black folk. Now that the Tec-9 claimed a Jenny, it needed a Rel. It was cosmic balance.

"What do you have to say now?" Spittle flew from Todd's crazed mouth. Rel had no words, only sobs. Again, Todd raised the Tec.

Ant threw open the bathroom door. He wildly let off shots in Todd's direction. Bullets ripped into Todd's shoulder, face, and neck. The well-intentioned white boy crumpled into a heap onto the floor.

"Ant," Rel said.

Ant followed the blood trail out the bathroom door.

"Oh fuck, nigga," Ant said. "I shoulda shot him before. I knew I shoulda."

"Ant," Rel said. "Ant, please don't let me die."

Ant stood over his lifelong homie, who leaked his life all over the floor of a white co-ed's bedroom, and knew he was dead already. He threw the duffel of guns over his shoulder. He then knelt to Rel and put his hand on his cheek with the same intimacy he placed the joint in his mouth.

"Happy birthday, my nigga," he said, tears in his eyes.

Ant bolted through the doorway. Rel sat in his own blood, shit and piss. The Drill mixtape still played.

His heels began to patter against the hard floor.

Ring of Fire

James Grady

Every step Cody took down that small town Montana alley brought him closer to murder. He willed himself to be invisible that Tuesday morning. There could be no witnesses to him using the backdoor of Jode Oil & Properties office. No one could know.

Except Nora, the soon-to-be-widow with a mouth to drop you to your knees that whispered the *whats* and *whys* and *hows* to Cody across white pillowcases.

Valerie opens the office at 8 so she can tell herself that when she takes off a 9:30 she's just going to coffee, though she never gets back from the hospital till 11.

The *nobody will miss it* silver key from Nora let Cody in the back door as he fought being haunted by what he'd told her.

You've got to keep Buck at your house. Alone with you. Until.

Cody shoved away visions of how Nora was keeping her husband from leaving the palatial prison they called home as he stood in the burgled offices' dark back hall.

Don't turn on the light: somebody might see that glow through the reception room's windows. If you don't hear anything, don't smell a cigar, turn the corner.

And he did, emerged in the *no one else's here* window-lit front office.

Cody plucked a tissue from the box on Valerie's receptionist desk, held it between the flesh of his hand and the old-fashioned landline telephone receiver he lifted to his face. He wrapped another tissue around a pencil on the desk, used its eraser to jab the landline's dialing buttons with those cell phone digits.

That's the easy way a cop could get us. Phone records—especially cell phone records. That's why we never talk on the phone, why we never get to call each other.

BZZZT rang in Cody's ear. BZZZT. BZZZT.

Buck's voice barked through the old phone: "What the hell is it, Val?"

His Caller I.D. will show his office called him, nothing unusual so nobody will check with Val, and if they do, a woman working on no sleep and less hope, she's gonna just shake her head, figure she did what the records say got did.

"Val's not here. This is Cody Stewart."

"The wind farm guy, right?"

Like it still meant something, Cody said, "Environmental Systems Engineer."

"Like I give a fuck. Why you callin' from my office?"

"Because you aren't here. It's about the land you lease us west of town by the wind farm, that Quonset hut. I figured I better call you before I call Sherriff Rudd."

"You don't call badges on nothing of mine without I say so."

"Figured you'd think like that. I'll meet you out there in, say, thirty minutes, then we'll work it out."

"Work what out? I'm the man who *tells*, not who gets *told*."

"Meet me out there in thirty minutes or I'll do all the telling."

Cody hung up.

Crumpled the white tissues and held that ball over Val's tan garbage can. Released that ball unfolded into two white sheets floating down to the maw of yawning sunlight as the front door opened.

Cody dove under the desk where Val's legs belonged.

Feet . . . can hear feet clunking into the office.

From under the front of the desk, Cody saw women's shoes walking toward. He curled into a ball under the desk. *Don't move, don't breathe, DON'T!*

Valerie's voice as she shuffled paper, objects clunked on the desktop above Cody's hiding head. "Put it here somewhere," she muttered. "I just know . . . "

She's moving around the desk, coming to the well where she sits and if—

"Yes!" Shoes turned and marched toward the door.

Opening, the door's opening and Valerie is saying, "Hey Paul, you're early."

"Yeah, well, not as much to carry since everybody's gone e-mail."

"You got some for us?"

Black shoes, blue pants, man's voice replying, "Just the usual. How are you?"

"Hell, sometimes I think that all this just can't be how things are."

"Ain't that the truth. How's Jesse doing?"

Thirty minutes! Only got thirty minutes!

"You know, day at a time. They say his numbers are good."

"That's great, Val. Here."

A beat, *she's walking back this way . . .*

Thump on the surface of the desktop above Cody's head.

Still got time! His eyes watch her shoes turn to face the door.

And the still-there shoes of the mailman, who says, "You know about Laetrile?"

Not moving! None of the shoes Cody can see on the office floor from under the desk's front are moving and it's lots less than thirty minutes now.

Val says, "Lay-a-*what?*"

"Tril," says the mailman. "Laetrile. Gotta get it out of Mexico because, well, you know the Fed. But you can find it on-line. Little white pills. They say they really work. Steve McQueen swore by 'em."

"Steve McQueen died."

"Oh. Well. Yeah. I just . . . you know. That's what they say."

The door swung open, black shoes, and the mailman was gone. The door shut. Val remained.

Go! Get out of here, just go! No time!

The desk groaned as Val slumped on its cluttered surface. Cody heard her sob.

Clock ticking, the ticking clock—

Val sighed. "God save us all from *what they say.*"

In the well of the desk, Cody felt the woman sitting on it stand, felt her turn and reach onto the desk for a tissue, blowing her nose and then stretching her arm back across the desk, over the gap between her empty chair and the well space for her legs *and if she watches what she's doing, looks down . . .*

Val tossed the wadded tissue where she knew the wastebasket would be. *Plunk.*

Her shoes marched to the front door, out, that exit slammed shut.

Cody uncoiled from under the desk, staggered into the chair draped by the brown sweater, rolled it back into its proper place. He ran toward the door, and then ran back, grabbed all the DNA tissues out of the wastebasket and stuffed them in his black jeans, slid out the back door, *check, yes it's locked*, hustled to the Jeep.

You've got to get there before him, be waiting for him, be ready.

Cody raced over the empty two-lane highway running west out of town like a gray scar through chessboard gold and brown fields, but it still took him seventeen minutes until his windshield filled with the occupying army of two-hundred twelve-feet tall, black-tower metal robots from outer space, each invader spinning three one-hundred sixteen-feet-long white blades to harvest this land's wind. He threw the silver key out the Jeep's window. Whipped the steering wheel left onto that gravel road. Kicked up a dust trail driving as fast as he dared.

No cars waited in front of the Quonset hut. The padlock hung securely from the door for that curved-walls warehouse on the prairie. Shadows of spinning white blades whipped across everything like the beats of a heart.

Cody jumped out of the Jeep. Looked back the way he'd come. His dust trail drifting over that gravel road settled. Vanished.

He grabbed the crowbar from the Jeep's tool chest, pried off the padlock, let it thump to the dirt. Cody ran back to the Jeep and locked the crowbar in its home like it had been there unused for weeks, slammed the tailgate closed.

A new cloud of dust rose over the gravel road.

Growing bigger.

Coming closer.

Cody darted into the Quonset hut, snapped on the dangling bare bulb. *He'll see the Jeep, know you're here, expect the light on, might not step into darkness.*

Cody's clean hands wrapped around that heavy baseball bat-sized metal pipe. He pressed his back against the wall by the Quonset hut's open door. Cocked the pipe beyond his right shoulder, kept his eyes on the rectangle of sunlight filling the doorway.

Blood, there'll be blood. Maybe not the first smash. That might just rock Buck in his tracks. Keep swinging. Gotta keep swinging.

Whacking him. Even after he's down. His chest, arms, his head even if his skull cracks open like . . . You've gotta go nuts on him, as nuts as a freaked-out and panicked-over-getting-caught meth-head; they've been busting into buildings to set up cook labs all summer long.

Tires crunched gravel outside the Quonset hut.

Blood will splatter all over and on you. Don't worry. You showed up, found him, rushed to help. Be sure he's dead but be like you don't know that. Drag him to your Jeep. Doesn't matter about the pipe: you tossed the pipe off him, fingerprints won't matter. Get him in the Jeep, race to town, 911 on your cell, screaming you gotta get him to the E.R. Honk your horn, bust traffic lights, crash into the E.R. glass doors, but get him there with you covered in blood, you found him, did your best, and so the why *and the* how *are there for the sheriff and everybody to believe.*

Outside the Quonset hut in the autumn morning, a car engine shut off.

Then it's the widow and the guy who tried to be a hero, it works and we're free.

Outside, a car door slammed.

Cody coiled every muscle to swing the pipe: *Do this and who you are dies.*

Again a car door slammed.

He's supposed to be alone!

Blur busting into Quonset hut. *Don't swing, it's . . .*

Staggering stumbling sprawling, Nora crashed onto the dirt floor, yelling, "No!"

The pipe sagged in Cody's grip.

"Don't fucking move!"

Buck filled the doorway, thrusting a silver pistol toward Cody. "What are you—drop that fucking pipe!"

What could have been falls from Cody's hands.

Buck's gun swings from Cody to Nora on the ground back to

Cody. "*Wait*: you two are trying to kill me *for real*? That's my plan! *You stole my fucking plan!*"

He threw a black purse to his wife huddled on the dirt floor. "You would have had that with you, *bitch*. They gotta find it on you."

The man with the silver gun shook his head in the dim light of this warehouse.

"Un-fucking believable. You two stole my plan and made it real! Now I can pass a lie detector test. Long as they don't ask me who pulled the wires on my truck so my wife had to give me a ride after you called. I wasn't even gonna do it today. Didn't have it all figured yet, how to get you two in a kill zone. But then you called and this is fucking America: you grab the opportunity you get, and *fuck*: you two actually got me out here to kill me! Now it's all true when I get self-defense!"

They made a triangle in that dimly lit Quonset hut.

Cody trembled a few feet away from the door.

Buck loomed on the other side of the sunlight flowing through that open gap.

That rectangle of light ended on the dirt floor where Nora struggled to her knees.

Buck zeroed the gun on his wife. "So *that's* why I had to muscle you into the car! Make you come when you tried to say *no*. Any bruises on you, *now* they came in the fight to get away from you out here, to get a shot at Mister Pipe Swinger over there."

He aimed the gun at Cody, frowned. "What the fuck did I ever do to you?"

"You're killing me and the woman I love!"

"Well *now*, yeah." Buck chuckled. "You *love* her? Oh man, you think she's got *love* in her? I might be an asshole, but she's a stone-cold bitch. Always thinking. Always scheming. Always playing. She's got moves nobody ever sees, sets shit up and pulls it off and she always ends up sitting pretty."

Buck swung the gun back to the woman clutching her black purse while huddled on the dirt floor. "Except for now."

Her husband smiled at Cody. "Weren't for me, you'd have to watch your back. What I don't get is what you got for her if she don't have me. And how will she use that? Hell, she's already got us all killing each other."

Buck shook his head and the gun wavered somewhere between Cody and Nora.

"What a day, huh?"

The waving silver gun took in the metal walls curving over them, the dangling light bulb and the sunlit open door to the world outside of golden prairies and blue sky.

"All this," said Buck, "who'd have thunk it? Your scheme, my scheme, both are true. As long as there's a good story for the cops, right. But the real question is . . ." The big man paused. "Who am I gonna shoot first?"

"Let him go!" Nora clutched her black purse like a prayer bag in front of her as she knelt on that dirt floor. "Don't shoot him!"

Buck loomed toward her. "You don't tell me what to do! Not anymore!"

"I love him!" said Nora.

Like he'd been waiting for her to say that, Buck leered and said, "Then looks like I finally get to take something away from you!"

The silver pistol swung toward Cody.

Nora's hand inside her purse blasted out jagged holes of flame *again* and *again* and *again* as Buck's gun roared a slug that screamed past Cody's right ear to crash through the metal wall.

Buck crumpled to his knees, his silver gun dropped to the dirt, his face turning to see his wife thrusting that purse, that damn purse she had, *she just had* to bring with her, that purse pointing at him and smoking through three jagged holes.

His face went slack, eyes emptying as the slab of meat hit the dirt floor.

Cody's ears rang. Gunsmoke seared his gasps. The woman he loved knelt on the ground, her hands enveloped by a black purse where she held the pistol that had never been part of anyone's plans.

She's always thinking.

And Cody realized his whole life had fallen into a ring of fire.

But were the flames the flash of a gun muzzle, or were they the circle of her love?

Thirteen

Renee Asher Pickup

When they tried me as an adult, I thought I was going to walk into a Scared Straight video, angry inmates, shanks, the looming threat of riot. Pendleton's minimum-security side looked more like summer camp. A cheap, bargain-bin summer camp, with paint peeling off the walls and metal furniture crammed into the smallest space possible. They stuck me in a room with Ricky, a Mexican guy from L.A. who called himself an "O.G.," talked real smooth, and walked like he owned the prison. He was a pimple-faced seventeen-year-old like me. I guess they thought we'd be safer together.

Ricky had never been outside of L.A. until six months before he got busted. The irony was, his mom sent him to live with an aunt out in Indiana, thinking she'd save him from the gangs.

"She Fresh Prince'd you?"

He laughed, ran his hand through hair held down with grease he swiped from the auto shop. "Yeah, holmes. She fucking Fresh Prince'd me."

Prison wasn't as scary looking as I thought it would be, but Ricky and I were still at the bottom of the pecking order. We ate last, did the shittiest jobs, and couldn't get the older guys to even bother giving us advice. If we had lunch money, they'd have stolen it. Two weeks in and Ricky was sick of it.

"I can't handle this shit," he said, after we failed to get one of the older guys to take our commissary money and buy us smokes. "Being here ain't that bad, but the fucking disrespect . . . "

We both had five years to get older and earn some respect, but Ricky wasn't willing to wait. "I got a plan," he said, pulling his shirt down and showing me the palm-sized tattoo on his chest. A bold "LA" like the baseball team, with a 213 over it. "I saw some *Sureños* here. They're gonna hook me up. They hook me up, I'll hook you up."

I didn't see him on the yard at all, but when he came into the shop later, where we'd both been assigned—to rehab us or reform us, or whatever, he had a big blue 13 on his neck, shining with Vaseline.

The threat of being sent "across the street" to Max was enough to keep me from stepping out of line, but Ricky was walking around with a big ass fresh tattoo on his neck, where anyone could see it.

"What the hell did you do?" I asked, while we reorganized a toolbox. Real life skills, for our real lives on the outside.

"I got myself some insurance."

Ricky's older brother was a member of some street gang in Los Angeles. He got jumped in when Ricky was still in elementary school. I knew that. The chest tattoo was the thing that spun Ricky's mom out, got him sent to Indiana where he got busted slinging pot. Tried as an adult because it was "gang related." But I knew that Ricky was never really in any gang. He just hung around his brother, got the tattoo in his own garage.

"I'm safe now because I'm *Sureño*. And you're safe because you're with me. This is how we do."

A couple days later, the guards hadn't noticed the tattoo, and I figured Ricky was in the clear. Then, the tattoo started itching, and Ricky couldn't stop scratching it. By the end of the week it wasn't a tattoo anymore. The thing that tried so hard to be a tattoo was now a bulging red sore that looked like a giant zit and stank so bad I had trouble being in our cell with him.

Ricky looked like shit, he wasn't sleeping because the thing on his neck hurt too much, he wasn't eating because the smell made him sick, and no one wanted to eat around him, anyway. When I woke up on Tuesday, the whole cell stank like B.O. and rot. His sheets were soaked in sweat, and he was sitting on the floor wrapped in his blanket.

"Man, you gotta eat," I said, extending a hand to help him up. He didn't take it.

"I asked a guard for a doctor last night and he said if I kept talking he'd send me to Max." His lips were dry and cracking.

At breakfast I tried to figure out what I could do. I couldn't get him food let alone something to help the tat. The guys that tattooed him sat together at a table across the room, from what I could tell, they didn't like white guys approaching them. I thought the whole point was they were supposed to look out for each other, but maybe when you're just somebody's little brother, some punk kid getting fucked in Indiana, you can't do much for them. So they don't do much for you. Maybe they didn't know he was sick.

That's the assumption that felt good, so that's the one I went with. I stuck an apple in my pocket and snuck it back to Ricky, begged him to at least bite into it and suck on it.

Ricky didn't bother getting out of his wet sheets the next night. He tossed and turned all night, moaning and crying to himself. All this for a tattoo. He asked for my blanket, shivering in his own. When I handed it to him, I could feel the heat coming off of him, the stench of the thing on his neck—growing larger every day, triggering my gag reflex.

Thursday was the Young Offenders group. Anyone in the clink under twenty-one was supposed to be there with Dr. Sherri, the cute blonde psychologist there to help us "process our feelings" and "make a plan for the outside world." The tattoo on Ricky's chest, the one he thought would save him in here? That's why he's in here instead of some juvie program that would put him on probation in a year when he turned eighteen. "Gang affiliation." There aren't any street gangs in Podunk fucking Indiana, but that didn't matter to the judge. I got tried as an adult because my dad wouldn't back me up. Because I swung on the arresting officer. Because I was smart.

The judge actually said that, like it was wrong to be smart. You could be an idiot and steal shit, but being smart? That's where shit really went wrong for me.

In Pendleton, though, being smart really did put me at a disadvantage. I knew that thing on Ricky's neck wouldn't make him so sick if it were just an infected wound. It was in him now, and it was fucking him up. If he didn't get some kind of antibiotic, or at least some peroxide, he was going to keep getting sicker until he died.

Dr. Sherri always talked about how much she cared about us. Cared about our futures. Cared about making sure we didn't end up back here once we got out. When she called Ricky's name, I thought, maybe I had a chance to do the right thing.

"Ricky's sick."

She frowned at her clipboard. "He isn't on my excused list."

"Because they won't let him see a doctor."

She pursed her lips and said, "Well if he's not sick enough to see a doctor, he's not sick enough to miss group."

That was it. Dr. Sherri cared so much, she wrote him up.

When I got back to the cell, the stench hit me hard in the face and I had to run to the sink to puke. Stuck in there with that smell, I was relieved to see that Ricky was at least sleeping. I thought about waking him up for yard time, but I didn't think he'd go. If nothing else, he needed the rest. The bulge on his neck had opened and was seeping green down into the blanket wrapped around him. The sad, sparse hair on his face was black against the gray of his skin and just standing next to him, I could feel his fever while he shook under the covers.

Out in the yard, I couldn't stop thinking about the way the tattoo was taking over Ricky's body. Someone had to give a fuck, but if it wasn't the guards, and it wasn't Dr. Sherri, who would it be? Even if I had the balls to go to anyone higher than the guards, he'd probably get shuffled over to Max just for having the damn thing. I didn't know what I could do, but I knew I couldn't spend another night in our stinking cell, listening to him whimper in his sleep.

The guys Ricky got the tattoo from hung out in a corner of the yard, away from everyone else. A mix of tall and skinny, and big burly Mexicans with tattoos covering every exposed part.

I got busted using my dad's locksmithing gear to steal beer. I hung out with football players, not gang members or criminals. The biggest guy was twice as big as a linebacker, and when he noticed me looking at them, the look he shot me made me want to piss my pants. I didn't have a plan, I didn't even know if these guys would help. I thought about looking for a couple guys from the auto shop or from Young Offenders, just forgetting the whole thing. But Ricky's smell stayed with me, burning my nose and tickling my throat. If I thought about it too long, I could taste the rot in my mouth. I thought about the way he cried the night before, when he was caught up in fever dreams, saying "Mama" in his sleep.

I took a deep breath and started walking toward them, one foot in front of the other, trying not to worry too much about what I would say, just finding the courage to say it.

"The fuck do you want, white boy?" the big one asked.

All five of them stared me down. My throat went dry, but I was standing there, now. I had to say something.

"I've got a problem," I said.

The guys who were sitting stood up. They all seemed taller than me, bigger than me. From across the yard, a couple of them were short, a couple skinny. Standing in front of me, they were all too big for a skinny white kid from the suburbs to talk to.

"You got a fucking problem?" the big guy said, laughing.

"You gotta do something about Ricky," I said.

My eyes were on the big guy, the one laughing at me. I didn't see the swing from whoever punched me in the ear. I hit the dirt, holding the side of my head and feeling tears burn in my eyes. The Mexicans laughed. One of them kicked me in the gut and another spit on me.

"You got a problem with Ricky, you got a problem with us," the big guy said, and it finally clicked as I took another foot to the gut.

I tried to correct myself but every kick to the gut knocked the air out of my lungs and I couldn't make my voice heard. I rolled over, trying to protect my stomach from their feet, but they just laughed and kicked at my back. Ricky could be dying alone in our cell and I was getting my ass handed to me for trying to save him. They stopped kicking me long enough for me to pull a loud, desperate lungful of air, which I promptly coughed back out, spraying blood from my mouth where one of them had caught me in the face.

They seemed to enjoy watching me writhe and cough, so they let me have a break from their feet pounding into me.

I sputtered out "No," trying to explain myself, but I couldn't get anything more out of my mouth.

A skinny guy pulled me up by the hair. "No, what?"

"No, I don't . . ." I couldn't stop gasping for air long enough to finish a sentence. "I don't . . ."

The skinny guy punched me in the face again. Maybe he was trying to help, trying to punch the hysteria out of me like on old TV shows. I bit my tongue on impact and spit out more blood. For the first time, I wondered where the fuck the guards were while these guys beat the hell out of me.

"Ricky's gonna die if he doesn't get some help!" I finally managed to say, tears streaming down my face.

One of the guys standing behind Skinny stepped forward. "Hey, put him down," he said. I fell to the ground sputtering blood, trying not to sob and failing. "That's Ricky's bunkmate."

My brain couldn't process the feeling of relief his recognition brought over me, paired with the embarrassment of sobbing in the dirt in the yard, so I just sobbed harder. Crying like a little kid, stuttering through everything I said. "Y-y-y-eah. Ricky's si-Ricky's si . . ."

"All right, homie, chill the fuck out," the big guy said, helping me to my feet.

I lifted up my scrub top and wiped my face on it, blood and snot smearing over the front. I couldn't stop the hiccoughing, couldn't man up and chill the fuck out like I was being told.

"What the hell is going on, kid?" the guy who saved me said.

I swallowed hard and told them about the tattoo, the guard threatening to send Ricky to Max. Dr. Sherri. I cried it all out like I was a kid talking to Mommy about bullies at school. They looked embarrassed by me, or worse, embarrassed for me. These hard-as-fuck guys who've probably been in and out of here, probably been to Max themselves, watching me cry in the middle of the minimum security yard.

The big guy finally spoke. "All right, whitey. Get the fuck outta here. You're making us look bad."

I made my way back to the cell, terrified of the stink and already feeling sick, but unable to stand being out in the yard red-faced, with snot bubbles coming out of my nose. I knew better than to ask for an ice pack. I crawled into bed and pulled the sheet up over me, wishing I hadn't let Ricky leak ooze all over my blanket. When dinnertime came around, I slipped off my bunk without letting Ricky see my face. I went through the chow line with my bruised face and blood caked in my nostrils and acted like it made me hard. I don't know who saw me crying like a bitch in the yard but that was over now.

When I got back to the cell with a couple pieces of bread stuffed in my pocket for Ricky, the room didn't smell so bad. My bunk had a clean blanket on it, and Ricky had a clean blanket wrapped around him. A microwave cup of ramen sat on the floor next to his bed.

"My boys came through for me," he said. "They got me some antibiotics coming tomorrow."

"Cool." I climbed up to my bed.

"I heard you got your ass kicked in the yard today," he said.

"Yeah."

"Well if you need something from medical let me know. One of the guys works in sick call. He can get it."

When Ricky's tattoo finally healed it was a warped and twisted scar on his neck that always looked a little redder than the rest of him, the gnarled 13 still visible inside it. His boys spread a rumor the scar was from a knife fight, some rival gang member trying to cut the tat off his neck.

Ricky got his respect. I got my smokes.

I never asked anyone in the prison for help again.

Ain't Gonna Work Tomorrow

Hector Duarte Jr.

Ed Gaynor saw it about to happen and did nothing because he wanted Manolo Poblete to get suspended. Manny was a dick and the girl he'd been targeting as of late was a genuine sweetheart.

Manny did nothing in class but joke around and refuse to work. Assistant Principal Thompson didn't want to suspend him because, "That's what he expects us to do. Let's be different. Kill 'em with kindness."

Now Manny was torturing Sandra Paez with his typical asshole behavior. Every Friday, they worked on an online reading program and Gaynor let them listen to music. It kept them focused, almost trance-like on what they were doing. Sandra didn't bother anyone, but here came Manny, yanking the earbuds off her head and pulling some hair along with it.

Sandra turned around and punched him in the middle of the chest. Gaynor smiled to himself as Manny's face went beet-red. The shoe had finally dropped.

"Don't touch me," Manny said. "Dumb bitch."

The room fell quiet. Everyone heard it. When Thompson ran

his inevitable investigation, there would be witnesses to testify. Middle school kids always folded like napkins at the first hint of pressure. Manny Poblete would have his day.

Gaynor remained stoic, reaching to the bottom desk drawer for a red referral slip. A couple of gasps scattered through the room. He filled out the form slowly, enjoying every loop and stab of the pen. In that moment, it did indeed feel like a sword.

"Manolo," Gaynor said. "Here you go, young man."

Manny didn't say a word until after he read it. Then followed the expected litany of stammered excuses. Sandra had bothered him all week. It was a delayed retaliation. If only he could really see what she was like outside the classroom. When Gaynor turned to Sandra, she was completely focused on her reading assignment.

"Just get to the office, Manolo. They'll hear everything you have to say down there." Manny had been a bug up every teacher's ass the entire year. Redemption was on its way.

Manny folded the referral and tucked it in his shirt pocket. He hoisted the book bag over his shoulders. "Sure thing, Mister GAY-nor." He slammed the door behind him.

Gaynor felt he had some power again. Ten years as an educator had only made him feel flaccid. Eighty-percent of his day was spent babysitting, prompting students to please take seats and raise hands.

He was lucky if they read a chapter of their assigned reading. Even if they did, most of them wouldn't understand it. On every single ride home from work, Gaynor wondered if he made a difference. With Manny, it finally seemed like a small victory loomed around the corner.

Gaynor felt himself professionally rotting over the years. In his twenties, he was the cool, hip, young teacher who kept up with pop culture, music, and movie references. At damn near forty, with the way society was headed, he didn't care to keep up anymore. Preteens searched for their place in the world, which made them so fucking unreliable. Monday morning, little Jane Doe was a cherubic angel, whispering her problems and asking for advice. By Wednesday, she might crack a joke at his expense just to prove to her crush or desired social circle how much of a bad ass she could be.

Allegiance was non-existent and so Ed Gaynor had lost connection with his students and, as time went on, the rest of the world. Parents were just as hopeless, stupid, and self-centered: a ME generation. If the trunk was cankered, what to expect from the branches?

At least he'd gotten rid of the headache by cutting off the head. Without Manny, the room was quiet as a funeral home. He could read and grade papers without pausing every few minutes to see who threw what across the room. It was amazing the effect just one student had on the rest of them.

Principal Thompson's surly voice piped in from the ceiling. "Mister Gaynor?" He forced his voice into a slow jazz-radio jockey lilt.

"Yes?"

"Can you please send Sandra Paez down to the office?"

"Sure."

Students bumped elbows and pointed as Sandra left the room white as a sheet.

There were five minutes left before final bell when Manny walked back in, followed by Sandra no more than a minute later. Manny walked in with a cocky smile across his face, while Sandra looked as if the weight of the world was hoisted inside her backpack and she couldn't possibly take another step.

"All right, ladies and gentlemen," Gaynor said, "let's stack our chairs and get ready to get going."

As they lined up by the door, Sebastian Scavuzzo crowded Manny in a corner. With stupid grins over their faces, they gesticulated wildly through their conversation. Sandra hadn't moved from her desk. Her head was entirely covered in the school hoodie.

Gaynor called her over.

She stared at the floor, trying not to let anyone catch her crying.

"What's going on?"

The question triggered sobbing so intense, Gaynor thought she might choke. Now everyone was at attention with the nicer kids pretending and the jerks, like Manny and Scavuzzo, smiling like cats that ate the canary.

"Can you stick around for just a couple minutes after the bell?" Gaynor whispered.

She nodded and wiped tears from her eyes. "It has to be quick, though." Her hands shook.

The bell clanged and the herd stampeded to freedom.

"What happened, Sandra?"

She couldn't speak over the sobs.

"Try to calm down. Explain to me what happened down there? Why are you so upset?"

"My mom hits me when I get in trouble. Principal Thompson is going to call my mom and I'm going to get into so much trouble." She stretched her arms out straight in front of her like they were locked in rigor mortis. Hers wasn't a fear of discipline.

Gaynor had developed an eye for abuse over the last decade. Sandra always wore the school sweater one size too big, even in eighty-plus weather. Mom never showed up for parent conferences. In the teacher's lounge, rumor had it she was vicious in her discipline. Sometimes Sandra didn't have lunch and Gaynor would give her some of his. He'd tell her to pretend she was going to the bathroom and she'd take a quick detour up to his room. At least once a week, she asked to stay and have lunch with him. He never agreed to that because if anyone on the faculty saw, it might come across as suspicious.

It was against the rules but Gaynor leaned in, hugged Sandra tight, and let her wail into his shoulder. "I'll talk to Mister Thompson and see what I can do."

"Thank you." She wrapped her arms tight across his back like she might never let go.

Principal Thompson sat behind his desk testing the battery life on a couple of walkies. Normally, Gaynor avoided the man who thought himself interesting, funny, and capable of selling Stevie Wonder glasses. Sitting on his patent-leather desk chair, Thompson made himself the biggest thing in the room. "Manny? Yeah, I had a talk with him and Sandra. Both parents are coming in tomorrow and we're going to have a conference."

"That's the thing. There's no need to bring them both in. He called Sandra a bitch in front of everyone so I sent him straight to you. I don't need that kind of behavior in my class. None of us do."

Thompson nodded his bald head. "I called Mom and he's having a lot of problems at home too. I really don't want to suspend him. That's not the answer with a kid like this. It never worked with me."

God damn it if the guy didn't always find a way to make it about him.

"Suspension would be good for him," Gaynor said. "Kid does nothing all day but stare at a blank paper. When I ask what he's up to, he just shrugs his shoulders and grins that cocky smile."

Thompson stood, walked around the desk, and placed a heavy hand on Ed's shoulder. "I understand but I really want to try and get him back on track."

"There are two weeks of school left."

"I'm aware."

"All right, fine. There is no need to bring in Sandra's mom, then. I can testify on every religious text the girl did nothing to provoke him like that. He's just a disrespectful jerk."

Thompson patted his shoulder. "It's done, Gaynor. I called both parents to let them know we have a meeting tomorrow morning. Let's wait until the morning to talk about it with everyone present."

Ed wanted to scream in his white, freckled face. He hadn't seen how fiercely she shook when she came back upstairs. How Sandra trembled in absolute terror at the thought of her mother being called. "She says her mom will hit her if she gets in trouble."

Thompson looked out the window, scanning the cars lining the front of the school. "I know every student and parent in this building. Every one. Sandra can be very dramatic. I mean, you've noticed she's not all right in the head, right? Two beers short of a six pack."

"Sir, I really—"

"I have to get out there. It's getting clogged. Let's talk about this tomorrow with everyone there. It'll be fine, Gaynor. You'll see." Thompson was almost out of the office when he turned and said, "Thanks for all that you do," and closed the door.

Ed Gaynor and his teaching efforts were an afterthought.

The ride home was cathartic. The first time in the whole day where he heard absolute silence. At the first light from the school, Gaynor stopped next to Sandra's mother's car. Sandra didn't see him because she was facing down, crying while her mother yelled into the space between them. Sandra was getting an earful. It would not be a good day for someone who had done nothing but get picked on.

When the light turned green, mom's open palm went up. Gaynor sped off before he could see where it would land.

What were the phone calls and discipline good for? What to expect from kids who came from houses like that? It was a miracle Sandra had fared as well. If standing up for herself to that asshole resulted in her getting a beat-down, what kind of good were Thompson, the school, or Gaynor himself, doing? The school was doling out customer service, not discipline.

His phone chimed a reminder about tomorrow's parent-teacher conference as he pulled into the driveway. Gaynor watched a duck cross from his patch of grass onto the street. A pickup truck slowly rolled toward it from the four-way intersection. As the duck slowly waddled its way to the middle of the street, the driver accelerated and the duck was trampled under the tires.

"What the fuck?" Gaynor shouted. He'd seen the too-big pickup hauling ass many times through the residential neighborhood. Stickers tacked to its back window promoted all manner of car racing and fishing accessories. "Fucking asshole," Gaynor yelled and threw his phone at the pickup's back window.

A screech of brakes echoed through the block. The driver got out. A long bushy beard pointed down to his chest. On his left shoulder, a devil clutched a pitchfork that stabbed at the guy's sun-tanned brown skin. A second generation Latino playing at redneck. "There a problem, faggot?"

"You just ran over that duck, you fucking prick."

The punch came too fast and hard for Gaynor to counter it. Next thing he knew, there was a pop and Gaynor was on the ground, spitting blood. The truck peeled out into the distance. Gaynor walked to the middle of the road where the duck desperately tried to lift its head like it might easily snap back into place. Drops of blood smeared its beak. Gaynor removed his sweater and wrapped the duck inside it. He drove fast as he could to his cat Felina's vet.

The vet assistant yelled he needed an appointment as he barreled through the door. The duck stopped trembling after Gaynor shot a rapid fire explanation about his sudden visit.

"It's not about my cat this time. It's about the duck. Call the doctor, please."

The veterinarian's eyes went wide. "Jesus, Ed, you're bleeding from your mouth." The doctor pulled out gauze from a drawer and shoved it in Gaynor's hand.

Gaynor had almost forgotten about the punch and was surprised by the size of his bottom lip, swollen like a grapefruit. He pointed to the duck as if the vet might be confused about who needed more immediate medical attention.

The vet examined the duck's limp body and snapped neck.

"Be careful," Gaynor said.

"It's dead, Eddie. Even if you'd brought him earlier there's no way to fix such a serious injury. I am very sorry."

Gaynor sobbed and blubbered like Sandra just a couple of hours earlier. "How much do I owe you?"

"Nothing. Just get to an urgent care and get that lip checked. It needs immediate attention."

There was a mom-and-pop sub shop in the same strip mall.

The pimpled sandwich jockey stared at his lip as Gaynor mumbled as best he could for a BLT. "Extra bacon."

"That costs more."

Gaynor slapped a twenty on the counter, "That's fine," and

dumped the change in the tip jar. The pimply kid thanked him profusely.

Remnants of his phone were still strewn in the street. Gaynor stuffed the split pieces in his pocket and walked inside his small, lake front, matchbox-sized efficiency. Felina purred and rubbed against his ankle. He left the door open so she could roam outside, get some sunlight on her tuxedo coat. From underneath his bed, he pulled out the white fireproof lock box and loaded the gun he kept in it.

Gaynor placed the sandwich and beer on the small plastic table facing the lake. He walked to the water's edge and pulled the phone pieces from his pocket. With an underhand arc, he threw them high in the air and squeezed out three rounds. All of them missed. A neighbor looked out from across the water and ran back in his house.

Felina hid under the chair.

A breeze kicked up as the sky turned the sunset a purple that always convinced him God was a painter. Felina chased ducks she would never catch. The sandwich was saltier than he expected and he could only finish half. The other half he put on the floor. Felina licked it once, sneezed, and pounced off to pretend-hunt.

A wail of police sirens echoed in the distance.

Ed Gaynor finished the rest of his beer in one pull, picked up the gun, and walked off in the direction the truck had disappeared. The police sirens grew louder and closer. Ed Gaynor walked down the middle of the street, gun in hand. It was a small neighborhood. He'd find that truck if it killed him.

Folsom Prison Blues

Ryan Leone

It is never dark in prison. There are gigantic stadium lights outside, with an orange glare that makes it impossible to see the stars while walking the yard's track. It illuminates your cell throughout the night, like a flame teasing a wick that never quite goes out.

Some men tie a T-shirt around their eyes but I've always found the horrors of the penitentiary brighter playing on a black screen. The way dry blood goes brown on a shank; the *tith-tith* of someone getting stabbed, *tith* sounding even longer when the wounds overlap; that sad and vacant look in a lifer's eyes when he has been completely hypnotized by routine.

My celly, a lofty skinhead named Boots, had put me up on prison politics while I was still in the county jail.

"No smoking with the Spades," he said. "No eating with 'em, after 'em, whatever. I try not to do any business with them for any fucking reason. I don't care if they got the best dope. They are animals, bro. California is racially divided 'cuz of all the dumb gangs and shit. If you're weak you are gonna get sniffed out. You gotta put in work for your own people. There's always going to

152

be some lop peckerwood that can't pay his bills who you can go after. And you *need* clean paperwork. If you snitched on your case or are some kinda sex offender, forget it, bro. You are the enemy and when you're discovered you will be murdered."

Murdered.

"One more thing," he said. "Don't mess with the punks. It's like illegal for the government to stop giving them estrogen, so they got tits and everything. They use Kool-Aid as makeup and have long hair. I'm not lying, bro. They look like broads! Years will start playing funny tricks on you, when you see some curvy broad walkin the fucking yard! I seen more people get whacked in the joint over punks than anything else. There are no chicks with dicks."

Boots paused then finished, "There are only dudes with boobs. Remember that. It'll save your life, kid."

I was designated to one of the most violent prisons in the country. Boots gave me some push-and-pull syringes before I left that I had to smuggle in my lubricated ass, an offering to my fellow white comrades.

It's hard smuggling six hypodermic syringes, especially when you have to travel for half of a day on a turbulent bus ride. With each bump on the road, your asshole is agitated and by the time you land on the prison yard, you're bleeding and your anal spokes have been permanently altered.

This is the great paradox: in a world measured by bravado and hyper-masculinity, you are at a favorable advantage by how much contraband you can smuggle up your asshole into the prison gates.

I don't care who you are, you can be doing fourteen months or a life-sentence, but you'll always remember that first night in prison. When those magnetic cell doors slam shut, the ceaseless light reminds you that you are in captivity, the small outside window acting as a hellacious postcard. Instead of palm trees, it is stamped with the silhouette of a gun tower and the ominous coil of razor wire.

It's a night that seems to loop in infinity.

My new celly was a heroin addict named Damien. He was serving a life-sentence for his involvement in an armed bank robbery where he had taken the lives of two innocent tellers. He was young like me but had all the symptoms of a lifer. He was overly friendly with the punks and had this careless stoicism, where he only cared about making each day more tolerable than the day before.

Damien's only hustle was cards. He was the best poker player in the whole yard. It didn't matter the amount of dope debt he accrued, he always managed to get someone to lend him money for a tournament in exchange for a split and he nearly always won.

In typical American fashion, he lived way beyond his means, juggling credit lines and always flirting with the danger of not being able to pay his debts.

His junkie eyes were so pronounced that it looked like he forgot to wash off eyeliner, sunken shadows completely void of life. His skin was jaundiced from years of bacteria-rich jailhouse wine and he had abscess knots and scabs festering on his arms, knuckles, and neck.

The chow-hall was where things really went down in prison because it was one of the only blind spots for the myriad digital cameras. It wasn't uncommon to be grabbing your food tray and see someone stabbed repeatedly in the back before they fell to the floor and go almost completely unnoticed for the duration of the meal.

The chow-hall was always tense.

The California prison politics separated all races in the cafeteria so you had to sit with your own people. It was like looking at a giant quilt of different skin colors. It was very uncommon for a Mexican man to walk over to the white section, so it was particularly troubling when one came up to Damien and leaned down and had a whispered conversation with him.

Later that night Damien told me that he was in trouble. He was in deep this time and the Mexicans were about to go to our people. In prison, if another race brings an issue to your own camp there is an obligation for them to clean it up to avoid the entire penitentiary going up in flames.

He owed $4,500 for heroin.

The Hispanic man that was responsible for collecting the debt was named Diablo. That's Spanish for "The Devil," and he had all the attributes of a demonically possessed man. Short and stalky, emblazoned in ashy Aztec tattoos that served as trophies for his many prison kills.

Damien told me that Diablo had proposed an offer—one last chance before he was reduced to a homicide statistic in the pen. The Mexicans had the heroin trade on lock, and one of the primary methods of smuggling the dope in was through contact visitation. Damien was to become their mule.

Diablo had girls that would come and see Damien. You're allowed an open mouthed kiss in the beginning and at the end of the visit. The girls would pass as many tightly packed balloons full of heroin into Damien's mouth as possible and then after the visit he would come back to his cell and eat a tablespoon full of shampoo to induce vomiting.

He smuggled as many as six grams of heroin in at one visit and he was now doing this three times a week. Diablo was selling the grams for $400 a pop and would reduce Damien's debt by

$100 a week, also providing him with scraps of dope to sustain his miserable and strung-out existence.

For Damien, it didn't matter if he was caught. He was doing life and he foolishly thought he had won some kind of junkie lottery because of all the free drugs he was now receiving.

Diablo was blatantly disobeying prison politics by employing a white-boy to help in the Mexican drug racket. If you're brown, all of the proceeds obtained from drugs are taxed by the "big homie," which is the Mexican hierarchy. This afforded Diablo a chance to circumvent the taxing process and do back-door deals.

The problem was that Diablo and his crew were terrible junkies themselves. They were always filmed in sweat, dope sick, waiting for Damien to get back from his visits.

He would be hunched over in our cell above the metallic toilet, sticking fingers down his throat as the Mexicans cheered him on. A balloon would plop out, one-at-a-time, and he would sit there with blue Head and Shoulders spittle caked around his mouth, panting from the shampoo vomit until the deed was finally done.

Then there was a problem. A young black convict had run up a sizable card debt and was taken into a cell by a bunch of black thugs who tried to make him suck their dicks. He refused and they killed him with an ice pick-style shank; it looked like a screwdriver but was about a third as big. He bled out of the holes poked in him. Then they fucked his corpse, wrapped him in a clear tarp, and dragged his listless bleeding body to the shower. A few other convicts found out that they had missed out on the necrophiliac session and he was taken back from the shower and more monsters had their way with him.

The guards eventually walked in and were so disturbed by what was taking place that they set the entire penitentiary on a lockdown.

The lockdown lasted a week and I watched Damien run out of dope and thrash in his bunk as the insidious drugs sweated themselves out of his pores.

The night before lockdown was over, we had received a kite from Diablo. He had some inside information that we would be off the following day and there was going to be a special visit.

In the note he said, "We are counting on you, Pero. We all sick."

Damien went to visit and came back to find Diablo and three of his crew waiting outside our cell. I was reading a novel on the top bunk when they came in.

They expertly mixed the shampoo with some water to make it more soluble in the plastic spoon and gave it to Damien to drink. It had always taken under a minute to make it come up but he had been projectile vomiting all morning from being dope sick and nothing came out.

They began to express frustration in malevolent Spanish. They made him another and much thicker shampoo shot—and still nothing came out.

You could see the dopesick fury in their faces; all this gringo had to do was puke out their precious antidote. And then the shanks were drawn and I put my book down, ready to defend myself and Damien. In broken English, Diablo explained that they would cut him open and get out the balloons if he didn't produce them. Damien stuck his fingers down his throat once more and nothing came out, just a few feeble suds from the shampoo.

Diablo made a gesture to his biggest henchmen and he rushed me before I had time to react. He pinned me down on my bunk as I struggled to see what was happening below me.

Diablo was holding Damien down as his friend took out the most serrated prison knife I had ever seen, it was over a foot long, like some dystopian weapon, jagged with swirling razored edges.

He stuck it straight into Damien's abdomen as he wailed in horror. He began to carve his stomach open; blood cascaded down his waistline and puddled around his body, intestinal wiring spilling out in a sick honey color you would never know existed inside of a human body.

Diablo stuck his arm into the freshly carved cavity and smirked as he pulled out a handful of multi-colored balloons.

They didn't even look at me after the guy let me go—they were too concerned about getting well. They left Damien's snarled corpse on the floor in the cell and eventually the guards came in because blood began dripping out of the cell and down the tier.

They knew Damien was a dope fiend and blamed it on a debt; there was no static, no investigation. **The guards knew better than to ask me. They knew I couldn't say a word even if I saw something. And of course I'd say I did not. Besides, what did I really see?**

Life is cheap in prison. Heroin is not.

Walk the Line

James R. Tuck

THE FIRST PART

"They always hire bums like me for jobs like this."

Darla turned further on the bench seat, putting her back against the door, ignoring the street passing outside the window. And the seat belt. He felt her near-silver spooky eyes on him like a Medeco lock on a chain. "Why *you* though?"

He shrugged, hoping between that and his studious watching where he was driving she'd be pushed off her line of questioning.

It worked about as well as he thought it would.

Those eyes kept boring into him, so sharp it felt like pressure.

"You have a problem with me being on this?"

"I've heard nothing but good things about Garrett McCabe so why would I?" The shake of her head pulled at the corner of his vision. "Just call me a curious cat, but Tony chooses people for reasons, so why you?"

"Yeah? Why'd he pick you?"

He caught the gleam of her smile from the corner of his eye, heard the snake hiss of stockings under her skirt over the hum of the engine. "Don't be silly, dear, you know why."

His throat went tight around a hard lump.

He swallowed it down and focused on the street ahead. "He said I'm trustworthy."

The laugh jerked her forward, hair spilling over softly rounded shoulders and more softly rounded cleavage. He didn't look, just let the blood auburn over pure cream float in his peripheral.

"Ah." Her bottom lip curved down in a frown of concentration "You're serious."

"It's what he said."

"Honey, you're in the same business we all are. Why would he think you're trustworthy?"

"The fuck does that mean?"

"Well, you're a criminal, dearheart."

"Doesn't make me a crook."

"Touché, I suppose. Still . . ."

"Still what?" Anger began to eat away the distraction of her, just the edges, but some relief.

"Why would he think *you* were trustworthy and *I'm* not?"

"He didn't say anything like that."

"I inferred it."

"Don't. I don't speak for Big Tony."

Her hand found her chin as she studied him. He turned right, and then left, following the route as he knew it in his head.

"New question."

He grunted his assent as he looked for a place to put the car.

"What are you packing?"

"I'm not."

"Not?"

"I don't carry. I'm on parole."

This made her sit straight. "You are the strangest person he has ever partnered me with."

He couldn't tell if that was a compliment.

"How are you going to do this without a gun?"

He lifted his hand off the steering wheel, letting it hang in the air between them.

"Are you kidding me? I have to rely on you and your . . ."

He clenched his hand into a fist.

"Oh."

His hand had become like unto a thing of horn-ridged callous and seamed leather, a hammer of flesh and bone, forged in a youth spent digging coal and bare-knuckle boxing.

She reached out and he unclenched, the movement stopping her. "Gimme." Her voice had gone petulant, all spoiled little girl.

He kept his eyes looking for an alley or a parking spot with access, driving with his left. After a moment he let his right drift slightly toward her, inviting. She shimmied forward on the seat, skirt sliding up sleek thighs. He specifically didn't look. Her hands were quick and confident, grasping his palm, tugging his hand toward her, separating his fingers, tracing the scar tissue that laced across each one.

Something hot and wet and tight slid over his thumb, clamping around the base with harsh suction.

He jerked his hand back as if it had been burned, thick knuckle scraping the undersides of teeth, ragged nail catching on soft lip as it pulled free from her mouth with a little *pop*. Her face chased after it for a second, moving forward, jaw working, eyes closed to slits.

The car swerved as he pulled it back into the lane.

"What the hell!"

Her eyes opened, the silver-gray gone dark tungsten with . . . something. Slowly, she slid back into her seat, turning to face the windshield. Spine straight and knees together primly she opened her clutch. "That's how I learn about new things." She pulled out a tube of lipstick, twisted it open, and raised it, stopping a half inch away. "I put them in my mouth," she said and began painting her now swollen lips.

Just in case he missed her point.

THE NEXT PART

"That was quite a thing!"

She tumbled into the car as he turned the key, shifted, and pulled away from the warehouse faster than it would appear to any onlookers. A glance in the rearview showed no one on the street but you could never tell. Smoke was just beginning to leak out of the top windows as he turned the corner and the building disappeared from sight.

"I've never seen anything like that!" She vibrated in the seat beside him, fingers working the clasp of the canvas bag she'd carried out.

Click-click, click-click, click-click, over and over and over and over again.

"Knock that off."

Her fingers stopped, hovering over the bag for a moment before clicking the clasp one more time and pulling the flap up to reveal a jumble of dark green and mint paper. She leaned over the bag and inhaled deeply, letting it lift her shoulders and throw her back against the door like it was a fat rail of Columbia's finest export. Her fingers plucked at the hem of her skirt. "God, I *love* the smell of ill-gotten gains."

He kept driving, feeling the blood on his hands and face drawing tight as it dried.

"You were amazing in there, darling."

He kept driving, feeling the blood on his hands and face drawing tighter as it dried.

"The way you dropped that guy with the shotgun, just POW!

And he was out like you hit him with a bat. I've never seen anyone move as fast as you." She rocked onto her knees on the seat. "It *really* worked for me."

"You should sit down."

She moved closer, a cat on the hunt. "Those guys back there aren't coming after us and we have time before we have to get back."

He kept his eyes straight ahead, even though the deep V of her blouse pulled even lower as she stretched.

"We can find someplace, pull off for a bit," fingernails trailed across his side causing a ripple of sensation that made his nipples harden. "We don't even have to get out of the car."

"You're Big Tony's girl."

"Big Tony has lots of girls."

Her hand skimmed lower. He shifted, dropping his elbow to block her before she could reach his belt.

"I'm driving, Darla."

"Pull *over*, Garrett."

"Sit back down."

"Pull over and I'll sit anywhere you want." Her voice was a purr, so close to his ear the moisture from her mouth was warm on the side of his neck.

"Sit down. I'm warning you."

"What are you going to do?" Her tongue flicked hot and wet across his earlobe. "Eh, big boy?"

His hand flashed off the steering wheel and slammed into the dash with a crack like a shotgun blast. The hard vinyl split under the blow.

Darla threw herself back in a streak of pale skin and locks of red hair like a tempest. "You'd hit me?!"

"Don't push me and I won't."

The bag of money lay in the floorboard, knocked there by her, loose cash fluttered on the floor pan. She didn't even glance down, crossing her arms under her bosom and glaring at him. "What's your fucking problem?"

"Right now? You are."

"That's insulting," she said "And stupid."

"You asked."

She shifted, planting one leg on the seat between them, knee against the back of it, the other up under the dash, that knee against the glove compartment. Her skirt hem draped between thighs that were all cream above dark stocking tops. "I can see from here that you want to, big boy, so you're not gay." She snarled, all the purring seduction ripped from her voice as it dropped. "You too fucking pussy for pussy fucking?"

His teeth hurt from clenching. "I won't warn you again."

"You're not going to help me out then tell me why."

He almost didn't answer, just shut his mouth and kept driving. He didn't owe her shit. Just deliver her and the money and the car back to Big Tony, get paid, and go home.

He rubbed his face; the callouses on his palm scratched his skin and felt good as he pulled thoughts together.

"You drink coffee?" he asked.

"You saw me with a cup when you picked me up."

"You ever have someone make *you* a cup of coffee?"

"You *saw* me *with a cup* when you *picked me up*." She spoke the words like he was an idiot.

"Not make coffee and serve it to you, but study you, figure out what your tastes are, what you like, and then work on it until they could make a cup of coffee exactly how it tastes best to you, even though you never knew yourself what that could be like. Make the coffee *specifically* just for you so that all their love and attention and care is distilled into one single cup that you then drink and ingest and it becomes a part of who you are and you carry a little bit of them in your belly for the rest of the day."

"No." Her face went sad, her knees drifting closer to each other. "I've never had that."

"I have. Every morning."

"Damn."

"Yeah."

From the corner of his eye, he watched her fingers move across her cheeks and then wipe off against her skirt.

He drove as she slowly turned and faced the windshield again. After a long moment she said in a still small voice, "So, you're going to walk that line."

It wasn't a question so he didn't give an answer.

She didn't expect one.

THE LAST PART

"It's all there."

Big Tony spun his chair around to look at Garrett over his desk. "We'll see."

"Sorry, just been a long day. Ready to go home."

"Yes," Darla piped up. "He has to go get a cup of *coffee*."

Garrett didn't say anything but his hand itched with the want to hit something and his ears felt hot and tight against his skull.

Big Tony looked from her to him and back again. "He can go have all the coffee he wants once Terrance finishes counting."

"Not much longer, boss," Terrance called from the corner, over the flutter and hum of the Safescan bill counter on the table in front of him.

Big Tony took a sip of mineral water from a bottle. "Any hitches?"

Garrett shook his head. Darla said nothing.

"Fire was a good idea." Big Tony lit a thin twisted cigarillo, puffing into the air. "That'll keep them scrambling, make them have to figure out a new place to hold shit."

"That was Darla," Garrett said.

"I have real good ideas." She glared daggers at him.

"You have an idea of doing something before getting here?"

The question was asked in the quiet, dangerous voice Big Tony sometimes got. Garrett had heard it once before when Big Tony thought the guy Terrance replaced was skimming off the top. It wasn't a whisper, but the lowest tone Big Tony's natural voice could effect, and it rolled across the room like a tide in a pool. The only sound left behind it the crisp flutter of the bill counter.

Darla's eyes went so narrow they were thin strips like tinsel. "You know better than that."

"Do I?" Big Tony asked.

Darla shook her head in anger not answer, and shifted her whole body away from him in her chair. Big Tony pointed at Garrett. "She proposition you on the way back?"

He just wanted to go home. "Mr . . ."

"Answer the fucking question."

He'd be home fifteen minutes after he left here. Fifteen minutes. Maybe he should be done with jobs from Big Tony. If the house were closer to being paid off he'd go straight, get a job in a little shop helping customers or in a factory somewhere nearby where he could go on autopilot for eight hours a day.

If only.

Yeah, right.

"Go ahead." Darla slid back around. "Answer his question."

Garrett dipped his head. "I said no. Never even thought about it."

Big Tony sighed. "It's okay. I knew you wouldn't. You're trustworthy." His hand came up from under the desk holding an ugly, blunt thing of wood and steel.

It took Garrett's brain a half second to realize it was a sawed-off shotgun, the barrels cut back till the tips of the shells were visible as thin green stripes. Darla realized what it was at the same time. Her mouth opened in a wild wail of a scream.

Big Tony cut her off with a squeeze of the trigger.

Both barrels spit fire and thunder into the small room, displacing all the air, making it concuss against Garrett's face.

Darla's chest folded in on itself and looked like someone had thrown a bucket of paint on her. The blast slewed her chair around, dumping her on the floor where her body rolled in a jumble of loose limbs and wild auburn hair.

Garrett stared down at her.

She don't even look real anymore.

Big Tony reloaded the shotgun.

"All the money is here, boss." Terrance said, as undisturbed by the gun violence and the dead woman on the floor as a butcher would be by a hamburger.

His voice was hollow in Garrett's ears, his hearing all jumbled from the shotgun blast.

"Jesus." Garrett's throat had closed; all he could get out after the Lord's name was, "What?"

The shotgun went back under the desk. "Nobody steals from me."

"Steal?"

"You said she propositioned you."

"She did, what's that got to do with money? I didn't fuck her."

"Wait," Big Tony's face creased so hard it nearly folded in half, "she propositioned you for *sex*?"

"Yeah."

Big Tony considered this as if it were a new thought. "And you said no?"

That drew Garrett short, cutting through the fog at watching a coworker killed in cold-blood in front of him. "You knew I would. I've got Jenny at home."

"Ah, yes, Jenny." He leaned forward, peering down from over the desk at Darla's corpse. "You missed out. She was a certifiable hellcat." Big Tony sat back down. "She wasn't stealing from me?"

"Not that I know of."

"Shame I had to let her go over a misunderstanding then."

Garrett didn't say anything.

Big Tony relit his cigarillo. "Your mess, you clean it up."

Garrett couldn't believe his still ringing ears. "Do what now?"

"You heard me."

I should just leave. Fuck the money. The image of Jenny hunched over the bills came into his mind. "I didn't do this."

"You weren't clear in answering my question. She got done because of it. It's on you to get rid of her."

Garrett considered Darla's body and the things he would have to do to make it disappear.

He thought about Jenny waiting at home.

He thought about coffee.

"I get her cut too."

Big Tony took a few puffs. "Fair enough."

"And I'm not cleaning your fucking rug."

Jackson

Angel Luis Colón

"What in the blue-blazing fuck have you been at?" Jesse pops up in my periphery like a cheap jump scare in a horror flick. There's at least two days' worth of driving in his eyes. "You promised me you weren't going to run off like some maniac."

Me? I'm nursing a three-day bender and a knot on the side of my head the size of a toddler's fist thanks to lipping off at a few truck stop hookers the night before. I instinctively pull closer the duffel bag on the barstool to my left. It's heavy with money, guns, and pre-packed sandwiches—my entire Canadian escape plan for when the deed was done.

Corrado chose a hell of a place to run.

I fight a burp that's threatening to provide rocket propulsion to my liquid breakfast. "You know damn well why I'm here."

Jesse sits and orders a beer from the bartender. I think her name's Stacy? She serves without asking questions. Permanent scowl on her face—the kind folks wear when they peaked in high school and see no future past the end of that counter. I envy that. I envy her ability to stand there and not want to move forward towards whatever awaits.

Jesse whispers between his teeth, "Let's finish up and get you home. I've been keeping tabs on the local police bands and TV. Ain't nobody seen your real face. Nobody knows you're in drag." He fidgets in the wobbly stool.

"I ain't done yet," I say. I avoid eye contact because fuck him, that's why. This was supposed to be a solo journey and I'm a little sore he's come along to ruin the general hopeless, aimless drive I was working on for so long.

"There's no way you're accomplishing this bat-shit plan without getting hurt or worse."

I burp into my fist again, motion to Stacy. "Sweetheart, you make Bloody Marys here?"

Stacy grimaces. "If you're cool with Clamato and some well vodka, sure."

"That sounds absolutely divine, my love."

Stacy winks at me. "I got you."

The perks of tipping big in no-horse town like Jackson, New Hampshire. I take a sip of the room temp beer in front of me. "Look, Jesse, I appreciate your concern, truly do, but motherfucker gotta pay. If you really wanna do me a solid, go back home and take care of Carl Weathers for me."

Jesse sighs. "Man, that old mutt's farting himself to death on Leigh's porch. He's fine. I worry about you. This ain't like you."

I laugh. "This is completely like me. I was fucking wronged, honey. How can I turn down the chance to get back at the cruel son of a bitch that broke my goddamned heart and took all my shit?"

That. Yeah. Corrado Ferrante. We met online—a subreddit providing tips and tricks for drag performers like me. He said he was from Italy and working on his visa. He didn't perform but he was a fan of the scene. We met a few times. He came to my shows at the burlesque hall since it turned out he was local. We played at the flirting thing, but I wasn't entirely out of the closet yet. Still, over time, I got used to him. I got used to those handsome features and that accent of his. Then the honey started flowing. He got me drunk on promises and cheap thrills—coke, ketamine, the occasional smash & grab. We partied well together.

So obviously, when certain federal mandates came to pass, he looked me in the eye and asked, "Will you marry me?" We'd only been together as a couple maybe a week or two at that point.

No ring. No knee. No pomp. It was the single most romantic moment of my life.

"Yes," was my immediate and unfortunate answer.

Three months later, Corrado needed some air after yet another argument. He never came back. When I got to my apartment, the place was gutted. Even the goddamn mantle—which came with the apartment—was gone. Our joint account was cleaned out, closed. The lease I thought he took care of? Non-existent. We were living month to month. Even the wedding license, something else I ignored since he was the one who handled those matters, didn't exist. Corrado Ferrante was a ghost, a man who literally lived in my memory.

It took a year of digging but I finally found another name for Corrado: Eric. More digging and Eric became James, became Francesco, became Piotr, and finally David Grimes. Ten years older than he said he was. Originally from Chicago. He had a habit of honey-potting men around the country and taking them for every single dime. It was a shot in the dark traveling to Chicago to the only address I found associated with him but it was worth it.

I met his mother in the rat hole apartment Corrado apparently spent his entire childhood as David. His mother had sharp features like him. She wore her makeup sloppy—like she gave no fucks. The housedress she wore was stained and at least three sizes too big for her. She took me through the story, about how David was a pathological con artist. He'd even taken her for a fair share of her social security, the poor mess. She said this was his disease and I said he could use a cure. It hurt her to hurt him but the woman was tired and the $10K I planted on her kitchen counter sure had a way of speaking my case better than I could.

So she told me all about Jackson. She told me about Corrado's love of hunting and fancy getaway vacations.

She gave me handwritten directions.

Jesse won't leave me be. He climbs into my rental car as I try to sneak off at four in the morning—the same time as every other slack-jawed hunter in the area. They're all in little groups chatting quietly and sipping coffee from massive thermoses.

"Made coffee," Jesse grunts as he hands me a thermos of my own.

"Thanks." I take a long sip. The coffee tastes like group therapy but it feels good to get the roof of my mouth singed. "There's no going back now." I fidget. I'm wearing rugged wear—hunting gear—and I'm utterly uncomfortable. It feels like I'm wearing someone else's skin.

"We're not there yet. Still plenty of time to talk sense into you."

I force a smile. Jesse's good people. He's taken great care to be a friend through and through. He was my best man, hell, he was the reason I met Corrado. I think Jesse overcompensates now after what happened as a means to deal with his guilt. I tell him I'm a big boy and made all these horrible, no-good decisions while wearing my big boy pants, but he never listens.

"You see him among these folks?" Jesse points to the wandering hunters with his chin.

"Nope." I take another sip of coffee. "Thinking he's in one of the fancy cabins up the hill. Seemingly has enough cash money to live the good life. Probably has a deer stand right outside the master bedroom so you can fuck and then murder something innocent before the afterglow fades."

Jesse chuckles. "Christ, you are one embittered fucking queen, ain't you?"

"Downright whiskey sour."

Jesse clears his throat. He's caught himself "enabling"—his word, not mine—and knows joking along will only make him guiltier than he was before. "I still think you can solve this with words."

"There'll be talking."

"That all?"

I press the ignition button on the dash and switch the car into drive. "We'll figure it out when we get there."

We pull up to a cabin after two hours of driving and stopping to talk to random hunters on the trails and roads. I feel like an idiot when I see the mailbox says "Grimes" on it in what looks to be handwritten calligraphy—how fucking tacky.

"Jesus Christ," Jesse says.

"What?"

"There's a fucking deer stand on the balcony."

I lean my head out the window and follow the poplar flanking the house up its side and sure enough, buried in the foliage is a fucking deer stand with easy access to a balcony. The house itself looks like something designed to serve as an LL Bean catalog backdrop. I imagine the inside being empty aside from a mattress in one of the bedrooms. The place seems too large for actual care.

"This doesn't feel right." Jesse seems to press his back into his seat as if he's hoping it'll cocoon him. "Walk away. All this will do is let him know he damaged you completely. He still wins this way."

I reach for my duffel bag. "It's not about winning."

"Then why not call and scream? Hell, just yell at him from the car." Jesse draws an arc over his head with both hands. "Make a scene. Embarrass the hell out of him."

I snort. "Embarrass him in front of whom? The fucking deer and rabbits?" I shake my head. "Nah. He needs to pay for what he did."

"So, what, you're going to shoot him? Make yourself a murderer over a thieving piece-of-garbage?"

"No, asshole, I'm going to rob him and bust his fucking head open. I'm going to do a tenth of what he did to me but maybe, maybe that'll be enough to teach him—to make him remember me." I needed to get out of this car before I lost my temper. "And fuck you for the judgement, Mr. 'Oh, it was totally my fault for introducing you guys online.'"

Jesse watches me. "You think he doesn't remember you?"

"All those other guys left behind?" I fight the urge to punch the dash until my hands go bloody. "In another year or two, I'm a memory. Maybe lucky enough to be the punchline of a story he tells his friends." I want to let more out—to open the floodgates—but I don't. Nobody deserves my anger more than David. It's the only real power I have anymore.

"You don't need to tag along." I yank the duffel to the front seat and move to get out of the car.

"Jesus," Jesse says as he grabs and holds onto the bag. "Can you not go in like you're in an action movie? Talk it out. Don't give him the satisfaction of being the one asshole to finally cross this bridge. Besides, if you're only going to rough him up, you don't need an arsenal."

I turn and look at this perfectly sane asshole. "Can you stop appealing to the better part of me?"

"I don't think there's another part beyond that. Just let this all breeze by. Brush your teeth, comb your hair or whatever platitude helps you process all these feelings." Jesse flashes me a smile and it earns a pinprick of guilt—more than enough.

"Fine." I let go of the stupid bag—I've got a revolver at the small of my back either way. "We'll do this your way."

"You holler and I'll be your personal Rambo." Jesse takes my hands in his. "I'm so fucking sorry about this, Junebug."

I hate that nickname. I pull my hands away from his and get out of the car without reacting.

The nerves hit as soon as I'm at the front door of the cabin. Maybe Jesse is completely right on this: what good does causing a scene do for anyone? It certainly won't help me. Fuck's sake, this is hunting country; what good is the little heater at my back going to do against rifles and shotguns and fucking crossbows? I turn to look at Jesse and I'm not entirely sure if I want him to give me a way out or to provide me with reassurance.

He does neither. Only stares at me like a kicked dog.

I take a deep breath and knock on the door with the gusto a jilted and betrayed lover should. I call out as loud as I can. There's no answer at first but I can hear footsteps from inside that house—his footsteps.

"Goddamn it, Corrado." I slam my fist against the door again. "Grow a pair and look me in the fucking eyes."

"I called the cops," the voice sounds nothing like Corrado, but I realize I never actually heard this bastard's real speaking voice. This is David, a namby-pamby-sounding con-artist piece-of-shit. "I called them when I saw you idling in the car. They'll be here any minute."

I am not having that so I start kicking the door. I start

screaming and shaking my head harder than Faye Dunaway holding all of the wire hangers in the world. "Open this fucking door," I scream with such a murderous edge that even I imagine myself as a perfect, emotionally abusive foster mother.

I hear the tumblers of the locks move and the door creaks open. The face that voice belongs to is pudgy—not Corrado. The man looks legitimately terrified. So terrified, I have to fight the urge to turn around because nobody has ever been that scared of me so there must be a bear behind me.

"Please," he says with a hand held up and out to stop me.

I ignore him and barge into the house. "David! Corrado! Whatever the fuck you're calling yourself. Come out." I turn and take in the space. It's gorgeously decorated, Teddy Roosevelt by way of Pier One. There are framed photos of the kind-eyed man with Corrado hanging on the wall in front of me. I snatch a picture and turn to the kind-eyed man. "Where is this son of a bitch?"

The man blinks. "Lawrence?"

"Oh for fuck's sake, is that the name he used for you?" I look up towards the second-floor landing. "Hey, Larry, get your ass out here."

"He's not here."

"Bullshit."

"I swear. He's out in Chicago sorting out family business." His voice doesn't tremor, his eyes don't twitch, and he doesn't even touch his face. No tells. I want to believe him but isn't believing what brought me all this way?

"Call him then." I pull the gun before I can tell myself that it's the dumbest idea I've ever had. "Call him. Prove to me he's in Chicago."

"I can't do that."

I nod. "Sure. You're living it up, right? Can't give up your cash cow, no?"

The man narrows his eyes. He makes a sound like a cough. "I'm the breadwinner." He points to the door. "I told you I called the cops. I wasn't lying about that and I'm not lying about Chicago. His mother died."

More lies. "I was just at her apartment three days ago. She told me all about this place. About your wonderful little life. His name wasn't Larry there, though, it was David Grimes."

The man's eyes go wide. He laughs. "This is ridiculous. You're crazy." He reaches in his back pocket and pulls out his wallet. He offers it to me.

"I don't want your fucking money, man."

He nudges the wallet towards me. "Take it. Open it. Please."

I reach over and take the wallet. Keep the gun leveled at him. I open it and look inside. "What the fuck am I looking for?"

"My ID."

I flip a fold over and spot his driver's license. The fucking name: David Grimes. "I don't understand."

David's eyebrows perk up. "You mind if I get something?"

I shake my head.

David walks to a small cabinet and slides open a drawer. He pulls a photo album out. "Is this the woman you spoke to?" He hands me a photo of Corrado with a squat woman. She's blonde, short, and very pale—nothing like the woman I spoke with in Chicago. Nothing like the woman that passed on so many of her features to her son.

"Oh my fucking God." It was Corrado I spoke to. How in the hell did I not see that it was him in front of me the whole time?

David's eyes are wet now. "I think I'm seeing where this was supposed to go." He sits across from me. "I woke up a few days ago and he was gone. He told me his mother passed and that he wanted to make peace with remaining family—see, he said things fell apart after he came out to them last year." David paces the room slowly. "Then this morning, I got an alert. Someone was trying to clear out my accounts. Thankfully, I never trusted him enough to give him full access to everything. The stories were always so weird, you know? Like, I loved him and trusted him when he was right there but when he was elsewhere, I felt the way a rabbit probably feels before a mountain lion leaps from the brush." He stops pacing and laughs—it's actually a bright, chipper laugh. "I can't believe this. I saw your car and said to myself, he sent someone to kill me. I wasn't wrong. I have no idea why that's so fucking funny right now."

"Smarter than me," I whisper, "I'm sorry." I walk to the door and open it. The car is gone. The money and guns are gone. The man who introduced me to Corrado and led me down the aisle with a smile on his face is gone.

I turn around. David is sitting down. He's staring at the floor the same way I did so long ago. We're both a pair of idiots, both taken because of love or pride or something else entirely. I can't find any space in my brain to work it out. "Hey, David?"

David looks to me. All that kindness in his eyes fading away. "Yeah?"

"The cops really coming?"

He shakes his head. "No. I was sort of hoping to appeal to your better judgment."

I throw the gun into the snow—my better judgment in full gear. "You have any liquor in the house?"

"Gallons."

I nod. Stare out at the snow-covered driveway and through the trees. "How about I make you a drink, David? I think we've got a lot to talk over." I close the door, leave my boots on the welcome mat, and walk inside.

I Don't Know Where I'm Bound

Jennifer Maritza McCauley

It was Mavis' last day in Nashville and he was ready to kick that city for good. Mavis, birch-brown, twig-thin and thick-maned, looking nothing like Nashville's postermen, was throwing back a shot at some blues joint in Printer's Alley. His half-sister Henrietta, a rust-colored santera, and Skitt, her painterboy friend, flanked him on both sides. They prattled on about nothing-stuff and Mavis wasn't listening. He counted the hours 'til he could get on I-24 and ditch Tennessee.

The city itself was fine. Mavis felt the same way about Nashville as he did most places: nothing. Mavis' father was a Greek-American theatre director who offed himself a year after Mavis was born, and his mother was a negra Dominican actress who died from melanoma soon after. Mavis spent most of his young life in Savannah with his half-sister and his mother's first husband, a Creole jazzman who toured the country and shuttled Mavis and Henrietta along with him. Whether Mavis was rumbling through the Deep South with his stepdaddy or in Miami and New Orleans for college, he felt dull connections to cities. Mavis didn't look like he belonged anywhere either: his skin was peanut-colored, his head box-shaped and boasting back-length coils of inky hair. All-colored folks frequently asked Mavis "whereareyoufrom" since he resembled any folk from any dark country.

Henrietta was Mavis' only real connection. She moved with Mavis to New Orleans after he set up JazzKidz, a non-profit with his grad-school pals. He followed his half-sister to Nashville, after his program lost its funding fast and she scored a part-time job reading tarot for a has-been CMT darling. Mavis re-opened his program at a TSU-sponsored prep school, but after two years, JazzKidz tanked a second time. When Mavis got offered a research assistant job at a museum on 18 & Vine in Kansas City, he took it. Henrietta stayed behind. He'd likely fail in KC, alone, but at least he'd be someplace different.

Still, Mavis was here now, in Nashville. Sitting at a short table on the second-floor of Bourbon Blues, looking over the iron-lace railing at the stage below. Here he was, prickly-feeling in this New Orleans-themed boogie bar, at this going away party thing Henrietta had planned for him, this thing she probably hoped would be tear-filled or frothy with laughter. It wasn't. Mavis didn't want to hang out in some faux-Louisiana club in Nashville. He didn't want to feel the weight of two failures and two cities he was sick of. He preferred to get wasted in the townhouse he and Henrietta shared, far away from the singer on the stage below, who Mavis loved.

The kid Mavis loved was called Beefie and he was on that stage, laughing loud. Black-skinned, nineteen and baby-faced, the boy was fiddling with his mic. Henrietta waved at Beefie, the bangles on her wrists clanging, near-hitting Mavis in the jaw. Beefie beamed big at them, showing off a row of milky teeth. His lavender eyes flashed, he pointed at Mavis and said, "I got you today!"

Mavis looked away. Only kid in Nashville who'd ever made Mavis' belly flip and here Beefie was grinning all angel-like for Mavis. Mavis glanced at Skitt, the plaid-shirted hipster and boyfriend of Beefie. Skitt was sitting too close to Mavis and watching the kid too. Skitt's face blasted so much pride, Mavis wanted to sock him in the fucking head.

Mavis massaged his temples. It was for the best he was leaving, he was shitty at romantic stuff anyway. He'd run through plenty of guys and girls in Nashville but nothing lasted past a month. Beefie was special, but not enough to make Mavis stay in the city.

Henrietta leaned over, whispered to her brother, "You should be proud. Beefie wouldn't be here if it weren't for you."

Mavis snatched her cranberry vodka and downed half of it in one gulp.

She was sort-of right. Two years before this "party," Mavis had walked in on one of Henrietta's cowrie readings in their townhome living room. Beefie was kneeling on the carpet, asking Henrietta about gigs, if he'd ever get one. This kid: night-colored, his nose crooked to the left, his skinny body layered with flat muscles. Mavis thought that boy was hella sexy. JazzKidz hadn't completely gone under yet, and Mavis knew some musicians on Broadway, so he just barged in, asked Beefie to sing a little something-something. Right there, Beefie belted out Otis Redding's "Tennessee Waltz," sang it so fine Henrietta clutched her neck and Mavis got stung with love. The day after, Mavis hooked Beefie up with a country guitarist who needed someone to front his Broadway band. Within a month, Beefie was singing at Tootsie's and Blue-Girl nightly and pulling in fat tips. For the next two years, Mavis couldn't shake his love.

Mavis wanted another drink. He turned around, checking for Hot Waitress. HW had been giving him some sweet eyes all night and he liked her. She had this blonde-rose wig, was pretty much all tits and she'd been bumping into tables all night, which he thought was kind-of cute. When the waitress bumbled over, the guitarist was already talking. He was going on about how privileged they were to play on the Jimmy Hall stage, where BB King and James Brown once performed. Blah blah.

Henrietta elbowed Mavis, tried to get his attention off HW and back to Beefie's show. Mavis ignored his sister and waved Hot Waitress over. The girl flounced to the table, pushed her fleshy breasts close to his face.

"What you need, cutie?" she asked.

"You think I'm cute?" Mavis grinned. He knew girls liked his little smirks. Nashville girls who weren't checking for Blake Shelton knock-offs thought Mavis was hot and swarthy. The smile worked on HW.

She smashed her pale, wobbling breasts together. "Maybe. You're exotic."

The tequila hit Mavis now, and he felt pretty damn dashing. "I'm black."

"Mixed?"

"Yeah."

"You straight?"

"I'm looking at you right now," Mavis chuckled. "Get me two more shots of tequila?"

She bit her bottom lip. "'Kay. But let's talk later."

Never mind, Mavis thought. He didn't want her rummaging through his life. He shot HW a naw kind of look and she stamped off.

Henrietta wrenched Mavis' shoulder back to her. "Show some respect to your friends. Please."

Mavis shrugged. He didn't want to see Beefie's goodbye show. Beefie didn't give a damn about him. Even if he did, Mavis couldn't do anything about it. That kid was one of those traditional Tennessee boys; he wanted a planned-out future, a bright wedding ring and a barn. Mavis wouldn't give him any of that.

Then, guitar strings sizzled. D7/AG/G7. A spill of keyboard. Long whine of sax. Of course, Beefie was doing that damn Otis cover. The kid had performed the Patti Page version at Tootsie's; the band mixed it spectacularly with Cash's "Tennessee Flat Top Box." Mavis liked Beefie's voice on Otis cover—it was Patti-high but scuffed with all of Otis' brusque pain.

Henrietta squealed. The waitress tossed Mavis' drinks on the table.

"Tip's on you," Mavis said to Henrietta, as HW walked off. He put down the shot and it scorched his stomach quick.

"This one's for my friend Mavis! Here's hoping he'll come back!" Beefie said. Some of the crowd clapped politely. Some folks drunkenly coughed Mavis' name like they knew him. Most folks leaned into lovers, murmured orders to the shuffling waitstaff, gnawed on Buffalo wings and alligator bites.

Beefie, glowing under orange light, killed that damn song. Tore Mavis up something awful. Sorority girls were hollering to nobody but the other folks stopped their talk; they wanted to see this kid croon about snatched-away love. Henrietta put her hand over Mavis' and he let her.

Beefie kept on singing. Rainbow lights streaked across the band. Skitt snapped photographs of his boyfriend with his pretentious-ass Rolleiflex. Mavis' insides toughened, softened. It was too fucking much. He leapt up from his chair and Henrietta got up too, said something like "Don't." Mavis held up a pack of Marlboro and ran down the spiral stairs, past the stage where Beefie was still singing him off.

Outside, in the alley, under a drooping string of lights, Mavis lit a smoke. He watched drunk folks turtle in and out of Bourbon's open doors. His wrists shuddered bad and he caught his lighter from dropping twice.

Mavis felt lonely as fuck, even though he had folks waiting for him inside. Girls with white-blonde hair curled to their asses wobbled along, tourists with white tummies shaking out of shirts waddled nearby, taut-bodied Alabama bros pumped their fists. These folks were going to parade onto Broadway, whining and brawling, upchucking all over the Elvis statue in front of the gift shop. How long had Mavis been looking at these folks? Too long.

Mavis finished his cigarette, flicked it to the floor. He looked at the star-specked spread above Printer's Alley. The sky was black, ancient, boring.

Mavis couldn't finish his second cigarette because, of course, there was trouble. Henrietta sprinted out of Bourbon, her patchwork skirt swinging, silver bracelets banging. She found Mavis, fell onto his chest and said, "Have you seen Beefie? Has he contacted you?" She stumbled back, out of breath.

"What's up?" Mavis said sharply. Knowing Henrietta, she was probably freaking out about nothing.

"We can't find Beefie."

Mavis raised his eyebrows.

Henrietta threw her hands on her hips and shook her head, her wild curls tumbling into her little face. "After you left, he ran off the stage. The band's just doing their own songs."

Mavis didn't understand why Beefie would run out. "He's probably fucked up. Throwing up in the bathroom or whatever."

"They checked all the bathrooms and the rooms backstage. You didn't see him run out?"

"No." Mavis shook his head. "He might have slipped out the back."

"And his phone is off."

Mavis rolled his eyes. "Of course."

"Beefie doesn't run out of shows," she said, the edges of her mouth quivering.

Sure, Beefie lived for his music. Sure, Mavis had watched Beefie spend nights on their apartment floor memorizing Tootsie's setlists. But that kid was ditzy as fuck. He lost his phone daily, had a staggeringly shitty alcohol tolerance and a penchant for sleepwalking. For all Mavis knew, Beefie had gone backstage to check on a sound glitch and tripped into a closet.

"We'll figure it out," Mavis said. His head throbbed.

As if the night couldn't get more annoying, Skitt showed up. The painterboy wandered into the group, nose to iPhone, his eyebrows knitted. "Hey guys," he said, without looking up. "Nothing. Called our landline at home too."

Mavis reached into his pocket for his lighter. When Skitt said "home," it stung a little, the word conjured images of Skitt and Beefie clutching each other under body-warmed sheets. "This isn't serious," Mavis said and lit the cigarette.

Skitt finally tore his eyes away from his phone. He snarled at Mavis. "Okay," Skitt said. "Let's take advice from Mavis, the guy who bailed on Beefie's show."

Mavis blew smoke into Skitt's face. Skitt coughed, put his phone down and lifted his weak ass fists. Mavis started, ready to come at him, but Henrietta punched Mavis' chest.

Fuck it. Mavis left the group. He fell down on a bench by the club door and finished his cigarette close enough so he could hear them, far enough that he didn't have to deal with their bullshit. The two threw out what they knew. Skitt was Beefie's ride, so the kid couldn't have gone home. Beefie might have

Ubered somewhere, but where? Home? He hadn't answered the landline. He could have gone to Broadway, where he worked and drank most weeknights, but there wasn't a clear reason why. Skitt didn't believe Beefie would have just left Bourbon Blues, so he decided to stay at the club. Henrietta didn't know what to do. They kept going on about how nervous they were, kept using words like "worried" and "anxious."

Mavis wasn't sure how nervous he was. His right eye was twitching but he knew, in his gut Beefie was all right. He just was. After Skitt was securely inside Bourbon, Mavis got up.

"I'll check Broadway," Mavis said to Henrietta. "Maybe the nerves got to 'im. Or he's drinking at Blue-Girl or something. You wait with Skitt or go home."

Mavis didn't know if Beefie was on Broadway, he just wanted to be alone. He turned and started walking off, but Henrietta floated to his side, hooked her arm around his. He smiled to himself, a little smile. He was fine with her there. Wasn't she always?

Mavis and Henrietta took a left on 4th Ave. North, got off Printer's. They pushed past wasted folks and weekend strollers, 'til the mouth of the street opened up to Broadway. There Broadway was: electric and country, old and city-like. Broadway, with its lit-up boots, classic record shops, and neon guitar cutouts. With its trinket-full gift shops, faux saloons, and live karaoke bars featuring singers ready for radio. There it was: fat with screeching folks who smacked BBQ-wet lips and wondered, endlessly, where to drink.

Henrietta zig-zagged through people-traffic. Mavis grabbed her wrist, got her to walk a straight line.

"You're frontin', May. You're not calm," Henrietta said over a bad cut of some Dierks Bentley song blasting from The Stage.

"Not in the mood for psychic shit," he barked and dropped her hand. He felt bad, again, for his words. Henrietta didn't deserve his foul mood.

The phone went off and Mavis scrambled to get it from his pocket. Beefie's real name "Jay Sarge" blinked on his phone.

Mavis' heart flew to his mouth. He cried out, "Hey? Hey?" Henrietta got close to Mavis' phone.

Then silence, glasses clinking, a chorus of drunk girls calling out each other's names.

The phone clicked off. Mavis called Beefie again but he didn't pick up. Mavis cursed and stopped himself from chucking his phone at the sidewalk.

Mavis ran his fingers through greased down curls. At least Beefie answered.

"He's on Broadway," Henrietta said, placing a hot palm on his Mavis' back. "Blue-Girl. Second floor."

Mavis wiped his face with the back of his hand. This was all so stupid.

Mavis spit on the ground, turned to Henrietta. "Guess the clairvoyance is working." Mavis suspected, after that call, Beefie was at Blue-Girl too, the only Broadway bar Beefie would frequent on his own. But might as well give it to the Orishas.

Henrietta didn't smile. She studied Mavis' face, her forehead wrinkling. "Let's see if I'm right. Not about where he is. But why he left."

"You know that?"

"Yeah, I do. No clairvoyance."

Mavis pulled his lighter out of his pocket and lit another cigarette.

In the Blue-Girl stairwell, Henrietta and Mavis shoved their way around wide-mouthed, booze-happy folks. Bumper chords and twangy strings throbbed in the wooden walls. If Mavis hadn't been so irritated, he might miss the sounds of live country, the ubiquitousness of Nashville's cowboy culture. Mavis and Henrietta got off the stairwell and fell into yet another sweaty, packed crowd.

Mavis pulled Henrietta through clamoring barfolks. He glanced down and saw his skin, a washed-out brown, and Henrietta's, bright olive, sprayed with freckles. He knew that wrist by heart. He squeezed her hand and released her when they got to Blue-Girl's bar.

Mavis waved away the first two bartenders, waited for a whiteboy named Clive. Mavis knew Clive, a muscle-heavy stripper who worked the bar during Beefie's evening shows at Blue-Girl. Clive showed up eventually, his slippery pecs tensed. He wiggled his torso.

"Hey, May. What can I . . ."

"Where's Beefie?" Mavis said.

Clive pointed to the stage.

Mavis turned and saw his Beefie hunched over, clutching his knees on the three steps leading up to the stage, where the band was finishing Hank's "Lonesome." Beefie looked smaller than usual in a huge leather jacket and tight grey jeans. The kid gazed dazedly at the singer, a gal in a green snakeskin dress.

When Mavis arrived at stairs, Beefie didn't notice him. Mavis called out his name; it tasted soft.

Beefie saw Mavis then. The kid's little lips fell open.

"I'm sorry," he said.

Mavis plucked his thumb at the door behind the crowd. "Let's talk?" he said. "Alley? Don't run off."

Beefie stood up.

Outside Blue-Girl, in another alleyway, Beefie leaned against the wall. He pulled out a Camel Blue, rolled it on his tongue. Beefie wasn't lighting the thing, just flipping it and triple-eighting it in his mouth. The action pissed Mavis off. Beefie didn't realize how dirty that whole performance was. Mavis reached into his pocket, tossed the kid a lighter and said, roughly, "Come on."

Beefie caught the lighter but didn't use it. He looked at Mavis defiantly, kept that cigarette weaving up and down his young tongue. Mavis got close enough to Beefie's face that he could feel the kid's cinnamon breath on his own lips. The tongue-rolling stopped. Beefie's eyes shook and Mavis reached over, yanked the cigarette out of the kid's mouth. Mavis lit it and started smoking, tasting Beefie's saliva all over the filter.

Beefie swallowed, audibly.

"Why'd you go?" Mavis said, pushing down his arousal. Beefie shoved his hands in his pockets and stared at a halved bottle on the ground.

"I couldn't finish the song."

"The band's gonna be pissed," Mavis said. "They gave this black kid a chance in this country band and you fuck it up. Now that's on you."

"I know," Beefie said. He squirmed against the brick. He reached into his pocket, pulled out his dead phone, drew circles on it with his forefinger.

Mavis didn't know what else to say.

Mavis could still hear the Blue-Girl singer. She'd moved on to some Cash song, an old one, back when the Man in Black was courting June. The folks on the street were laugh-crying and everybody, somewhere, was singing something.

"I spent all week practicing," Beefie said to his Converses.

"Sorry," Mavis said, and took another drag from Beefie's Camel. "I'm an asshole."

"No. I wasn't singing good enough. That's why you left."

Mavis blew smoke from his mouth. He said, gently, "Naw. You were beautiful."

Fuck "beautiful." Mavis wasn't the kind of guy who used "beautiful" unless he was acting sarcastic or trying to get in somefolk's pants. He wanted to shove the word back in his mouth.

Still, Mavis saw it, the red flash in Beefie's eyes, the chin twitch. The story Henrietta knew without telling him. So that was the story: Beefie ran out because he was hurt Mavis took an impromptu smoke break during his show. Because Beefie loved Mavis too.

"There's too much changing," Beefie said softly.

"Nothing is changing for you."

Beefie's lips trembled. "When you leave, it will."

Mavis stepped away from Beefie. He yearned to yank the kid to his chest. Or run out of the alleyway, never to see Beefie again.

"Hey, man," Mavis said. "I'm leaving. And I love you."

Beefie's dead phone smacked the ground. The kid's eyes stretched wide as China plates. Beefie didn't say anything. That unreadable look made Mavis feel naked, ugly. Mavis straightened his face; he tried to look tough.

"Why didn't you say anything?" Beefie mumbled. "For two years."

Mavis shrugged one shoulder. "I don't know."

Beefie kicked a pebble. The rock hit Mavis' shin, lightly. Yeah, Mavis could just rush over, bury his nose that kid's velvet neck, but he wouldn't. This was all pointless.

"There's Skitt," Beefie said. "You're not coming back."

"Yeah," Mavis said. Beefie opened his mouth but Mavis turned from him. Mavis looked out at Broadway's hot streets. A German-looking family strode by in plastic pink boots. A few coils of brown-blonde Henrietta hair stuck out of the alley mouth. His sister was waiting for him, as she always was. Mavis pulled out his wallet, counted two hundred dollars and pulled his phone out. He pushed the money and cell into Beefie's hands.

"Call Skitt. Let him know you're alive," Mavis tore the Camel out of his mouth, tossed it to the ground. He stamped the thing out. "Apologize to your band. Give them that two hundred bucks, say you thought I got sick or something and that's why you ran out. I'm gonna snag Henrietta, get plastered in my own place."

At Mavis and Henrietta's townhome on Hillwood, Skitt, Henrietta, and Beefie drank hard. Skitt invited some hipsters over from East Nashville, and Henrietta brought out a twenty-buck karaoke machine so Beefie could sing '80's pop. Mavis fixed a pot of chunky gumbo for everyone, but didn't drink. He watched the boy he loved butcher shitty music, Henrietta wow hipsters with her cowrie, he watched all those folks finish off his stew.

The group fell asleep, drunk and warm-bellied. Mavis thought about rousing Beefie but he was snoring in Skitt's arms. Mavis dozed off on the leather couch and woke up early, when the sky turned pink. He took two packed bags to his '98 Sentra and climbed inside. How fine a feeling: the thud of ass to carseat, the swift rush of freedom that came from sitting in a small space alone. Mavis started the engine.

Henrietta opened the door. She stood on the yellow porch in bunny slippers and cotton robe. His sister-friend: looking like some kind of home. Mavis raised a hand and loved her. He pulled out of the driveway and got back on the road.

I Still Miss Someone

Steven Ostrowski

Harmon Bush pushed aside the curtain and peered down the steep slope of pines to the road. No one drove by. In the sky above the tree line hung a smudge of pink dusk. He thought of the girl and the need started its yammering: *this time, this time, this time.* But he had no faith that this time would be any different than the first two. From the sofa, Corrine aimed the remote at the TV and switched channels from a show about exotic snakes to a game show. Like always, she maxed the volume for the game show, and Harmon flinched at all the yapping and laughing. What the hell could be so funny? He saw the television set as a box of noise and colors that he'd just as soon blow the guts out of. Except what the hell would Corrine do without it?

It had been thirteen days since Harmon spotted the girl with blonde hair and a plump behind walking alone on Mill Street in the dark. He'd never been on Mill Street—it wasn't the way home from the bar—but there he was, driving down it slowly. He thought it must be meant. The need that night, like a pounding headache that ten aspirins couldn't relieve. Yet even as he slowed the truck and pulled up beside the girl, he didn't really think he'd do it. That is, he didn't think *he* would, but the *need*, which was like someone else altogether who lived inside his skull, the *need* might.

"Excuse me, honey," he heard himself say. It was dark with just a grin of a moon, and there was nobody anywhere. The girl came right over, a readiness for mischief on her face, and in twenty seconds Harmon had her in the truck, hands tied behind her back and kerchief covering her mouth. He drove the backroads toward the shack—though almost every road in the county was a backroad. The girl's blue eyes looked terrified, but she didn't try to kick the door open or squirm her way out of the cord. It was almost like she expected this would happen to her sooner or later, just the way Harmon expected Corrine to turn her back to him every time he came into the house. He wanted to tell the girl not to worry, that he needed something from her and then it would be over with, but just like always his voice got dammed up in his throat and he said nothing.

He needed to get out there to her now—part of him did—but he'd wait for full dark. When he felt a sudden stinging sensation in his hand, he looked down to realize his long left thumbnail had been screwing itself into his right palm. There was a dollop of blood where he'd torn the skin, and he looked at it a long few seconds before he wiped it on his dungarees.

"What the hell are you doing over there, Harmon?" Corrine said. She kept her eyes on the TV.

He passed quickly in front of the set and went into the kitchen. Shutting the door behind him, he opened the fridge and took out the last can of Bud, snapped off the lid and drank. Through the television racket and the closed door, Corrine called, "That's right. Drink the last goddamn beer, too. Keep taking everything I ever had away from me."

Harmon tried to think of the last time they'd talked civilly to one another. He tried to recall the last time they'd actually touched. The thought itself was intolerable and he walked to the back window and drank the beer and looked out at the sky going blue to black. He remembered something his father, who didn't like talk, told him the morning he married Corrine. "Show a woman weakness and you're a dead man for life."

Harmon touched his back left pocket to make sure the piece of paper was there. He touched his left front pocket and felt his keys. He didn't have to touch the utility knife to know it was hanging off his belt. His mind could not tolerate the idea of trying again with the girl, much less failing. When he brought his thumbnail back to his palm, he felt a sting and a new smear of greasy blood. He wiped it on his dungarees.

Okay. Dark enough.

Pushing open the kitchen door, Harmon told Corrine he was going to drive over to Marvin's to look in on his Aunt Marnie. Even as the words mumbled out of his mouth, he thought he should probably have come up with something else this time.

"*Again,* Harmon?" she squawked. "*Again?*" She kept her eyes on her program, and despite himself he looked at her. She always was a slender woman, but since what happened to Lucy last spring she'd gone to bone. Little by little her face was being sucked into the black hole of her mouth. She said, "Your brother and Jenny take good enough care of your damn aunt. Why do you need to visit her again? Your old man dies and you barely go see her for three years, and now you're going over there every other night."

Harmon wondered if he was capable of hurting Corrine, if that was the next thing he'd feel hounded by the need to do.

"Back in a while," he muttered.

"Wouldn't bother me if you weren't."

*

He drove the truck down the hillside and turned left onto Highway 661. He was glad that there were no cars on the road but he drove slowly anyway. He averted his eyes when his headlights found the posters stapled to every third telephone pole. Just that morning, at work, Ed Morgan had mentioned to Kevin Thompson that the state police had been putting them up all over the county. A girl from Belton. Sixteen. Runaway. "Chubby thing," Ed had laughed. "Hell, she's in California by now if she's got half a brain. Laying on the beach. Anyway, that's where I'd a gone. What about you, Harmon?" Harmon said he didn't know and walked back to his station. Behind him, Morgan said to Thompson, "That's one strange hombre, ain't it?"

At 8 Mile Creek Road, Harmon turned left and flicked on the high beams. The night sky was full of stars that looked like eyes. The woods on both sides curved over the deeply rutted road like a nightmare tunnel. He drove the six miles to where the road ended in a muddy turnaround, and he angled left onto an even smaller road—a path, really, packed dirt just wide enough for the truck to scrape through.

It wasn't until he was twenty or thirty yards away that the shack came into view. It blended into the woods so well that it didn't look like anything at all. He shut the engine off and sat, heart slamming against his ribs.

In all his life, Harmon had never felt so desperate and pathetic, a stranger to himself. Before what happened to Lucy last spring, he'd always known himself to be a man, like his father had been, who took it for granted that you got born into life's troubles and lived with them without fretting or whining. A man of even keel who did what was his to do. Except that after what happened, he became a man who couldn't stop his mind from hearing the cracking of skull bones, or of seeing the picture of long blonde hair soaked dark in a pool of blood, a body under his truck wheel right there in the place where he always parked it behind the house. He couldn't stop himself from hearing his own voice coming strange and high out of his throat, saying to his daughter, "Lucy, what the hell you doing laying in the mud in the goddam dark? Lucy. *Lucy*, you answer me, girl." Then seeing the empty fifth of Jack Daniels beside her leg. Corrine came running out the back door screaming "What the hell did you do, Harmon? Did you kill her? Did you kill my baby? My only baby?"

And he heard himself think, *she's mine, too, Corrine. Goddammit, she's mine, too.* She'd been hard to tame and influenced by too many wrong-headed kids. She defied him and she'd run away more than once, and she didn't give a good damn about the punishments she got, harsh as Harmon made them to try to save her from making bigger mistakes later on.

But she was his, too, dammit. She was the only one he had, too.

After they buried her, Harmon discovered himself to be a man unable to sleep more than a few hours a night, and whose workday went on and on like some sadistic torture. He'd become a man desperate for relief, a man who needed an alternative to the hammering memory of what he'd done.

Suicide was not an alternative. After his mother had killed herself with her head in the oven when Harmon was eleven, his father had spit on her grave and called her a goddamn coward, the words twisting out of his mouth with disgust and conviction.

Many times in the last two weeks Harmon had asked himself if what he'd done was premeditated. He always answered that it wasn't. It wasn't, even though on the Sunday morning before he took the girl he drove out to the shack with a month's supply of food and water packed into a cooler, and even though he boarded up the one small window, and made sure the old padlock still worked, and cleaned off the toilet seat and threw down into the hole five or six packets of air freshener—even then, he didn't believe he would do it. Come on. Do *what?* His mind preferred not to answer, even as he placed a three-foot length of cord and a somewhat clean kerchief on the passenger seat.

In the two weeks since he took her, he'd tried twice to do it. Four other times he'd driven all the way out, then turned back without going into the shack.

But the need said do it or suffer what nobody can suffer forever.

Stepping out of the truck, Harmon sucked so much piney air through his nostrils that it stung deep in his skull. He walked slowly, and he slowly unlocked the padlock. As he opened the door, a few inches at a time, he thought that maybe the girl would try to shove him and run for it, or jump him and claw him and bite him—*something.* But just like the both times before, she stayed sitting on the floor in the corner, wrapped in blankets, one of the flashlights he'd left there for her lying in her lap, turned on. Harmon closed the door. Even in the dark, he couldn't look in the direction of the girl; couldn't bear the sight of the blonde hair a tangled mess or the eyes raw as winter.

He stood near the door, looking at the floorboards, until the girl tried to say something. Except she started to cry instead. "Just do what you came to do and get it over with," she sobbed. "Just do it. Just do it and let me go. Please, mister, but don't kill me. If you let me go I won't tell. I promise I won't tell anybody."

Harmon thought, *so do it.*

He felt for the piece of paper in his back pocket. He took a few steps toward the girl. Humiliation filled him like a dirty trough. Humiliation was like the need, but worse. It had its own voice and the voice said *don't do it.* It said, *get out of here now.* Go slap that goddamn wife of yours across her sour puss and throw her goddamn TV set down the hill. Or slide your knife across her throat.

Harmon shut his eyes to the voice, tugged the paper out his pocket. Hands trembling, he unfolded it.

The girl said, "I already know what it feels like."

Harmon looked at her shadowed silhouette.

"My daddy," she said. "My daddy and my uncle . . ."

He failed to understand, until he did. "No," he said, and his head shook. Good God Christ almighty, how he wanted to disappear. To not exist. "No," he said again, softly.

"But then . . ."

He thrust the piece of the paper at her. "Read this."

The girl's eyes blinked. She reached up and took the paper. "What? What do you want?"

"Read it to me. Out loud." He added, "Please."

She looked at him, her eyes blinking wildly. Finally she glanced down at the piece of paper. She adjusted the flashlight in her lap to see what it said.

"Read it please," Harmon said again.

The girl read. "Daddy." Her voice was unsure, watery. "I know you feel bad that you killed me." She stopped and looked up at Harmon.

At her glance he shut his eyes. His body shook and his left thumbnail twisted, back and forth, into the ripped skin of his palm.

"I forgive you, Daddy," the girl went on. "I know you didn't mean it. I know it was an accident."

She stopped reading. The silence pressed down on Harmon's skull. "Please finish," he said.

"But I'm in heaven now and I forgive you, Daddy."

All he knew was that what he felt was unbearable in too many ways. He touched the keys in his pocket. He touched the knife.

"I'm sorry that happened," the girl said. She lifted the piece of paper toward him to take back.

"I don't need it."

The girl said, "Can I, can I go?"

Harmon hadn't thought through what should happen next. He never thought he'd get this far. He nodded.

"I, I don't where we are. Will you bring me back?"

His right palm was smeared with blood and he wiped it on his dungarees. "We'll need to go to the police station first."

"*No*," the girl said. "Please, no. I'll say I ran away. I've done it before lots of times. They'll totally believe me. Please, mister. You didn't do anything that bad."

Without meaning to, Harmon looked into the girl's eyes. He thought for a second that he knew her, and he looked away.

Man in Black

Terri Lynn Coop

I hate elevators. The idea of locking myself in a soundproof metal box kept aloft by cables is absurd. However, since my knees like twenty flights of stairs even less, when the doors slid open I stepped inside and pressed my back to the mirror lining the rear of the car. It adds an extra step if I need to escape the confined space, but I can keep an eye on my fellow passengers. A small monitor embedded in the wall over the control panel proclaimed the "Elevator News Network" and cut to a scene of a street protest complete with signs and chants.

"There oughta be a law."

The voice didn't match the man. The accent said downtown, but the suit had an uptown air. Nice close-weave wool, muted colors, and the cut worked on his large frame. On closer inspection though, the edges of the lapels and pockets were worn and shiny, indicating many homegrown or low-rent cleaner ironing jobs. The years had taught me to look past the surface and concentrate on the details.

It's probably his one nice suit. Maybe to see his lawyer or real estate agent.

His tone demanded an answer. "I don't know. We have plenty of laws. Some days it seems like we have more than we need."

"Yeah, but this ain't right. These shitbag judges are letting scum walk right and left on technicalities."

"Is that what the protest is about?"

"Yeah, they're calling for all the judges to be impeached. Those perverts they're freeing should all be frying instead of eating steak."

"I heard something about that mess. It's terrible. Seems there's no justice anymore."

"Damn criminals got all the rights. Nobody cares 'bout the victims."

"I'm not so sure about that."

The elevator's ding relieved me of the duty to participate in any more conversation. A beefy hand held the door open while he motioned for me to exit. Despite my mood, I had to smile at the unexpected courtesy. The city never ceased to surprise me.

Two bus rides later, I grabbed a cup of coffee in a busy Starbucks and cached the ski mask in the men's room trash. A place like this changed out the bags often and tomorrow was trash day.

Since it was a nice afternoon, I bought a bag of buttered popcorn from a pushcart and smeared the greasy kernels all over the black calfskin gloves as I fed the pigeons. After a quick stop by an overflowing park dumpster to toss the leather gloves wrapped in the red striped bag, I was down to the membrane thin surgical ones I always wore when I was performing an errand. Those went inside-out into the most fetid storm sewer I could find. Locard's Principle was in full force. The leather might have the errand's blood and the latex might have my genetic markers, but never in the same place at the same time.

My prints were on file, but not my DNA. Still, no one had ever died of an over-abundance of caution.

Calm spread through me as sunset highlighted the churning water behind the ferry. It's not only beautiful, but also critical to my next task. We're not crepuscular animals. Our eyesight is poorer at dusk and the day's fatigue is settling in to dull our curiosity. The other passengers didn't disappoint. Every pair of eyes was locked on the screen of the phone they each pointed toward the last pink and purple clouds spanning the horizon.

A stretch of my shirt cuff and the knife slipped into the dark water. I'd bought three from a street hawker and this was the last one. For ten dollars each, I got solid no-name knockoffs of my favorite four-inch Schrade fixed blade tactical knife. Tantos are the perfect shape for penetrating the spinal cord in the sweet spot between C1 and C2 and the thick blade isn't prone to breaking if my aim is off center. Although the cheap steel would never have held an edge, I only needed it to be sharp once.

The gentle bump of the boat meeting the dock reminded me that I had one more thing to do before wrapping up my errand. When I got to the parking lot, I extracted the plastic bagged package from my vest pocket. The throwaway phone still had the clear vinyl stickers over the screen and keypad. Even so, I wrapped it in a handkerchief before I punched the three numbers.

"This is 911, what's your emergency?"

I intoned the address and hung up. Prying off the back panel, I extracted the SIM card and battery. It was five blocks to where I'd left my car. Along the way, the phone and battery found their way into two separate trash cans. The card would meet the heel of my boot after spending some time on the barbeque grill.

The decision to make the call came easy. It was Friday before a holiday and a good chance that my errand wouldn't be discovered until Tuesday. By then the foulness would be well underway. A body in a warm, closed office decomposes at an alarming rate. It's not the fault of the police and paramedics or the minimum wage workers who'd be forced to clean it up. And the single puncture wound would be more visible on fresh flesh.

It's my signature.

That means it's time to change it. One body is an anomaly. Two are a puzzle. Three are a pattern. Falling into a pattern invites laziness and mistakes, even by a professional. On the flip side, anything that falls outside the pattern is dismissed, so I'll get at least one free one in the next round. Plus, three is just a good round number.

The hot shower mixed well with the cold bourbon. Two handfuls of dish soap scrubbed most of the temporary black dye out of my hair and a cheap over-the-counter product put the gray streaks back where they belong. All my clothes, right down to the thrift store boots, went in bags for disposal. I always enjoy coming back to myself after an errand. It's a rebirth of sorts. The steak sizzling in my favorite cast iron frying pan made me smile. It smelled like justice.

The lack of media coverage on Saturday and Sunday told me that not only had my errand been found, but also that a bunch of cops were pulling overtime hustling to hook it up with the previous cases. Come Monday, since it was a holiday, I still didn't expect to see much. At my favorite bistro, I flipped through a stack of newspapers after I asked for coffee. A third of the way through, I found out I was wrong about the media. My photo, a grainy still off a security camera, covered the front page of a tabloid rag. It was a bad profile and the bill of my cap covered everything but the tip of my nose and chin, but it was still me.

I hate elevators.

"What?"

I jumped when the waitress spoke. Turning, I half-expected to see shock and revulsion. Instead, she gave me the same warm smile I saw week in and week out. Even though my stomach had turned into a churning volcano, I ordered my usual pastry. This was no time to freestyle.

When she left, I folded back the photo and read the article. It was thin. Turns out the big guy in the dark suit on the elevator was named Albert and he worked for the Transit Authority. All he remembered was a tall man dressed "sort of like a soldier" who kept his back to the wall and didn't have much to say. The rest of the article was Albert saying that I was a hero. One thing it was short on was details. The physical description fit about thirty percent of the population. After I finished the article, I paged through the rest of the paper in between sips of coffee and torn-off chunks of cinnamon roll. It was acid and sawdust in my mouth, but this was about normalcy. It was just another weekend breakfast at my favorite place.

"I'd like to give the guy a medal," the diner at the next table said as he dumped ketchup on perfectly good eggs. "Did you hear the whole story?"

"Nah."

"It's a doozy. Bail bondsman was taking out his fees in trade. Turns out it was rough trade, if you know what I mean."

You have no idea.

"I remember that. He killed a couple of them. About a year ago, wasn't it? I thought he was in jail."

"Yeah, he was, until some pansy-ass judge threw out the case. Said the cops didn't tie his shoes and tuck him in at night. Damn liberals. There was a time when shit like this got taken care of."

"Uh, it looks like it got taken care of pretty thoroughly to me.

Knife to the neck. One cut. Probably one of those Special Forces guys."

"I wish he'd speak up. Man like that would never pay for a drink again."

I'd heard all this before in other restaurants and bars. But I hadn't heard it from someone holding a paper with my picture on the front page. It was time to get out of here. I finished the dregs of my coffee, left cash on the table, and folded the paper under my arm, cover in. As usual, my natural camouflage—salt and pepper hair with an outfit so bland and casual that it had to be expensive—didn't raise any alarms. Not a single diner gave me a second look as I left.

I ambled another fifteen blocks, no need to hurry, to an Internet café that prides itself on not being nosy. Along the way, I picked up a baseball cap and some passable rip-off designer sunglasses. A lot of people hate the street vendors, but not me. I can get just about anything I need with no receipts or hassle. At the café, I paid cash for thirty minutes and did some quick searching. I wasn't the only one interested in the photo. The tabloid article already had five hundred comments, most of them complimentary. The general consensus was that a rogue veteran, the sort of character that exists only in action movies and cookie-cutter thrillers, was out re-balancing the scales of justice. I scanned the serious news outlets and didn't find much more. Someone had leaked the name of the errand and the security photo, but no real specifics.

Detective Sinclair, this has you written all over it. Sorry, I don't have any appetite for bait today.

This wasn't the first time I'd gotten press, but this one landed closer than I liked. Definitely time to change my look and my MO. It was a damn shame; the blade had been the best. The screen grayed, telling me my time was up. I'd learned what I needed to know so there wasn't any reason to stick around. I already had the next errand picked out. Prosecutorial misconduct had led the appellate court to vacate two hundred sex crime indictments. One of the defendants, released by Elevator-Albert's shitbag judge, was out on an OR bond. His crime made the others on the list look misunderstood. But it wouldn't be today. The weather was perfect and I still had several bags of incriminating material I needed to dump. The leaves were past their prime, but a drive along the coast was just the ticket for thinking and planning.

Climbing the seven flights of stairs on Tuesday morning got my knee humming and my blood pumping. I hesitated at the door. Once I opened it, I was committed.

You've got no choice, Ace. This is your duty.

Out of habit, I moved carefully to minimize the sound. Evidently, I'm not as slick as I thought, because a woman's voice cut through the air as soon as I'd latched the door behind me.

"Good morning, sir. You're late."

"And I missed you too, Yvonne."

"Time and tide waits for no man, and with your vacation day and the holiday, the tide is coming in even heavier than usual. You're going to need your waders. They're lined three deep in the hallways."

"Crack the whip, my dear. Crack the whip."

"What can I say? You're the most popular show in town. And everyone out there has a ticket. Here, put out your arms."

I let her slip the light wool-silk blend black robe over my shoulders and adjust my tie. A knock on the door and a bailiff poked his head into my chambers.

"Your Honor, you should have been on the bench five minutes ago. You know what they say about justice delayed . . ."

Yvonne brushed a bit of lint off my shoulder. "I'll bring you coffee. This will be a long one. Sorry I can't do anything about that."

"There oughta be a law."

With a wink to my clerk, I opened the connecting door to the familiar refrain of "All rise."

Understand Your Man

Max Booth III

Later that night as my spine developed oblong knots against the metal cot and my feet numbed from hanging inches above old, piss-stained linoleum, my thoughts returned to where they always ended up when everybody in the world was bound to be asleep but me.

I thought about Joanie.

I thought about what she might be doing. Had she managed to salvage a few hours of sleep or was she also awake, her mind curious about what I was up to? It made me feel better to think about her tossing and turning in bed or pacing back and forth in the kitchen with the sink light on and the faucet dripping, cursing herself for calling the cops and making me spend another night in county for no good reason at all. The rage inside me only started bubbling when I pictured her sleeping soundly. When I pictured her relieved of my absence.

For my own survival, I needed her to feel as bad as I did about me being locked up in here.

Otherwise I would break.

I would explode and destroy everything in my radius.

The next morning I called my mom on the jail phone and apologized for accusing her of not loving me and for saying the things I shouldn't have said. I could tell by the tenderness in her voice that she'd been crying most of the night because of the names I'd called her. I barely remembered what I'd said. The anger had taken over and it was like I'd blacked out. Whatever left my mouth after that could not be my responsibility. We talked about my younger brother, Jordan, for a spell, who had escaped Ohio five years previous and moved down south with some woman he'd met on the computer, and I pretended I gave a shit until I felt enough time had passed before I could bring up the subject of bail again.

She paused and responded with a sigh heavy enough to collapse the jailhouse roof. "You said you wasn't gonna ask me about that again."

"I'm sorry. It's just that I'm going crazy in here, Mom. I feel like I'm losing my mind."

"Maybe this is what you need. Some time alone to clear out your head. I was talking to Jordan and he thinks—"

"I don't give a shit what Jordan thinks. And neither should you. He abandoned all of us, in case you've forgotten."

"He didn't—"

"Mom. I need to get out of here. Now."

"Honey, I can't—"

"Then why the fuck did you even answer the phone?"

"Andy. Stop it."

"Stop what? You're at your house free to do whatever the fuck you please while I'm rotting away in this goddamn box and you don't even give a shit. And who knows what Joanie's up to, given that it's her fault I'm even fucking in here. You say you love me but we both know that's a goddamn lie. You don't love shit except Jordan and the grandkids. You've never felt an ounce of compassion for me, not even when I was a baby."

"Andy—"

"Admit it. I was a mistake and I still am and nothing I've ever done has been enough to erase that fact. I'm nothing to you."

"I'm trying to help you—"

"You want to help me?" I started laughing and I feared I would never stop. I bit my tongue until a warm liquid soaked into my gums. "Go fuck yourself. How about that, Mom? You go right ahead and fuck yourself."

I didn't know who hung up first. It was likely a tie.

The cop sitting at the end of the hallway looked up from his cell phone and rolled his eyes. "Man shouldn't talk to his mother that way."

I debated saying something that'd probably end with my nose broken. I swallowed the rage instead. "I need to make another call."

The cop shrugged. "It's your money." He returned his attention to the mobile game on his cell.

I dialed Joanie's number. The digits were engraved deep in my heart. It rang until the automatic voicemail answered. If she would have just picked up the phone and allowed me to explain myself, I knew she would have forgiven me and dropped the charges. She'd done so before, she'd do so again. I wasn't no goddamn wife-beater. I'd just lost my temper, was all. Any man could. She had to understand that. She *had* to.

I told the cop to take me back to my cell. He held up his finger and said to give him a second, that he was almost finished with the level on his game. I stood next to him and leaned against the wall and realized how easy it'd be to strangle this fat asshole and take his gun and shoot my way out of the jail. What then?

I didn't want to think about what then.

An hour later, the cop slapped the bars with his baton. I remained motionless on my bunk, sleep finally catching up with me.

"Come on. Get up. You gotta go."

"I made bail?"

"No. But we received a bomb threat. We're cutting you loose."

I sat up and groaned. Everywhere ached. "What are you talking about?"

"Legally we can't keep you here. We gotta sign you out." He paused, keys in hand. "But understand, you'll be expected to sign yourself back in tonight by seven. Otherwise we'll have to issue out a warrant."

"Someone called in a bomb threat…?"

He nodded. "Probably some fuckin' kid, but we gotta treat these things seriously."

The guard led me down the hallway and told me to stop at the yellow line while he collected my possessions. I stood at the edge of the line and stared at its fading paint and thought about that Johnny Cash song my grandfather used to sing while he cooked pancakes on the weekends I slept over as a kid. I wondered if I walked the line, if I could justly call myself a man. Was I made of the same substances as him? Would he be proud of the paths I'd followed? He would've understood. He would've rubbed my hair and told me it was okay, that men can't be expected to keep it together twenty-four-seven. That's why wives existed, he might've said, to absorb the stress a man collects during the nine-to-five. Although in my case, it hadn't been a nine-to-five but a whenever-the-hell-I'm-needed. Except now it probably wasn't even that, considering I was scheduled to work the evening shift last night and instead of clocking in I was playing with my pecker in a six-by-eight. I doubted Joanie had considered how we would pay rent now. I doubted she considered much beyond herself.

The guard brought me a clipboard and a pen and told me where to sign, then coughed over my belongings. Not much. Shoe strings, a belt, my wallet, and a dead cell phone. He reminded me when I was due back and sent me on my way. I looked at my reflection in the black mirror of my phone and wondered how far I could throw it. Then I slid it in my pocket and started the hour walk back home and thought about my grandfather singing Johnny Cash in his underwear while flipping pancakes and wished desperately to be back in his kitchen when life didn't seem so goddamn impossible.

I hadn't thought about that Cash song in years. It seemed appropriate to have it stuck in my head during the walk home. I couldn't remember the majority of the lyrics but when did that ever matter? The important bits stayed with me. The rest was filler, anyhow.

I'd never cheated on Joanie. Sure, sometimes my eyes looked where they shouldn't have looked, and sometimes my imagination took me places far away, but I hadn't touched another woman besides her since we got together. But dirty thoughts were expected. Even popes couldn't control their dreams. I only wanted her. Nobody else. If walking the line meant never straying from the person you love, then I walked the line straighter than anybody. I was true through and through.

I stopped at my mom's house on the way home. The look on her face when she saw me could have raised the dead.

"Oh no. Tell me you didn't break out. Oh my God."

I sat down at the kitchen table and explained what happened. She frowned. "They just let you go?"

"I guess so."

"Hmm."

"What."

"I've never heard of no jail ever letting everybody go because of some phone call."

"Fine, don't fucking believe me then. I got shit to do, anyway."

"I don't even recognize you anymore, Andy."

I stormed out of the house without responding, but not before snatching a couple cigarettes from the pack on the table and pocketing her lighter. She yelled my name from the front door. I refused to give her the satisfaction of turning back and seeing her face. She could chase me if she really gave a shit.

We lived two streets over, which was convenient whenever a babysitter was needed. I took my time walking home, smoking both of the cigarettes I'd taken along the way. Nicotine had never tasted better. If I turned myself in tonight, who knew when I'd get another chance to smoke. Some people might have looked at jail-time as an opportunity to quit, but I had no desire to give up cigs. I liked that they could potentially kill me. It made them sexier, somehow.

My boy was playing in the front yard in a pile of dirt. Both of his tiny, chubby hands held a toy car and they smashed into each other like they'd rather die than let the other live. Six years old and not a guardian in sight. Nobody would have given a shit back when I was a kid but nowadays they'd send a S.W.A.T. team after you for something like this.

"Andrew. Where's Mommy?"

He looked up and drool dripped down his chin. Dried snot and dirt was smeared across his face. He shrugged and returned to his cars. I patted him on the head as I passed him and he growled like a dog paranoid someone was after his bone. I found Joanie in the bathroom, standing in front of the mirror while applying makeup to her swollen, bruised face.

"You look like shit."

She paused only slightly, then continued without looking at me. "Wonder who I got to thank for that."

"What did you do, hit yourself with something once I left?"

This time she turned toward me. "What?"

"No fucking way I hit you that bad. Whatever . . . *this* is, you brought upon yourself."

"Are you fucking serious right now?"

I shook my head, amused. "Like you've never hurt yourself and placed the blame on someone else. Milking that sympathy card is what you do best."

"Jesus Christ, you're such a piece of shit. Get out of my way."

I blocked the doorway with my arms. "Ain't you even one bit curious how I'm out already?"

"Nope." She ducked under my arms and went into the kitchen. By the time I caught up with her, she already had a beer open. I thought maybe it was for me but she raised the can to her own mouth instead.

I retrieved another beer from the fridge and tried to disguise my disappointment. She always got me a drink when I came home. It was one of our "things."

"What do you mean—'nope'? My mom thought I'd broken out. Should've seen her face."

She eyed me as she drank, then belched. "You ain't escape from nothin'."

"Then how do you reckon I'm free?"

"Because I called and told them a bomb had been left somewhere in the building."

I almost spat out my own beer. "No you fuckin' didn't."

"Yes, I fuckin' did."

"Jesus Christ, Joanie. Why would—"

She pointed at a paper on the kitchen table. "Tax refund came in. I tried to cash it but those sons of bitches at the bank turned me down since my name ain't on it."

"Oh."

She grabbed her purse. "So I thought we'd go get it taken care of, considerin' that motherfucker slapped another eviction notice on our door this morning."

"Let him try. I'll kill him."

"That seems to be your solution for everything lately."

"I didn't hit you that hard."

She laughed. "My face is practically a goddamn horror movie, Andy."

"I didn't do that."

"Sure you didn't."

She tried to walk past me but I set my beer down and grabbed her wrist and squeezed until she looked at me.

"Let me go."

"Not until you admit you're a goddamn liar."

"Only after you admit you're fuckin' crazy."

"I didn't make your face that way. I barely touched you."

"Whatever you say, Andy."

"No, it's not whatever I say." I squeezed tighter. Why was she being this way? After everything I'd done for her. "It's what *you* say."

She sighed and lowered her head. "You barely touched me."

"You made those marks yourself."

"Okay, Andy."

"Say it."

"I made these marks myself."

I released her arm and she rushed outside. I lingered in the kitchen and finished off my beer and threw the empty can against the wall. We loaded Andrew in the backseat and drove across town to the bank and deposited the tax refund. We'd been looking forward to this check for a couple months now. I'd lost count of the bills we owed. Everything added up. Everybody wanted something. I wanted to take Joanie and the boy and live somewhere in the woods where the water company couldn't find us. We'd hunt deer and rabbits and fuck in the mud and life would be perfect. There was plenty of water in the lake and none of it cost a dime.

After the bank we drove to our landlord's house, but nobody was home, so we drove to Wal-Mart instead. Joanie held my hand as we walked in and life felt worth embracing again. We bought a new TV that cost three thousand dollars and a new Blu-ray player. As I drove to pick up some lunch, Joanie squeezed my thigh. We ate like royalty at McDonald's while the boy played in the jungle gym area.

I ate my cheeseburger and thought about how goddamn beautiful simple things could be. "We're going to be okay."

Joanie cleared her throat. "I gotta go to the bathroom."

"So go."

My phone had finally charged enough to turn on, so I browsed social media as she excused herself. The first thing that popped up on my newsfeed was a picture of Joanie's face, bloody and swollen, staring straight into the camera.

The caption read: "my husband decided to give me a makeover #blessed."

It had over a thousand shares and hundreds of comments. I wasn't positive what "viral" meant, but I suspected this might've been it.

I scrolled through the comments as the boy laughed on the slide. Friends and strangers were calling me every name in the book, and some I wasn't even familiar with. People I thought would always have my back. Even my younger brother, Jordan, had ugly things to say about me. Apparently I was a monster and

I didn't deserve to keep living. If the commenters on Joanie's picture had their way, my balls would be ripped out from my scrotum and shoved down my throat, and even that wouldn't have been a severe enough punishment. It would've only been a start.

When Joanie returned from the bathroom, I was shaking. She took one look at me and backed away. "You saw it, I gather."

I nodded, trying to squeeze my phone hard enough to shatter it. Nothing happened.

She tensed. "Well, now what."

I wanted to drop my phone and replace it with her throat and never stop squeezing. I wanted to murder her in the middle of McDonald's with the whole world as my witness. The rage inside me begged to spill her blood, to break her neck, to make her scream an eternal scream.

It would be so easy.

I thought about my grandfather and wondered how he'd react in a situation like this. Would he keep walking the line, even after everybody else had long abandoned it? Maybe the line had never existed. Maybe Johnny Cash didn't know what the fuck he was talking about.

I rose from the booth and Joanie looked at me with genuine terror in her swollen eyes. She backed away, cowering in anticipation. I stepped forward and hugged her and told her I loved her with all my heart, then turned around and dropped my wallet on the table and left out the side-exit carrying the knowledge that if I ever saw her again it was likely I'd kill her.

She didn't try to follow me.

I walked down the road, careful not to step outside the yellow line dividing lanes, embracing the gusts of wind conjured by passing traffic. When I made it back to the jail, the cop at the front desk seemed shocked to see me.

"Thought for sure we'd have to come collect you in a few days."

I told him to shut the fuck up and take me to my cell.

I was tired and ready to sleep.

Were You There When They Crucified My Lord?

Heath Lowrance

Maybe you want to hear about how this church started, how our founder Jeff Jankey came to start it, and what sacrifice he ultimately made for our sins. I know you have a lot of ideas about what kind of man JJ was, as the Spirit Son of Johnny Cash, and you may not like the meager origins of our faith. But knowing the truth, and still maintaining your belief, is essential to reaching the Next Stage. And I feel like you're ready, like your conviction is strong enough to please the Man in Black and carry his Word far and wide. So listen, and I'll tell you. And you can not, repeat, can not, share this story with the Cash novices. They aren't ready for it. They wouldn't understand it.

The idea to start the Holy Church of the Man in Black Our Savior Johnny Cash came to JJ over the course of two horrible weeks, two horrible weeks in which everything went to shit and he knew all his stupid dreams were a bust, and the only way to make it work was to exploit a legend. He wasn't a religious guy. But he did worship Johnny Cash, so maybe that counted? But he knew, really, it wasn't about his own feelings on the subject. It was about everyone else's.

It started at the karaoke bar.

When JJ stepped up onto the little stage, he heard a few people laughing already, and one mildly drunk guy said to his friend, "Oh great, a Johnny Cash, what's a night out at karaoke without a Johnny Cash or ten," and his friend said, "Well, at least this guy's gone all out, hasn't he? Check out the duds on this guy," and JJ wasn't sure if they knew he could hear them, but he flushed and gripped the neck of his beat-up guitar. The guitar didn't have strings; it was solely for appearance. His belt buckle thumped against the back of it and the microphone picked it up and it echoed hollow against the far walls of the karaoke bar.

The stage was tiny, elevated only a few inches above everything else. It was too bright, and JJ winced. Almost everyone ignored him, as they ignored all the karaoke singers except their own, and they drank and laughed and carried on at the bar along the back wall. Closer to the stage, though, at the tables, people were paying attention, smirking, not expecting much, getting ready for a solid laugh.

JJ's throat was dry; he'd left his beer at his table. The karaoke machine was to his left, and with a quick practiced hand he scrolled down to the C's, to the meager Johnny Cash selections. Normally, his first selection of the night would be "Sunday Morning Coming Down," but the last few days he'd been practicing "I Still Miss Someone," and he felt pretty good about it, and "Sunday Morning" had that slightly higher octave in the third verse and JJ wasn't feeling confident enough to try it with this crowd. He tapped "I Still Miss Someone."

JJ was twenty-eight years old, thin, with a long, sad face that looked nothing like his hero's. He had dyed his hair jet black, but it lacked Cash's thickness and so hung lank and dead over his forehead. He dressed in black jeans, a black button-up shirt with fake pearl buttons, a black suit jacket he'd sloppily embroidered himself on the shoulders with red guitars. He didn't own boots, but he'd painted his sneakers black using Magic Marker. In the harsh light, they looked more blue than black. He looked more like a Salvation Army Dracula than Johnny Cash.

Over the sound system, the opening guitar and backing vocals started up and JJ suddenly didn't feel ready but it had started and he had no choice now and he felt this every single time, without fail, the nerves, the fear, it never went away and he never felt confident and he knew he would crash and burn as always, and his brain said why, why do you do this, you are no good, you're the worst, you're an idiot for trying, but it had started, the smooth back-up singers on the track singing, "I still miss someone . . ." and now here it was, the part where you sing, and it's too late, you have to do it.

JJ pretended to strum guitar strings that weren't even there, and moved in close to the mic and sang, "At my door, the leaves are falling . . ." and he was off key and his throat felt dry and closed, and he sounded awful.

He performed the entire song, not hitting a single right note, he was way off from the get-go, and the worst part was he knew it and couldn't seem to find the right key, but he kept going. He tried to not look at the crowd. He kept his eyes on the back wall. But he couldn't help it—every few seconds his eyes shifted downward. Almost everyone was ignoring his performance, laughing and talking and drinking amongst themselves. The two mildly drunk guys in front were watching, though, big stupid smiles on their faces, the kind of smiles you have for a stupid child or a puppy doing something cute. Indulgent smiles.

JJ performed the song, he stuck it out until the end, even though everything in his brain screamed to stop, to just leave the stage and get out of the bar as quickly as possible. He did the entire song, strumming his pretend strings, trying in vain to summon the spirit of Johnny Cash, and failing.

When it ended, there was no reaction, as if he hadn't even been there, except for the two guys in front. Both of them laughed and clapped, and one of them said, "Fuck, man, if I close my eyes, it's like Johnny Cash himself is in the room!" And at the far end of the bar, someone let out with a loud, "Woooo!" And there was the clatter of glasses and the cash register ringing up another drink and nothing else.

JJ cleared his throat and mumbled, "Thank you," and left the stage. He headed immediately for the exit.

On his way out, he saw three other Johnny Cashes waiting their turn.

He thought about those three other Johnny Cashes all night. He couldn't sleep for thinking about it. All of them had that same fervent look in their eyes. All of them had that fire of devotion. It was clear not just from their half-assed attempts to dress like their hero and emulate him in their posture, but from that look in their eyes.

They worshipped Johnny Cash. Just like JJ did.

And why? Why this country/folk singer who'd been dead for years now and never got played on the radio? What was it about him that spoke to so many people across the generations? Was it the sincere loneliness of his gravel-stressed voice? Was it the mythic quality of his life? Was it the simplicity of his songs?

Whatever it was, Cash's music had struck a chord with JJ from a very early age, when his stepfather used to play his records. Something about the Man in Black got right into JJ's guts and heart, and he was not just a fan; he was a fanatic. And JJ wasn't the only one.

JJ wanted to be Johnny Cash. He'd tried to take guitar lessons when he was a teenager, but had given up quickly, as his clumsy fingers couldn't form even the simplest chords. But it didn't matter; the crux of Cash wasn't his guitar playing after all. It was that voice. So JJ had focused on that, trying over the years to emulate that voice. He had no more success with that than he did with the guitar playing, but he kept trying, telling himself that maybe, with age, with maturity, it would come to him.

But that night, sleepless, tossing and turning in his bed, he knew at last it would never happen. He'd never sound like his hero.

He thought about those three other Johnny Cashes at the karaoke bar, and he thought about the idea of worship, and he thought about a church.

The name of it came to him quickly. It wasn't a great name. It didn't have to be. It only had to say what it was, that's all.

JJ looked up at the ceiling and said out loud, "The Church of the Man in Black, Our Savior Johnny Cash," and he laughed a little to himself.

He went to sleep thinking of it, and he dreamed, and in that dream Johnny Cash came to him and blessed him.

Maybe at this point you're thinking all of this is a damn cynical beginning to the founding of our religion. I know it sounds that way. It sounds like the Spirit Son did all this to exploit something he saw in others, or to find some path for himself. But it's not like that. JJ saw a need in others, just like he saw his own need. And after all, the Man in Black himself appeared to him and blessed him, and what more evidence of his divinity do you need than that?

Over the next few months, JJ studied. He read up on the Mormons, on the Jehovah Witnesses, on the Scientologists. He

Googled the hell out of state laws about religion. He got fired from his job at the auto parts place but collected unemployment and focused even harder on his research.

In the meantime, he still hit the karaoke bars two or three nights a week, doing his Johnny Cash songs. He auditioned to be the lead singer in a rock band, started singing the lyrics to "Mean Eyed Cat" when the band played some pompous riffs, and they stopped playing after a minute of uncomfortable glances at each other and the bass player said, "Are you, um . . . are you singing a Johnny Cash song? That's, you know, man . . . that's not really what we're looking for."

But mostly JJ was distracted with his research.

It took a year to get it together.

I was there for that first meeting of the Church of the Man in Black Our Savior Johnny Cash. There weren't many of us, sad to say, and the Spirit Son hadn't quite developed himself to be the perfect vessel he was at the end. Really, it was about the message at that point. A few people showed up because JJ had posted flyers all over town, and you have to admit, the idea was at the very least an entertaining one. A church dedicated to Johnny Cash? Wacky, right? If I'm being completely honest, my own initial attraction to it was that it was funny. It was a novelty. This was early days, though, before I or anyone else understood the purity of JJ's message.

That first meeting, JJ talked about the Man in Black's life, and he made an argument for Johnny Cash's divinity, and we sang songs. There was no songbook; we all knew the lyrics. JJ had hired a little three-piece band to play the music, and it was fun. Not inspiring, but fun.

We all came back the next Saturday, all of us, and many more. Word of mouth, you know. "Y'all gotta come see this, it's all about Johnny Cash as God and we sing songs and drink soda and it's fun."

Over the course of a few months, JJ got better at orating. His singing never improved, he never did sound like Johnny, but he sure did find his calling in singing the praises of the Man in Black, and the more you listened, the more . . . right it sounded. Johnny Cash was God.

And the idea that JJ was his Spirit Son, that developed gradually. But it made sense. Who else had such passion for Johnny Cash? We all loved Him, of course, but there was something about JJ's utter devotion that inspired us all, and when someone said, "JJ . . . are you Johnny Cash's kin?" JJ stopped what he was doing and stood there at the podium and his eyes shone and he said, "I am the Spirit Son of Johnny Cash," and there was such a rush of emotion through that hall and we broke out into "Johnny Yuma" and all of us knew the Truth.

We donated money every week to pay rent in the hall, and we all dressed in black, and the men dyed their hair black and the women wore pearls and flower-print dresses like June, and our numbers grew. We started an outreach program, going door to door and putting up flyers, and the Church just kept getting bigger and bigger.

After two years, we had enough to buy a new building, a really beautiful place with custom-made stained glass windows with images of Johnny and June on them, and the place had a nice rustic look, the kind Johnny would have approved of. JJ grew into a charismatic leader, and every week he laid out the gospel of the Man in Black, and what He wanted from us, and how we couldn't allow JJ, as his Spirit Son, to go without the finer things, and we sang songs and felt enormous peace of mind.

The Church brought people into the fold, not just Johnny

Cash fans, but for everyone who suffered. We brought happiness and enlightenment.

By that time, I had become one of JJ's most trusted confidants. One day, he called me on the phone and asked me to come see him at his home.

He sounded scared.

He was sitting at his big, ornate desk when I got there, with the portrait of the Man in Black behind him, guiding him, and I sat down and JJ said, "It's the I.R.S. They've been investigating the Church." He had a Southern drawl now, even though he was from Detroit, but it wasn't an affectation; it was Our Savior speaking through him.

I asked him why the I.R.S. would be interested in the Church, and JJ said, "Well . . . apparently there's some question as to whether or not we're legit. They want to take away our tax-free status. They want to put me in jail."

"In jail? For what, in Johnny Cash's name? That's insane."

"Fraud," JJ said. "They think I'm a fraud."

I hadn't seen JJ so shook up. He explained to me how his lawyer had visited, told him about the charges the government was getting ready to press against him, how, if he didn't pay back taxes he'd be facing serious prison time.

This was a serious problem. There was nothing I could do to help, obviously. I worked at a car wash at the time. But I did my best to bring comfort to the Spirit Son and we sat around his office for a few hours, singing songs and reflecting on Our Savior.

By the time I left, JJ seemed considerably more at ease. When I was at the door, he said, "I need you to do something for me," and I said, "Anything, JJ, you know that. Anything at all," and he said, "Let it slip, just a little, to the congregation. Let it slip a little that evil forces have targeted us and our faith will soon be put to the test. Will you do that for me?" And I said, "Sure, I guess, if that's what you want, JJ," and he said, "Don't give away details. Just . . . let it slip. Do that for me," and I said, "Sure," again, and he nodded, and I left, feeling uneasy about it.

I didn't know it at the time, but he had come up with a solution to the problem. One that would change everything about our faith, and make us all stronger.

It happened three days later, during our Saturday sermon. None of us saw it coming, but when it happened, it just seemed inevitable. It seemed like the next logical step in the Church's evolution.

It started normal, with a couple of songs, JJ sermonizing about our Savior the Man in Black. He even allowed a couple of the children to come up to the podium and testify about how Johnny Cash had saved them and changed their lives, and the women sobbed and the men nodded sagely and it was a lovely sermon.

And then JJ took to the podium again, and his voice was grave.

He said, "Brothers and sisters. Today is . . . well, it's a trying day for our church. Evil, dark forces are rallying against us. I know you've heard some rumors, and I am sad to tell you the rumors are true."

A murmur went through the pews, uneasy, and JJ said, "You all know there is evil in this world, and it was inevitable that sooner or later, as our faith grew and our Word spread, that evil would settle in on us, turn its vile attention to us. They can't allow us to grow, you see. They can't allow the Truth to shine, or else they'd lose their power."

Talk of good and evil, plain and simple, is at the heart of any faith, and the congregation responded with amens and praises.

His voice growing stronger, JJ said, "But our Truth is too great for them! Our light shines too bright! They can never snuff out the glory of Our Savior the Man in Black!"

"Never!"

"Praise Johnny!"

"Amen!"

JJ nodded, said, "Johnny bless you all. We are all His children, and He loves us. And He has a plan, revealed to me, to share with you."

At the far side of the stage, there was a cart filled with little plastic cups of some orange-colored beverage. We'd all noticed it, but thought nothing about it until JJ spoke to the children in the front pew, "Kids, do me a favor. Those drinks over there? Take them and hand them out to everyone. Everyone. Everyone gets a drink."

The kids, about fifteen of them, snapped to it, rushing to hand out the orange drinks.

Everyone in the congregation took one. They held the cups, looking at each other uncertainly, not sure exactly what was going on, but there was a creeping realization that most of us couldn't quite grasp, and a sense of growing dread in the hall.

The kids handed out the cups to everyone, every single person in the church. JJ took the last cup himself. He raised it, said, "This we do in the name of Our Savior. Don't be scared, brothers and sisters. There's nothing to fear. Johnny awaits us on the other side."

Someone in the back of the church whispered, "Jesus Christ," and in the sudden silence it sounded like a scream.

JJ took a deep breath, brought the cup to his lips, and drank.

He dropped the cup to the floor, smiling, gazing out upon us all.

But his smile faded when he saw that no one else was drinking.

He said, "Brothers . . . brothers and sisters . . . you have to . . . you have to drink . . ."

The last couple of words were slurred. He stumbled backwards away from the podium and dropped, and within seconds he was dead.

The rest of us dropped our cups on the floor like they were . . . well, poison, and stared at JJ's dead body on the stage, half-obscured by the podium.

Our faith in the Man in Black is strong, stronger than anything, but killing yourself over it? That's just dumb. That's fucking stupid.

There was a long criminal investigation after that, and it eventually ended with the Church retaining its tax-free status, and we had a rotating staff of ministers before I eventually took over as head of the Church. We still meet every Saturday, and we sing songs and praise Johnny Cash, and we eulogize his Spirit Son, Jeff Jankey, who died for our sins so we wouldn't have to, because that was how it had to happen, and it made us stronger, and the newer members of the Church are always asking those of us who were there what it was like, and the only answer I can give is: "It was scary, but the Spirit Son saved us, he died so we wouldn't have to, and Johnny Cash loves us, and everything is okay."

About the Authors

Micah Schnabel is a singer/songwriter/writer from Columbus, Ohio. He plays in the band Two Cow Garage and also releases solo work under his own name. You can catch him singing songs and telling stories in and from the dark corners of the world.

Rob Hart is the author of *The Woman from Prague*, picked by *Publishers Weekly* as one of the best reads of the summer. He is also the author of *New Yorked*, nominated for an Anthony Award for Best First Novel, *City of Rose*, and *South Village*, picked by *The Boston Globe* as one of the best books of 2016. Short fiction has appeared in publications like *Thuglit*, *Needle*, and *Joyland*. Non-fiction has appeared in publications like *Slate*, *The Daily Beast*, *The Literary Hub*, and *Electric Literature*. You can find him online at @robwhart or www.robwhart.com

Jen Conley's short stories have appeared in *Thuglit*, *Needle*, *Crime Factory*, *Trouble in the Heartland: Crime Fiction Inspired by the Songs of Bruce Springsteen* and many others. She has contributed to the *Los Angeles Review of Books* and is one of editors of *Shotgun Honey*. Her story collection, *Cannibals: Stories from the Edge of the Pine Barrens* is available now. Visit her at jenconley.net

David James Keaton's work has appeared in over fifty publications, and his first collection, *Fish Bites Cop! Stories to Bash Authorities*, was named the 2013 Short Story Collection of the

Year by *This Is Horror*. His second collection, *Stealing Propeller Hats from the Dead*, received a Starred Review from *Publishers Weekly*, who said, "Decay, both existential and physical, has never looked so good." He teaches composition and creative writing at Santa Clara University in California.

Lynne Barrett's recent fiction can be found in *Mystery Tribune*, *Necessary Fiction*, *Fifteen Views of Miami*, and *Fort Lauderdale Magazine*. She's received the Edgar Award for best mystery story, and her collection *Magpies* won the Florida Book Awards gold medal for fiction.

David Corbett is the author of five novels. Patrick Anderson (*Washington Post*) described *Done for a Dime* as "one of the three or four best American crime novels I've ever read." George Pelecanos remarked, "Corbett, like Robert Stone and Graham Greene before him, is crafting important, immensely thrilling books."

Tom Hazuka has published three novels, over sixty short stories, a book of nonfiction (*A Method to March Madness: An Insider's Look at the Final Four*), and has edited or co-edited six anthologies of short stories, including *Flash Fiction*, *Flash Fiction Funny*, and *Sudden Flash Youth*. He teaches fiction writing at Central Connecticut State University. Links to his writing and original songs can be found at tomhazuka.com.

Mike Creeden is the author of the rock and roll noir thriller *All Your Lies Came True*. His work has appeared in *Tigertail*, *Miami Living*, *Everything Is Broken*, *The Florida Book Review*, and *Trouble in the Heartland: Crime Fiction Inspired by the Songs of Bruce Springsteen*.

Nik Korpon is the author of *The Rebellion's Last Traitor*, *Queen of the Struggle* (January 2018), and *The Soul Standard*, among others. He lives in Baltimore.

Sarah M. Chen juggles several jobs including indie bookseller, transcriber, and insurance adjuster. She has published over twenty crime fiction short stories with *Shotgun Honey*, *Crime Factory*, *Betty Fedora*, *Out of the Gutter*, and *Dead Guns Press*, among others. *Cleaning Up Finn*, her noir novella with All Due Respect Books, is a 2017 Lefty finalist and IPPY award winner. http://sarahmchen.com

Terrence P. McCauley is an award-winning writer of crime fiction and thrillers. His third novel in his University Series, *a Conspiracy of Ravens*, will be published by Polis Books in September 2017 and is available for pre-order now. The other novels in the series, *Sympathy for the Devil* and *A Murder of Crows*, were also published by Polis Books. In 2016, Down and Out Books also published Terrence's World War I novella, *The Devil Dogs of Belleua Wood*. Proceeds from sales go directly to benefit the Semper Fi Fund. Terrence's short story "El Cambalance" has been nominated for Best Short Story in the ITW's annual Thriller Awards. A proud native of The Bronx, NY, he is currently writing his next work of fiction. Please visit his website at www.terrencemccauley.com

S.W. Lauden is the author of the Greg Salem punk rock P.I. series including *Bad Citizen Corporation* and *Grizzly Season* (Rare Bird Books). His Tommy & Shayna Crime Caper novellas include *Crosswise* and *Crossed Bones* (Down & Out Books). Steve lives in Los Angeles.

Gabino Iglesias is a writer, journalist, and book reviewer living in Austin, Texas. He is the author of *Gutmouth*, *Hungry Darkness*, and *Zero Saints*. His work has appeared in the *New York Times*, *Verbicide*, *Electric Literature*, and other print and online venues as well as in a bunch of anthologies. Find him on Twitter at @Gabino_Iglesias

Danny Gardner enjoys careers as a comedian (HBO's Def Comedy Jam) actor, director, and screenwriter. He is a recent Pushcart Prize nominee for his creative non-fiction piece "Forever. In an Instant," published by *Literary Orphans*. He is a proud member of the Mystery Writers of America and the International Thriller Writers. Danny lives in Los Angeles by way of Chicago. His debut novel, *A Negro and an Ofay*, is published by Down & Out Books.

James Grady was named "one of 50 crime writers to read before you die" in London's *Daily Telegraph* in 2008. Grady's first novel *Six Days of the Condor* became the iconic Robert Redford movie (minus three days). He's since published more than a dozen other novels, twice that many short stories, written for CBS and HBO dramas. Grady's received France's Grand Prix Du Roman Noir, Italy's Raymond Chandler medal, Japan's Baku-Misu award for novels, and a Mystery Writers of America Edgar nomination. Grady's also been a muckraking national investigative reporter and columnist. Born and raised in Shelby, Montana, he now lives inside Washington, D.C.'s Beltway.

Renee Asher Pickup is a mellowed out punk rocker living in Southern California. Renee writes fiction about bad things happening to flawed people, nonfiction that is critical of the status quo, and truly believes *From Dusk Till Dawn* changed her life. You can find her blogging at *Do Some Damage* every Friday, facilitating classes at *LitReactor*, or on any podcast looking for a host that likes to blab and have a beer. Her novel with Andrez Bergen: *Black Sails, Disco Inferno* is available now from Open Books.

Hector Duarte, Jr. is a writer out of Miami, Florida and current co-editor at *The Flash Fiction Offensive*. His work has appeared in *Flash: The International Short Story Magazine, Sliver of Stone,*

Foliate Oak, Shotgun Honey, Shadows and Light: An Anthology to Benefit Women's Aid UK, The Whimsical Project, Spelk Fiction, HorrorSleazeTrash, Pulp Metal Magazine, and *The Rumpus.* He also teaches English-Language Arts to seventh graders and listens to (as some friends might argue) too much Phish. He is very grateful for his wonderful girlfriend, Samantha, and his pampered tuxedo cat, Felina.

James R. Tuck has written a number of books and will write many more. He used to throw people out of bars for money.

Angel Luis Colón is the author of the *Blacky Jaguar, No Happy Endings,* and the upcoming short story anthology Meat City on Fire (and Other Assorted Debacles). His award-nominated fiction has appeared in multiple web and print publications including *Thuglit, Literary Orphans,* and *Great Jones Street.* Keep up with him on Twitter via @GoshDarnMyLife

Jennifer Maritza McCauley is a writer, teacher, and Ph.D. candidate at the University of Missouri. She is presently Contest Editor at *The Missouri Review,* associate editor at *Origins Literary Journal* and reviews editor at *Fjords Review.* She has received an Academy of American Poets Award, and fellowships from CantoMundo, SAFTA and the Knight Foundation. Her most recent work appears in *Vassar Review, Columbia Journal, Passages North, Jabberwock Review* and *Puerto del Sol* among other outlets. Her forthcoming poetry collection *Scar On/Scar Off* will be released by Stalking Horse Press.

Terri Lynn Coop is a recovering criminal defense attorney turned antique dealer and writer. When she's not digging through thrift shops or standing her ground at an auction, she writes legal thrillers and dystopian sci-fi. Her first novel, *Devil's Deal,* is available through Amazon.

Steven Ostrowski is a fiction writer, poet and songwriter. His work appears widely in literary journals, magazines, and anthologies. He is the author of two chapbooks of poems and one of stories. A collaboration of poems he wrote with his son, Ben Ostrowski, is due out in 2017.

Max Booth III does not know how to play the guitar, but he does have a Twitter account, which you can follow @GiveMeYourTeeth.

Heath Lowrance is the only person in this anthology who actually met Johnny Cash. And June Carter too. It was in the parking lot of a Wal-Mart outside Nashville. Yes, Heath is the author of *The Bastard Hand*, *City of Heretics*, *Hawthorne: Tales of the Weirder West*, and some other stuff, but none of that is relevant. He met the Man in Black. And he will tell that story at any given opportunity. Also, he worked as a tour guide at Sun Studio.

WITHDRAWN

CPSIA information can be obtained
at www.ICGtesting.com
Printed in the USA
LVOW12s1629210518
577951LV00001B/136/P